HOPE CITY

THE ALASKAN ADVENTURES OF PERCY HOPE

BOOK ONE

NEIL PERRY GORDON

Cover Artist: Erica Miller, Hope Alaska - ericamillerart.com

To the Miller Family of Hope City, Alaska,

whose friendship and love inspired this

novel

"I would rather be ashes than dust! I would rather choose that my spark burn out in a brilliant blaze than be stifled by dry-rot. I would rather be a superb meteor, every atom of me in magnificent glow, than a sleepy and permanent planet. The proper function of man is to live, not to exist. I shall not waste my days in trying to prolong them. I shall use my time."

—Jack London's Credo

HOPE CITY, 1898

Table of Contents

CHAPTER ONE—REPORTS FROM FARAWAY

"Did you see the morning paper, Sam?" Liam, red-faced, held up the early edition of the *San Francisco Examiner*.

I shook my head. "No, I haven't had a minute since we've opened," I said, standing on the second to the top rung of the sliding wooden ladder, and reaching overhead to put away the back stock of coffee beans.

"The headline says," he began, lowering his voice, trying to sound like one of our teachers from school, "JUNE 6TH, 1898—REPORTS FROM FARAWAY LAND, WHERE THE EARTH SEEMS LINED WITH GOLD."

"Wow, that's something," I said, trying to sound interested, and pointed to the bags on the floor. "Hey, Liam, do me a favor and hand me one of those."

Liam put down the newspaper, bent over to grab a ten-pound burlap sack of beans, and lifted it up to me.

"Sam, we should go to seek our fortune. You'll never get rich working in the store for your dad, and I'll never make a living slaving away in that saloon, cooking and cleaning tables for those drunkards."

"Sounds good, Liam," I whispered, "but please stop talking about it. Father doesn't like conversations unsuitable for customers."

Liam looked around. "There's no one in the store," he said, picking up the newspaper again. "It says people are flocking to Alaska by the thousands. So far they found more than a ton of nuggets."

"You believe that crap?" I said, climbing down the ladder, and grabbing a broom to sweep up the errant coffee beans scattered across the floor.

Liam tapped the paper with a finger, and said, "If it's printed here, it must be true."

I shook my head and exhaled. "You're naïve."

"Doubt me at your own peril. But when I'm rich and living in one of those mansions up on Nob Hill, you'll be stuck here helping customers."

"That's right, Liam. But you're forgetting that this will be my store when Father retires, and maybe, if you're nice to me, I'll give you a job sweeping the floor when you return from your silly dreams of seeking your fortune."

Just then the bells on the front door rang. I raised my eyebrows to Liam, and whispered, "I'll see you later."

"Good afternoon, Mr. Hawthorne. How may I be of service," I said, keeping my gaze upon Liam, and jerking my head toward the door, encouraging his departure.

Liam smiled at the schoolteacher, and said, "Good day, sir," and pushed the front door of Rothman's General Store open, and exited onto Market Street.

Mr. Hawthorne glared suspiciously at me, and said, "Good morning, Master Samuel."

I leaned the broom back in its corner and approached Mr. Hawthorne. "How may I be of service, sir?"

"Do you spend much time with young Liam?" he asked, removing his hat and placing it on the counter.

I furrowed my forehead at the derogatory phrase *young* in front of my friend's name—after all we were the same age. "Liam and I are buddies," I replied with an honest shrug.

Mr. Hawthorne leaned over, bringing his hawk-shaped nose close to mine, and wagged a finger at me. "Stay away from that boy, Samuel. You have a future. I assume that one day this store will be yours, and your *buddy* will work for wages, somewhere in the city," he said, flicking his fingers, like he was dismissing a servant.

I forced a smile, and said, "Is there something I can help you with, sir?"

Mr. Hawthorne squinted his eyes to emphasize his words. "You're seventeen years old, Samuel, and graduating high school in a few days. It's time to think about your future, not fraternizing with people beneath your station."

"Good morning, Mr. Hawthorne," came the words from my father, Benjamin Rothman, who was walking down the wooden staircase from our rooms above the store.

"Ah, Benjamin, I was just telling your son about socializing with people who can help elevate his position in life."

"I heard what you said, John, and I would appreciate if you would stick to your subjects of schooling, and leave his life's lessons to me," Father said.

"Of course, Mr. Rothman," he replied, with reddening cheeks.

"Now, please tell me how I may be of service," Father said with a smile.

CHAPTER TWO—GRADUATION

Just before I took my seat among the sea of wooden chairs, I scanned the audience beyond the rows of my classmates, searching for my parents.

"Do you see them?" asked Liam, who was also gazing outwards, hoping to glimpse his father.

I shook my head. "No, but I'm sure they're out there, somewhere."

"I don't see my father either. But he wouldn't miss this for anything. He insists on visual proof that I'm graduating."

Once seated, our school principal, Mr. Lionel Bullworth, stood before the podium and began. "Parents, siblings, relatives, and friends, this has been a rewarding year for our students. They've worked hard, and every one of them has earned the right to step upon this stage and receive their diplomas," he said, gesturing to the wide wooden platform, where the tenured members of the faculty were seated, trying their best to look like learned scholars.

Mr. Bullworth smiled, and added, "But before we do that, I'm pleased to have the honor of introducing a special guest to offer a few inspirational words to our graduates." He turned and gestured to a young man seated at the end of the stage. "I trust that many of you who were in Mr. Hawthorne's reading class will recognize this man's name. You have read several of his short stories this past year, and as I was told, much to your delight," he said, with a smile. "Our commencement speaker is not only a writer, but he's also an explorer. Just last year he journeyed into the wilds of Alaska with his brother-in-law, to join the Klondike Gold Rush. I'm sure his future stories will draw upon his once-in-a-lifetime experience from those exciting adventures."

Liam elbowed me and nodded quickly with his eyes opened as wide as his mouth. I patted Liam's knee and smiled.

"Students, parents, friends, and faculty, I'm pleased to introduce: author, explorer, and a native of our great city, Mr. Jack London," he said, to a robust round of applause.

Jack London rose from his chair, and pulled down on his brown linen jacket, trying to smooth out the stubborn creases. He wore a black silk cravat, tucked into a white shirt that seemed to have yellowed over the years. He hurried across the stage and reached out to shake hands with Mr. Bullworth. His blue eyes looked over the audience, and he took a calming breath before he began.

"I was born just a few blocks from here," he said, pointing in the direction of his childhood home.

"Did you know that?" Liam whispered to Sam.

I shook my head.

"I'm curious. How many of you have ever ventured beyond the borders of our great city?"

A few hands rose in the audience. Neither mine nor Liam's among them.

Mr. London nodded slowly. "Graduates of Mission High School, you're about to embark upon a new chapter in your lives. Actually, many new chapters." He smiled at his writer's reference.

"Once you step through those doors," he said, pointing to the back of the auditorium, "free to roam the world, what will you do with your life? Will it be worthy of an adventure story, or will it be another sad tale of a wasted life?" He paused, allowing his question to marinate, before he continued. "Perhaps you'll make do by reading about a life worth living through my books, instead of experiencing a full and exciting one of your own."

I glanced over to Liam, whose right leg was bouncing up and down.

"I had a rough time of it in the Klondike. I developed scurvy. My gums became swollen, and I lost four teeth. And I have replaced them with these," he said, opening his mouth and tapping on his false, brownish-colored teeth with a finger.

A buzz of conversations washed through the audience.

"I have a constant pain in my hips, and in my legs, that reminds me of my struggles," he said, patting the source of his apparent discomfort. "But if you ask me if I regret my decision of venturing into the unknown, my answer would be a resounding no. I'd do it again, even knowing what I know now. Life's too short. We need to squeeze whatever we can out of it."

Mr. London paused and turned to look at the faculty seated behind him. "What I'm about to say, may sound blasphemous to the adults in the

7

room. But I believe that when I'm dead, I'm dead. And I believe that with my death, I am just as obliterated as the last mosquito I squashed," he said, smacking his hand hard onto the wooden podium, giving me and the audience a jolt.

"Perhaps some of you will find my words inspirational"—he shrugged and continued— "and others may find them upsetting. But either way, it doesn't matter, the result is the same," he said, and pointed with an outstretched arm. "Wake up before it's too late and live a life worthy to be remembered."

With that, Jack London nodded, and returned to his chair. The faculty, most likely expecting a more traditional speech, such as one expounding upon the virtues of hard work, sat stunned, with near-identical expressions of shock, while the students rose to their feet and applauded vigorously.

CHAPTER THREE—BERTHA

"It's huge!" shouted Liam, gawking at the steamship docked at San Francisco Harbor.

I pointed to a page in the guidebook, published by the Alaska Commercial Company, and said, "She's called the *Bertha*."

"Yes, and she's leaving for Alaska tomorrow," Liam offered, his tone heavy with suggestion.

"I know you all too well, Liam. What are you getting at?"

Liam shrugged. "I don't know, except that maybe we should go too."

I squinted at Liam and said. "Are you serious?"

"Sure, why not? We could buy two tickets and go."

I looked into Liam's bewitched eyes and said, "I don't know . . ."

"Come on, now. You heard Jack London. We're only on this earth for a short time. When we're dead, we're dead like a squashed mosquito. We need to live for today, Sam."

I shook my head. "My father needs me to work in the store. I can't just abandon him. It's not right."

"Your father ran the store for many years before you came along— I'm sure he'll manage."

I listened, and continued to stare at the enormous steamship jutting beyond the length of the docks.

Without waiting for an answer, Liam continued, "Let's do it, Sam. Let's book our passage and leave tomorrow."

I watched as dozens of workers load crates of supplies into the cargo hold. The docks were filled with men milling about. Some were making purchases of mining supplies at wooden shanties.

"But what would I say to Mother and Father?" I asked Liam.

Liam frowned and said, "If I told my father, he wouldn't be pleased. Who would cook and clean for him? So, we just don't tell them anything."

"Have you lost your mind, Liam? We can't just disappear. They'll send the police looking for us."

Liam just laughed, and said, "Come on, Sam, let's go on an adventure."

I shook my head. "This is a crazy idea. What do we know about prospecting for gold?"

Liam shrugged. "We can learn quickly; we'll figure it out."

"It's not just that. Alaska is the wilderness, and we're city kids."

"Jack London was a city kid too. Now look at him," Liam pleaded.

I couldn't deny that Jack London's words inspired me to do more with my life than to work in a general store, at least for the summer. "I suppose we can buy a book about mining."

"So, you agree to go?" Liam said, grabbing my shoulders, and shaking me back and forth.

I looked at the guidebook advertising the goldfields of Alaska and smiled. "I do want to go, but I must tell my parents. We can't just leave without a word."

CHAPTER FOUR—THE PARENTS

"I think I need to lie down," Mother said, patting her forehead with one of her delicate hankies.

"Don't be so dramatic, Sara. It's just for the summer," insisted Father. "The boy needs to strike out on his own, make a name for himself. And who knows, maybe he'll find gold and we'll be rich," he said, cutting a piece of meat, and placing it in his mouth.

I nodded vigorously, trying not to show my sudden dismay at having shared my potential discovery with Father, though his reaction didn't surprise me. To him, everything was a business deal. If I did bring home any gold, he would probably use it as a lesson to teach me about the importance of *squaring up* with him for the spending money he allotted me.

"I suppose you're okay with letting him go into the wilderness? A bear could eat him," Mother cried and reached for the pitcher of water to refill her glass.

"Stop it, Sara. Neither a bear, nor anything else, will eat him," Father said, and turned to me. "You need to promise to write to us once a week with updates on your wellbeing, and your progress," he said, taking his napkin off his lap, and wiping at a piece of food stuck to his salt-and-pepper colored beard.

"I will, Father. I promise."

"I'll support this summer's adventure, with an understanding that if you strike gold, I expect to be paid back, with interest," he said, pointing his index finger into the air.

Mother dropped her silverware onto the table, causing me to jump. "All you think about is money, Benjamin. What about your son's safety? What will he eat; where will he sleep? Who will do his laundry?"

Father waved his hand at Mother dismissively. "It's about time the boy grows up."

I stood up, walked over to Mother, and wrapped my arms around her from behind, while she remained seated. "I'll be fine. I'll write to you each week, I promise."

She got up from her chair, put both of her soft hands upon my cheeks, and said, "You're my only child, Samuel. If something should ever happen to you, I don't know what I'd do."

"Nothing will happen, Mother, I promise."

Tears rolled down her cheeks, and I looked over to Father, who smiled and said, "She'll be all right. I want you to know that I'm proud of you, Son."

"Thank you, Father."

"Now what about Liam? You think his father will let him go?"

"I don't know. I'm heading over there after dinner. I guess I'll find out soon."

After dinner, I walked down the street to Liam's house. He and his family moved to the neighborhood at the same time as our family. We met when we were both seven years old and have been best friends for the past ten years. Liam is an only child, just as I am, and last year his mother had a sudden heart attack and died. She was only forty-four years old.

Liam had a tough time adjusting, which resulted in several episodes of serious misbehavior. He was constantly getting himself in trouble at school, and there were a few times where I needed to protect him from the older boys who wanted to beat him up after he insulted them. Good thing Father sent me for boxing lessons these past three years, giving me the skills to knock those bullies on their butts.

When I arrived at his house, Liam was sitting on the front steps of the wooden porch to his house.

"I can't go," he said, the moment he saw me.

I sat down next to him. His chin was propped up by his two palms.

"Why, what happened?"

"Father went crazy."

"What did he do?"

"When I told him I wanted to go to Alaska, he started screaming hysterically. 'Who will cook for me? Who will take care of me?' You should have heard him—it was pitiful."

I turned to look at the front door of the house, worried that Liam's father could be listening. "Where is he now?"

"I think he's in his bedroom, hopefully asleep."

"What are you going to do?"

"I guess I'm not going," he said, shaking his head. "It's probably not a good idea anyway. Father needs me, especially with Mother gone. He relies on me to take care of him."

A silence hung over us, until Liam added, with a burst of enthusiasm, "But that doesn't mean you shouldn't go."

"Without you?" I paused, and said solemnly, "I don't know if I want to."

"Did you ask your parents?"

I nodded.

"And what did they say?"

"Of course, Mother was against it. But Father saw it as a chance to make some money, so he was for it. But if you're not going, I don't want to go either."

Liam shot up to his feet, and pointed a finger at me, inches from my face, and said, "You're going with or without me. I couldn't live with myself if you didn't go because of me."

I shrugged and shook my head.

"No, you listen to me, Sam. You'll be on the ship tomorrow, even if I have to drag you there myself."

Later that night, back in my bedroom, with my head propped upon my pillow, I gazed through my open window into the cloudless, starlit night, and thought about what I had told Liam. I said I would go to seek my

15

fortune in the goldfields of Alaska without him, but I wasn't happy about it. Going alone would certainly test my courage, and I was excited to give it a try.

When I finally said goodbye, I gave him a hug, and said, "I promise whatever gold I'm lucky enough to discover, I'll share it with you, even though my father has already claimed a share."

Liam pushed me away, and said, "Don't be crazy. All I want you to do is write me of your exploits, and don't leave out the juicy details, if you know what I mean."

I glanced over to where my valise was sitting on the floor. Mother had folded everything perfectly, including the best of my warm clothes. As much as I tried, I couldn't deny that she was right in her earlier remarks regarding how she took care of me. I wasn't much of a cook and never had to do my own laundry. But I wasn't worried, as I knew I would figure those things out. What concerned me more was the unknown world of the Alaskan wilderness which I was about to embark upon.

I imagined people living in remote towns far from any big city, constantly aware of the bears, moose, and eagles who shared the land with them. Did the people live by lanterns, use outhouses, have running water, and clean their laundry with washboards in streams? And what about their clothes, would they freeze stiff when they were hung out to dry?

I thought about all the comforts of my bedroom, especially my soft bed I was lying in. I couldn't help but chuckle as I considered the crazy prospect of leaving all this behind to strike out into the wilds of Alaska.

While I wasn't afraid of sacrificing my regular routine for an adventure, I did wonder what it would be like standing in a frigid river day after day, bent over panning for gold, like I saw pictures of men doing in the books I borrowed from the library. Was I cut out for such a difficult trade?

Then I remembered the words Jack London shared with Liam and me and several other boys, when we gathered around him after the graduation ceremony.

One of my fellow graduates asked, "Weren't you afraid to go to such a remote place as Alaska?"

Mr. London shrugged and said, "Why would I?"

The boy replied, "Because it's dangerous—you could have been attacked by a bear, or frozen to death."

Jack London smiled. "That all depends on what's inside you," he said, poking a finger into the boy's chest. "I believe that a man without courage is the most despicable thing under the sun; a travesty in the whole scheme of creation."

It was that statement that ultimately made me decide to spend the summer in Alaska, and as I recalled these inspirational words while I lay in my bed, I dismissed any of my cowardly thoughts.

CHAPTER FIVE—BON VOYAGE

I didn't sleep well the night before my departure. I awoke hours before sunrise and was dressed and waiting for Mother and Father with my valise on the front porch. They wanted to see me off, and purchase my passage to Cook Inlet, Alaska.

When we reached the ticket office, we learned that there were three types of tickets, depending on class. Obviously, there was the first-class ticket, which was two-hundred dollars—way beyond Father's price range. Second-class tickets which provided 'a step-down in luxury, but still very nice,' as the ticket agent explained, were only one-hundred dollars.

Mother insisted that we purchase the second-class ticket. "I don't want him sleeping with riffraff," she said, under her breath.

But we ended up buying a third-class ticket, commonly known as steerage, for $25. Father said it was only a six-day voyage to Alaska, and I could keep the difference for spending money when I got to Alaska, which gave me a total of $150 and doubled the money in my pocket.

When we turned the corner from the ticket office and walked onto the dock, Mother let out a shriek that turned all the heads of the people within earshot. "Oh, my Lord, I've never seen something so big in my life."

I raised a finger in the air and said, "The *Bertha's* over two-hundred and forty feet long. I read about it in their advertisement."

Propped up toward the back third of the ship was the gangway where passengers were now boarding. Before I could take a step in that direction, Father grabbed me by my wrist and said, "There's something I need to tell you."

I looked at him with a puckered brow and said, "What is it, Father?"

He jerked his head, and led me to a quiet place, next to an old, abandoned shanty. "Let's talk here."

I looked over to Mother, who just shrugged.

"Listen to me," Father said, putting both hands upon my shoulders, and gripping them tightly. "You do not want to tell anyone that you're a Jew. You should change your name to something that's very plain."

I wasn't sure what Father was implying, and I supposed my facial expression communicated my confusion.

"These types of people," he said, gesturing to the hundreds milling about, "don't think well of our kind. Trust me, I know of which I am speaking, Son."

"Your father's right," Mother whispered.

I had heard stories that my father shared with his Jewish friends of their life in Poland before immigrating to America with Mother, of events that took place before I was born. I knew what being a Jew meant in these faraway places, but never imagined that I would be witness to it.

"What should I change my name to?"

"I don't know"—Father shrugged—"a common *goyim* name, maybe something like Percy."

19

"Percy, I like it. But what about my second name?"

Mother lifted a finger in the air and said, "Make it hopeful, uplifting."

"How about Hope?" I said, standing taller upon the announcement.

"Perfect," Father said. "You'll be Percy Hope."

When we got to the gangplank, we waited in a long line. The clerk, in the official uniform of the Alaska Commercial Company, was holding a clipboard, checking passengers in. Mother and Father wanted to wait and watch me board. While we were talking, standing in line, I heard my name being called.

"Samuel Rothman!" rang out across the harbor for all to hear.

I stood on my tiptoes and looked for the source. It was Liam, waving his arms and running towards me.

"It's Liam," I said.

"Liam?" Father queried. "I thought he wasn't coming."

"That's what he said, but I think he's with his father. They're probably coming to say goodbye."

"Sam," he shouted again as he approached.

Father shushed him. "Quiet, Liam, why are you yelling?"

"I'm coming with you, Sam."

I leaned closer and whispered, "Don't call me Sam. My new name is Percy, Percy Hope."

Liam shook his head, confused.

I motioned with my hand and said, "Don't worry about it. What do you mean you're coming?"

"Father changed his mind," Liam said, turning to him, and smiling.

Liam's father Wade shrugged and said, "It's high time I took care of myself for once in my life."

"Oh, this is wonderful," Mother said. "I was so worried about sending my Samuel alone."

I grimaced at Mother and reminded her, "It's Percy, Mother."

"Who's Percy?" Liam chimed in.

"Oh, for God's sake," interjected Father. "Can we all keep it down?"

"This is wonderful," I said, giving Liam a hug.

"Are you bringing your cooking supplies?" Mother asked, pointing to the cast-iron skillet tied up to the handle of Liam's valise.

Liam shrugged and said, "Someone will have to cook for us. I'm sure you don't want your boy to go hungry."

Mother grabbed Liam and kissed him on his cheek. "Wonderful, I'm so happy you'll take care of my Samuel."

Wade patted his son's back. "Hopefully, I'll figure out how to cook a few things," he said, sounding pitiful.

"Oh, don't you worry, Wade. We'll be happy to have you over for dinner, from time to time," Mother said.

Wade tried to smile, and said, "That would be nice."

Liam and I stood on the passenger deck of the *Bertha* and waved goodbye to our parents.

"Goodbye, Percy," Father shouted, sounding convincing.

I waved and yelled, "Farewell, Father, farewell, Mother."

"So, Percy," Liam said, with a heavy emphasis on my new name, "let's find our berths in steerage."

CHAPTER SIX—EARL WHITMORE

It took me a while to get used to the motion of the ship. I once read about a phrase called *getting your sea-legs* and thought this must have been what the author was referring to.

They directed Liam and me to our berths in the lower levels of the ship. We descended a metal staircase, made our way through narrow corridors and squeezed through tight hatches.

"We're below water level," Liam said loudly, over the humming of the ship's engines.

"This must be it," I said, entering a large space, filled with hammocks tied to metal posts bolted into the ceiling and floor. The air was thick with the pungent smell of unwashed men, many of whom had already claimed their berths.

"Let's take these two," Liam said, pointing to a pair of empty hammocks, swinging side-by-side.

I put down my valise and lowered myself into the canvas hammock. The stiff fabric wrapped itself around me like a cocoon. The first thing I noticed was the sour stench of vomit. Whoever slept here before, on a previous voyage, must have gotten seasick and thrown up. Apparently, it was not an odor that washed away easily, if the ship's hands even laundered these hammocks at all.

As I lay there, looking out in between the rolled edges of the fabric, an old man's face appeared.

"Comfortable?" he asked.

I pushed away the fabric flaps and wiggled myself out of the hammock and jumped up to my feet. Standing there was a large man, with a long, scraggly black beard, and equally black, beady eyes.

"Hello, sir," I said, extending my hand, "my name's Percy Hope."

The man nodded and gripped my hand hard. "It's good to meet you, Percy."

"I'm Liam Kampen," Liam said, climbing out of his hammock.

The man stroked his beard, and said, "Percy Hope and Liam Kampen. Where you boys from?"

"Right here, in San Francisco," I said.

"Either of you have experience in prospecting?" he asked, scratching at something on his ample belly.

We both shook our heads.

"There's nothing to worry about. This will be my second season placer mining along Turnagain Arm. You boys know what placer mining is, don't you?"

I nodded. "Yes, I read about in a book at the library. It's an ancient method of using water to discover heavy minerals, like gold."

"Yeah!" Liam blurted. "We're going to placer-mine for gold."

The man let out a hearty belly laugh. "You're one hundred percent correct. But you make it sound easy, and trust me, it's anything but. That's why you two should agree to work with me. I'll show you the tricks of the trade. You'll find gold faster if you know how," he said, with a smile that displayed black gaps in his mouth, where several teeth used to live.

I looked over to Liam, whose wide eyes expressed his enthusiasm at the offer.

My first reaction was to be reluctant and suspicious of such generosity from someone we just met. "That's a kind offer, mister . . ." I paused, waiting for the stranger to tell us his name.

"The name's Earl Whitmore," he said, shaking our hands again. "It's encouraging to meet two young men like yourselves, who are not only eager to discover gold but also making something with their lives. I wish I could turn back the clock and be your age again. I would have done things differently, that's for sure."

"Thank you, Mr. Whitmore. But before we partner up with you, or anyone else, we would like to get to know the person," I said with a smile, trying not to insult the man.

"Perfectly understandable," he said, swinging his arms outward. "Let's get to know each other. We have six days until we reach Cook Inlet; that should give us plenty of time."

I nodded, even as I asked myself why I was willing to trust a stranger.

"Well, let's get ourselves topside. It stinks like death down here," he said, gesturing to the hatch leading back to the stairwell.

I looked at Liam, who shrugged.

"Very well, Mr. Whitmore, please lead the way," I said.

It took a while for Liam and me to find the opportunity to distance ourselves from Mr. Whitmore and speak freely. The grizzly old man was friendly enough, but I wasn't sure if he was a trustworthy fellow.

"We just met the man," I said.

Liam held out his hands. "I don't know, he seems okay."

"I'm just saying that we proceed slowly before we consider a partnership with him."

Liam shrugged. "All right Sam."

As we stood at the starboard side of the ship, observing the diminishing California coastline, I asked Liam, "How did you get ever get your father to agree to let you go?"

"After you left last night, he came out onto the porch."

"He heard us?"

Liam nodded. "He did, and he must have been moved by what we said, because he told me I could go."

"It's incredible that he changed his mind," I said, leaning my elbows along the long wooden railing wrapping around the deck.

"He said it wasn't fair to expect me to give up my life to take care of him, and he would manage without me, at least until we returned in September."

"That's great, Liam."

"I've been meaning to ask you about this *Percy* thing."

I lowered my voice to keep my words private and told Liam what Father had said about being a Jew in a strange land.

"Percy Hope, that's a funny name. But I like it," Liam said, wrapping his arm around my shoulder. "All right, Percy Hope, let's go see if we can get something to eat."

CHAPTER SEVEN—THE COMPANY

It was the next day that my opinion about Mr. Whitmore changed.

The men in steerage ate together on the stern end of the upper deck. Most sat cross-legged, leaned their backs against the railings, and scooped out stew and boiled potatoes with pieces of crusty bread and shoved it into their mouths. While we ate the lukewarm concoction of what I figured were the cheapest foods the shipping company could provide, Mr. Whitmore conducted a spontaneous orientation meeting.

"How many of you have ever been to Alaska?" he began.

Only a few hands among at least the forty men tightly gathered on the downwind end of the ship rose into the air.

"That's what I thought," he said, stroking his dusty beard. "This is my second trip."

"Have you had any luck?" a voice shouted from behind an obstruction that blocked my view of the man.

"I have," he announced boldly. "And last summer I did well. I don't want to brag about what I deposited into my Wells Fargo account, but if I can duplicate my earnings, I'll be set for life. That's why I'm heading back for more. But I'll tell you," he said, pointing his finger to emphasize his forthcoming words, "you should all know that the gold is not just sitting there, waiting for you to come and pick it up. It's hard work, and when we get to Turnagain Arm and disembark in the mining village, there will be no one there to greet you, except maybe the whores in Sunrise," he continued to a rumble of guffaws.

Liam looked at me with an expression that spoke volumes. Though we never discussed it, neither of us had ever been with a woman before. I'd never even kissed a girl, though Liam had a girlfriend when he was fifteen, and he confessed they kissed a few times.

I wondered what it would be like to be with a woman who knew what she was doing, because I hadn't a clue. This was something I might consider a worthy experience to splurge upon. But I knew if I behaved so crassly, allowing my cravings to get carried away, my money would run out quickly.

"What I'm offering," Mr. Whitmore continued, "is an opportunity to work with the Alaska Commercial Corporation as a prospecting partner, with something commonly called, a *grubstake*."

An orchestra of chatter rose among the men. He had captured their interest.

"When you sign your grubstake agreement, each of you will receive your own set of professional mining equipment, and an education in the techniques of placer mining," he said, nodding along with his enraptured audience.

"But that's not all," Mr. Whitmore continued, raising his arms into the air. "The Alaska Commercial Corporation, which we call the Company, will also stake you in your own exclusive claim in a prime, pre-scouted location, where gold has been discovered."

I had to admit that Mr. Whitmore now had my total attention. In fact, he had everyone's attention and we were all salivating at each word.

"What's the catch?" someone shouted.

"Catch?" Mr. Whitmore repeated, feigning surprise. "There's no catch, but there is an agreement. The Company is out to make a profit, just like all of us here. This is how it works," he said, and paused for a moment to build up the anticipation. "You will receive the equipment, the knowledge of how to use it, and a stake of where to mine it, along with a room in one of our bunkhouses to live in; all this in exchange for you earning twenty-five percent of whatever you discover."

Laughter swept across the deck. Several of the men were doubled over. Someone shouted, "That means the Company keeps seventy-five percent. How's that a good deal?"

Mr. Whitmore raised his arms to silence the belligerence. "You can quickly dismiss this as a poor deal, and you're free to do so. But remember one thing, twenty-five percent of something, is a hell of a lot more than one-hundred percent of nothing."

Upon that last remark, the din of multiple conversations ceased. By the time the group of men broke up, Mr. Whitmore had signed up fifteen as partners with the Company, including Liam and myself.

CHAPTER EIGHT—BREAKFAST

That night, Liam and I stayed topside until we couldn't keep our eyes open any longer before we retired to our hammocks in steerage. As we stepped into our quarters, the air was thick with the smell and taste representing the nearly four dozen men, their hammocks swinging back and forth in rhythm with the rocking of the ship. Sounds of snoring, coughing, sneezing, and farting, echoed off the walls like a symphony of the human condition. If I wasn't so exhausted, the assault on my senses would have kept me from sleeping.

When morning came, I reached over and shook Liam, who mumbled something about letting him sleep. I said fine, and that I would meet him topside, but first I needed to relieve myself. I found my way to the latrine, which was a long wooden bench with cutouts to piss or shit into. Whatever hideous smells lived within the steerage quarters was now a fragrant relief from the odorous concoctions simmering below.

I quickly did my business and found my way topside, where fresh buckets of water were available for washing ourselves. The crisp invigorating air of the early morning, along with a splash of icy cold water upon my face, offered a rebirth of my spirit.

I waited for Liam to join me before tempting fate with breakfast. I was fearful that the poor quality of the food would loosen my bowels once again, and force me back down to the latrine, more often than I would have liked.

"Good morning," Liam said, emerging from the hatch leading from the lower decks. He rubbed his eyes and took a breath. "I don't know about you, Sam, but I can't spend another minute in that shit hole."

I opened my eyes wide, and said in a whisper, "You mean Percy."

"Yes, sorry. Good morning, Percy. How did you sleep?"

"I slept fine," I said, shaking my head, "let's get something to eat."

A few men were already in the food line, holding out their wooden bowls for the servers to plop in the morning fare. I looked over to Liam, who offered the same expression of disgust he made at dinner last night, which made sense, since breakfast resembled a similar, if not the same concoction.

The unshaven, and probably unwashed servers, wore aprons with food stains that I imagined were from the hundreds of previously served meals. They scooped out a stew with lumps of mush as big as eggs, along with a boiled potato, and some indistinguishable meat. To wash down this slop, they offered us what someone called a *belly-wash* coffee, which I think referred to the quality of the brew as barely drinkable, which it was.

When we found a place to sit along the deck, Liam stuck his nose into his bowl and pulled it out as fast as if he were smelling the waste in the latrine. "This is disgusting. When we get to Alaska, I'll get a job as a cook and show these people what good food is."

I jerked my head to gawk at Liam upon his surprising comment. "What about seeking your fortune prospecting for gold?"

Liam shrugged. "Why can't I do both?"

"How do you plan to do that? All you have is that dirty skillet of yours."

"A dirty skillet and an eager stomach are all you need," he said, with a smirk.

"Morning, Percy, morning, Liam," said Mr. Whitmore, approaching us with his breakfast bowl in hand.

"Good morning, Mr. Whitmore," I said. "That was quite a presentation you gave us yesterday."

"I'm glad you two saw the validity of the offer. You won't be sorry."

"Hey, Mr. Whitmore, what's with this slop? It's not suitable for a pack of wild dogs," Liam complained.

"Your torture will end soon. When we drop anchor, and boat over to the mining town, I'll show you a place that will delight your sophisticated palates."

I cocked my head to Liam. "He's the cook, not me. I'll eat anything. Well, almost anything," I said, looking into the unidentifiable assortment of glop in my bowl.

"You're a cook, Liam? We always are looking for someone who knows how to be innovative with our limited supplies," Mr. Whitmore said, with a mouthful of mush.

"I didn't leave home to become a cook, Mr. Whitmore."

"You can do your prospecting during the day and get yourself an evening job," Mr. Whitmore said, wiping off a piece of potato stuck to his beard.

"You make it all sound so easy, Mr. Whitmore," I said.

"Well, nothing is easy in Alaska. You must never forget where you are, nature can offer some nasty surprises."

"Like bears?" Liam asked with a mouthful of breakfast stew.

"Sure, there are bears, and we had a few attacks last summer. But besides the ferocious animals, you also need to know that there's no law where we're going, and some ruthless men like to take advantage of that. In fact, there is someone I should warn you about. His name is Magnus Vega. He uses his gang of thugs to pressure local businesses into giving him a share of their profits, in exchange for his so-called *protection*, as he likes to call it."

"Protection?" I asked. "Protection from what?"

Mr. Whitmore laughed. "You mean from who. If you don't give Magnus Vega a *piece of the action*, he'll cause trouble for you."

"Magnus Vega?" Liam repeated.

Mr. Whitmore nodded. "He's the cruelest man I ever met. Best to keep your distance from him, if you can."

CHAPTER NINE—THE ALASKAN COAST

On the morning of the sixth day, with the rain blotting out the view of the sun beyond the eastern backdrop of snowcapped mountains, we sailed from the vast Gulf of Alaska into Cook Inlet. Our last breakfast onboard the *Bertha* was served topside as usual. But unlike the previous days, we ate today's meal under a relentless downpour.

Liam and I squeezed against the hull of the deckhouse, which offered some protection from the winds and driving rains. Other men too huddled together, trying to stay dry, which was proving to be a futile effort.

Just as I was thinking of heading back down into my odoriferous steerage berth and wait out the bad weather, shouts from the port-side railing caught our attention.

Liam and I stood up, walked over to the other side of the boat and saw a snowcapped peak rising out of the inlet, blowing a stream of white steam from its spout, and creating a spiral-shaped cloud formation under a gray, rain-soaked sky.

"Is that a volcano?" Liam asked.

"It is," said Mr. Whitmore, standing alongside us at the railing. "It's called Mount Saint Augustine."

Liam's jaw hung open, and he asked, "Is it going to erupt?"

"You never know. From what I heard, the last time it erupted was fifteen years ago. Perhaps it's due," Mr. Whitmore said with a smirk.

Liam looked at me wide-eyed, then over to Mr. Whitmore, who just laughed. "I'm just kidding with you, Liam."

I had never seen a volcano before, active or dormant, except in our geology textbook. It was a spectacular site, an island, rising from the depths of Cook Inlet with an inverse, cone-shaped, snow-covered mountain, spewing steam into the atmosphere.

While the sight of the active volcano was thrilling for me and the hundreds of other passengers who were now squeezed topside, it was quickly dwarfed by the palatable excitement by the hundreds upon hundreds of Beluga whales, suddenly swimming alongside the *Bertha*.

As I gaped at the array of bright-white humps breeching the icy waters, one of the older men standing beside Liam and me said, "There are thousands of them in Cook Inlet. They flock here to feast on the salmon."

The sight brought tears to my eyes. That some of God's greatest creatures were greeting us upon our entry into their domain was nothing short of a religious experience.

For someone who had only seen such examples of sea life in picture books at school, this was an invigorating lift to my spirits as we cruised the last day up Cook Inlet, planning to anchor just off Fire Island, which was close to the mouth leading into Turnagain Arm.

*

"Sam, did you hear those men talking last night about how hard it was to get to the gold?" Liam asked.

"I did," I said, although I tried to reassure both him and myself as I continued, "but we're not going to the same place. From what Mr. Whitmore said, we're heading to a small town; it will be nothing like getting to Dawson City in Canada."

Fueling my private worries were the stories we heard from men who had been to the Klondike—the world's main draw for gold. The journey to get there was an ordeal of unfathomable proportions. Men and even some women sailed on steamships like the *Bertha* to a small town in Alaska called Skagway. Once disembarked, the *stampeders*, as they were called, needed to climb a fifteen-hundred-step staircase of frozen snow, known as the Golden Steps, through the Chilkoot Mountain Pass.

Thousands of souls struggled hauling their loads upon their backs over the treacherous terrain. The Canadian government required that each man provide for themselves at least one ton of supplies, in fear that without the basic necessities, the prospectors would never survive for long in the wilderness. Of course, no one could carry two-thousand pounds upon their back in one trip, meaning that several grueling, round-trips were required.

Even for those who weren't injured or killed along the way, their journey was far from over. They still needed to build or acquire a sea-worthy craft to transport them, their equipment, and supplies, five-hundred miles down the turbulent and rapid Yukon River before arriving at Dawson City, a bustling metropolis of forty thousand souls, who were there for one reason only.

Among these *stampeders* were famous and important people trying to stake their claim to a fortune. John McGraw, the former governor of Washington, was rumored to have journeyed to where the Yukon and Klondike Rivers meet, along with the mayor of Seattle, and twelve men from his police force, all of whom returned home with their pockets lined in gold.

A most disturbing story was told by an older man named Scott Jenkins, who boasted about killing the outlaw by the name of Soapy Smith. As we were told, this Soapy fellow was a conman, cheating prospectors out of their money through various schemes. One of which was setting up a phony telegraph office in Dawson City, where he tricked people by charging a fee to send their messages to the states.

Mr. Jenkins accused Soapy of cheating in a poker game, while several of his gang members were looking on. Soapy challenged Mr. Jenkins to a duel where he ended up shooting Soapy dead, right on Main Street while hundreds of people watched.

Other seasoned miners shared tales of prospectors spending outrageous sums on amusements. One such man was Jimmy McMahon who, apparently, spent twenty-eight thousand dollars on whores, gambling and whiskey.

It wasn't unusual for the dance-hall girls to earn large sums from these frivolous men. The dancer Gertie Lovejoy was said to have a genuine diamond inserted between her two front teeth.

We heard from many onboard the *Bertha* that the gold was not nearly as plentiful as it once was in the Klondike, and that the journey to Turnagain Arm was much easier and offered less competition than the hordes who had poured into Dawson City. Once I knew that getting to our destination didn't require risking our lives, like the *stampeders* had, I could breathe more easily again.

CHAPTER TEN—MAGNUS VEGA

"Isn't it about time, boss, that we give this town a name?" suggested Stan Smith, my head of security.

I scratched the three-day-old grizzle on my neck, which reminded me I needed a shave. But that would have to wait until I got back to Sunrise. I had received word that the *Bertha* had just dropped anchor out in Cook Inlet. The shallow waters and lightning-fast tides of Turnagain Arm wouldn't allow the large steamship to enter the inlet, so the steamer, the *LJ Perry*, shuttled the passengers and their supplies onto shore.

I patted Stan on his muscular shoulders and said, "You know what, Stan, you're right. I will ask the first person off the *LJ Perry* his or her name, and that will be what we'll call our town."

"Are you serious?" Stan asked, exhaling a long stream of cigar smoke into the rain-soaked, gray Alaskan sky.

I shrugged and said, "You got a better idea?"

"I suppose not," Stan said, shaking his head.

We walked down to the drop off point where Resurrection Creek emptied into Turnagain Arm and spotted the steamer approaching. I saw Captain Austin Lathrop, or Cap Lathrop as he was commonly known, at its helm. Cap had designed and built his steamer, the *LJ Perry*, to maneuver the sudden shallow waters of the Arm, according to the swift, shifting tides. He was an expert in predicting the tide schedule and was now coming in to tie-off along the embankment.

"Okay, boss, here we go," Stan said, as one of the ship's mates jumped off and tied up the steamer.

The first man that stepped from the boat looked young, only seventeen or eighteen years old, I presumed. He was a tall, brawny lad with shoulder-length brown hair and wide-spaced blue eyes that sparkled from the reflection of light off the water.

The moment he stepped from the boat and put his right foot upon the grassy embankment, he looked directly into my eyes, and smiled.

"What's your name, boy?" I said.

He paused for a moment, as if he wasn't sure how to answer, and said, "Percy."

"Percy." I nodded and asked, "What's your surname?"

"Um," he replied and paused again before answering, "Hope. My name's Percy Hope."

I clapped my hands together and turned to Stan and said, "Hope! That's the perfect name—Hope City, Alaska."

"And you are, sir?" Percy asked, extending his hand.

"I'm Magnus Vega."

"Magnus Vega?" he replied, sounding fearful in his tone.

"You've heard of me?"

"Yes, um, on the ship, your name was mentioned," Percy said, sounding convincingly nervous.

"Ah, you must have met my good friend, Mr. Whitmore. He likes to frighten the greenhorns about me. I hope you didn't agree to anything with him."

"We sort of did," he said, clumsily.

"Hi, my name is Liam," said another young man, stepping from the boat and introducing himself. "Percy and I are friends."

"Well, Liam and Percy, why don't you boys come with Stan and me. We'll see about finding you a place to stay and get you set up. I gather you're here to seek your fortunes."

"Oh, we're good, Mr. Vega, thank you," Percy said.

"Is that so?" I offered, with a touch of sarcasm. "Be careful who you make friends with. Survival in these parts can be a tricky thing if you're not connected to the right people."

The boys smiled, said their farewells, and headed into the newly named mining town of Hope City, Alaska.

CHAPTER ELEVEN—HOPE CITY

"That was Magnus Vega, the man Mr. Whitmore told us about," I said to Liam.

"He didn't look so bad," Liam replied, turning his head to look behind him.

"You're right, he didn't. Do you really think he was serious about naming the town after me?"

"Oh, you mean that made-up name of yours, Percy Hope?" he said, nearly singing the words. I stopped walking, pushed a strand of my rain-soaked hair off my face, reached out to squeeze Liam's forearm, and said under my breath, "Don't kid around with my name anymore. I doubt these people would appreciate my deception."

Liam nodded. "All right, I get it. But what if it's true and they plan to name this place Hope City?"

I shook my head. "He couldn't have been serious. Now let's do what Mr. Whitmore said, and find the Company offices, and report in."

My first glimpse of this mining town, whatever its name was, was one of a dirty, singular muddy-brown color, placed before a majestic backdrop of deep evergreen mountains, still covered along its peaks with snow, and encompassed by dark-gray, heavy rain clouds.

It took a moment to make out the scene through the heavy downpour. Every living thing: men, women, and a few dogs, oblivious to the weather, appeared to be covered in a glistening coat of mud.

Liam and I stood staring for a few silent moments, absorbing the stunning sight under the pouring rain. We were both drenched. Rain was running off the brim of my hat like a waterfall. My clothes were soaked through and through. I elbowed Liam to get his attention and cocked my head as a gesture for us to move on.

He nodded, and as I stepped from the grass into the silver, glistening mud, my right foot was swallowed into the muck up to the top of my boot. "Shit," I said and pulled my foot back, returning it to the firm earth. But as I did, my boot remained buried deep in the clay-like mud.

"I can't believe this," I said, and got down onto my hands and knees to reach into the mud-hole and pulled out my boot, that required greater force than I expected.

Shod once more, I stepped upon the previously unseen boards laid out as a walkway. This was no doubt an active town, made clear by the hustle and bustle of its residents making their way to and fro. No one paid Liam or I any mind, as we made our way along the wooden boards on what must have been Main Street, though there were no street signs that identified it.

Just as I was about to suggest that we ask for directions, Liam pointed and said, "There it is."

I followed the direction of his arm and saw the sign, swinging wildly in the sharp winds that read: THE ALASKA COMMERCIAL CORPORATION.

44

Fifteen minutes later, Liam and I exited back onto Main Street, with our grubstake financed by the Company. With that and the money provided by Father, I felt financially secure, at least for the time being.

They gave us a room to share at the Company's bunkhouse, which we found by being directed to take a left from Main Street onto B Street, and then a second right onto Second Street. Each road was just another river of mud, with boards laid out for the pedestrians.

Along the way, we passed the general store, which naturally caught my interest. I would make sure to peruse this establishment and include my findings in my first letter to Father.

When we reached the steps of the bunkhouse, it was apparent that it would not be much of an improvement over our steerage accommodations upon the *Bertha*. Similar to the rest of the wooden structures we passed by, this three-story building looked like its exterior cladding would barely survive another brutal Alaskan winter.

We entered through the front door into a large room littered with an assortment of pickaxes, shovels, pans, among other unfamiliar pieces of equipment that I assumed were for mining. This must have been the holding area for the prospectors residing here.

"Who are you?" a deep, resonating voice said surprising me.

I turned and saw emerging through a darkened hallway, a tall, shirtless, muscular man, towering over six feet in height with a bushy brown mustache.

"Hello, sir, the Company sent us here," Liam offered.

"You two just arrived off the *Bertha*?" he asked, looking down to the growing puddle of water encircling us.

I nodded. "Um, sorry about that," I said, gesturing to the mess we made. "My name is Percy Hope, and this is Liam Kampen."

"Don't worry about it," he said, gesturing to the floor. "My name's Rolf Carson. It's good to meet you boys," he said, extending his large hand.

We shook hands, and both Liam and I stood frozen in place, not sure what to say or do next.

Rolf took the initiative and said, "I'm the bunkhouse-boss. Come on, I'll show you boys to your room, and you'll probably want to get out of those wet clothes."

Liam pointed to the gear scattered on the floor, and asked, "Is there no mining today?"

Rolf shook his head. "Not on the sabbath. I trust you boys are Catholic and have no problem attending services?"

I glanced over to Liam, who was Catholic, while I was masquerading as one. "Yes, Mr. Carson we would attend services," I said, trying to sound convincing.

"How come you're not at church?" Liam asked.

I looked at Liam with wide-open eyed surprise at his bold question.

"I'm Asatru. I honor the Norse Gods," he said, pulling back his shoulders to stress his impressive physique. "We attend church on Sundays."

"You mean like Odin?" I asked.

"I'm impressed, Percy. These dimwits know nothing of this ancient belief."

I shrugged. "I didn't know there was a religion worshiping the Norse Gods."

"There is, albeit a small congregation of just me and a few others, we like to think of ourselves as Vikings."

"My family's from Norway," Liam blurted out.

"Ah, there you go, Liam. Perhaps you may want to join our small group?"

Liam shrugged. "I'm not sure, but I would like to learn more about it."

"We'll talk about this later. Come on now, follow me and I'll get you boys situated."

CHAPTER TWELVE—SUNRISE CITY

"You get those boys to lay more boards on the roads, Stan. I can't spend half a day traveling between Hope and Sunrise."

"I'll get on it right away."

The road from our newly named town of Hope, to the more established town of Sunrise, was normally a three to three-and-a-half-hour ride by wagon. But with the recent unrelenting rains, and consequential knee-deep mud, the horses took over five hours trudging their way through the muck. For commerce to prosper between these two towns, it required reliable roads.

With Stan on his way to manage the road repairs, I walked along the newly constructed, elevated wooden decks toward the Gold Digger Saloon. Tonight was our grand opening, and I wanted to make sure everything was in order for my new venture.

The town had grown to over eight-hundred people, enough to support a new drinking, gambling, and social establishment. Plus, with my business savvy, along with the prettiest whores in Alaska, I made a bet that the Gold Digger Saloon would soon be the most popular playground in Sunrise.

"Good day, boss," Suzie greeted me as I pushed my way through the swinging saloon doors.

"Well, good day to you, Suzie. You're looking lovely today," I said, walking over to the house madam, and placing a gentle kiss on her freshly blushed cheeks. "Are the girls ready? Tonight, will be a madhouse, and I don't want anyone with even a bit of gold-dust in their pockets leaving here disappointed."

"Don't you worry, boss. Their pockets, along with their seeds will be as empty as the love in Satan's heart."

I stopped and turned, surprised at Suzie's wit. "I like that," I said with a broad smile, "you're the clever one."

Suzie tilted her head, and offered me a smile—which never failed to stir my desire for her—and said, "Thank you, boss."

"Have you seen Henry?"

"Yea, he's in the stockroom, taking inventory on the whiskey," she said, pointing to the door in the back of the saloon.

I took a good look around. Everything appeared in order. A fresh layer of sawdust was being spread, coating the wooden floorboards, ready to soak up the frequent spills.

Things were working out well, especially now that we had names for both towns. In a way, they were like sisters. Hope was the good sister, with its residents insisting upon no liquor, gambling and definitely no whores. This was due to the influential pastor of the Catholic Church, Reverend O'Hara. It was he who governed the people, and it would be him who would need to christen the town Hope before its residents would accept it.

Then, on the other end of the spectrum, was Sunrise City, the bad sister. She had no religion, nor did she want one, as far as I was concerned. Life in Sunrise was a wild, unbridled ride, and with the opening of the Gold Digger Saloon, I would be its master, guiding its gold into my pockets.

"How's it going, Henry?" I asked, walking into the stockroom.

"Oh hey, boss," Henry said, rising from his crouching position where he was counting bottles.

"Have you checked on the still?"

"I was just there. All looks fine, but I hope we don't run out of corn."

"Don't worry about that," I said, flicking my wrist. "I'm expecting several crates to come off the *LJ Perry*. Cap should make a delivery sometime today."

"Then we should be set for a while."

"That's good to hear. I'll be back later. I have a few things to attend to back in Hope."

Henry looked up with one of his dumbass looks, and said, "Hope, what's that?"

"That's the name of the town, down the Arm. It's grown large enough to earn a name."

"Hope," Henry said, nodding. "I like it, sounds reassuring."

I nodded. "It does, doesn't it?"

On my way out I perused the new wooden tables arranged throughout the saloon floor and was reminded of the conversation I had last night with Scott Oppenheimer, the owner of the Sunrise Lumbermill who built them. He told me that Simon Wible, undoubtedly Sunrise's most successful miner, was introducing something revolutionary.

Mr. Oppenheimer rubbed the back of his neck and twisted his mouth while he thought. Then he wagged his finger and said, "That's right, he said it's called *hydraulic mining*."

When I questioned him further about it, Mr. Oppenheimer said that was all he knew. But this sounded like something I needed to find out more about from Mr. Wible.

Just as I swung the saloon doors open and took a step onto the front porch, I nearly tripped over the crates of corn stacked right in my way.

"What the fuck?" I shouted.

A head popped out from behind the crates. "Sorry about that, Mr. Vega."

"Oh hi, Cap, sorry about that. I didn't mean to yell at you."

"It's okay, I shouldn't have piled them right in front of the entrance," said Cap Lathrop, owner, and captain of the *LJ Perry*.

"Thanks for bringing this yourself. We can't make whiskey without it," I said, grabbing an ear from one of the crates.

"I hear that tonight's the big night?"

"Indeed. I hope you can make it, though you'll probably be busy running back and forth along the Arm shuttling my customers."

Cap nodded and removed his hat to push back his thick red hair. "Need to keep the transportation moving. You know that road is useless in this weather."

"It's knee-deep in mud and doesn't look like it will dry up anytime soon. But don't worry Cap, I'll keep you busy. The best way to get anywhere around here is by your steamer."

CHAPTER THIRTEEN—HOPE GENERAL STORE

Rolf showed us to our room, which was up at the peak of the three-story house, in the A-framed attic space.

"Sorry, this is all I have available for now," Rolf said, bent over because of the low-ceiling. "But don't worry, we have people packing up and leaving all the time. The life of a prospector sounds glorious to those in the Southlands, but once you get a true taste of what placer mining entails, many run back home to wherever they come from, and before you know it, you'll have a regular room just like the rest of us."

"Where do we sleep?" Liam asked.

"I'll get you a few blankets. You'll be fine," he said, and descended the wooden ladder back down to the third-floor landing. "Oh, I nearly forgot," he said, looking back up at our faces, peering down at him through the square hole in the ceiling, "Report to me tomorrow morning after breakfast, and I'll introduce you boys to the men at the Company office. There you'll get your equipment and your first lesson in placer mining."

We thanked Rolf, set down our valises, and I said to Liam, "So what do you say we change out of these wet clothes, and take a look around?"

Liam peered out through the dormer window. "Looks like the rain has let up. Yea, let's see what life is like in this town called Hope."

"You know what I've noticed, Percy?"

"What's that?" I said, trying to get used to my new name, while Liam did his best to try to remember to say it.

"Look around you," Liam said, gesturing to the people about town. "What do you notice about the men?"

The town was bustling with men, along with a scattering of women dressed in their church clothes. I took notice that the men wore suit jackets, with buttoned-up vests, and dress pants. Some even sported a pressed crease, and bowler style hats. "Is it the hats? They are all wearing hats?"

"That's true, but there's something else," Liam teased.

I shrugged, tired of Liam's game.

"It's the mustache. They all have one. Look!" he said, sweeping his arm across the vista on Main Street.

"So they do," I said, noticing the healthy growths of hair under nearly every man's nostrils.

"I want to grow one too," Liam said, placing a finger beneath his nose to imitate what one would look like.

"I've tried, and so have you, Liam. Maybe when we're older, we'll be able."

"I suppose you're right," he said, his voice trailing off.

"Hey," I said, pointing, "let's go check out the general store. Maybe we can pick up a few things."

Liam shrugged, and replied, "Sure, why not."

I was thirteen years old when I started working regularly at Father's store. My hours were after school, and on holidays when I had no classes. He taught me everything about running a general store. He would say our purpose was to always have the essential items in stock, so as to never disappoint our customers. Father created something he called a *want-book*, which was a notepad where we wrote down items customers asked for. They could be anything from an unusual food item like a tropical fruit, to a specialty such as a Cuban cigar. One time a good customer asked for an elixir that was said to cure rheumatism, and to my surprise, father was able to provide it.

One of Father's favorite amusements was to visit similar type of stores to Rothman's within our city. He called this a *busman's holiday*, which he said came from professional bus drivers who would take long bus rides on their vacation. He enjoyed taking me with him on his reconnaissance missions. He pointed out things we did better and noted the good ideas or places to improve upon.

The first thing I noticed when Liam and I entered the store was a large black, cast-iron wood stove, which of course was inactive this time of year. But I imagined what a mess it caused in wintertime, producing a perpetual layer of soot covering the merchandise, the shelves, and floorboards.

"What can I do for you boys?" said a middle-aged man, with a white beard in striking contrast to his jet-black hair.

I extended my hand and said, "My name's Percy Hope and this is Liam Kampen. We just arrived from San Francisco."

"Ah, it's good to meet you boys. My name's Russell Jones," he said, shaking our hands.

"My father owns Rothman's General Store in San Francisco. I used to work for him before Liam and I came to Alaska," I said.

"Rothmans?" he asked, with a dubious look. "I thought you said your name was Percy Hope."

I felt my face flush. "Um . . . well . . . that's because father purchased the business from Mr. Rothman years ago, and kept the store's name because the customers loved the man."

"I see. Smart decision," said Mr. Jones, nodding. "I would like to give my store a name too, but Jones' General Store sounds unimpressive. I thought of using the name of this town. But so far we haven't come up with one."

I looked over to Liam, and back to Mr. Jones with a smile. "Well, I don't know if this is true, but when we came onshore a few hours ago, we were greeted by two men. One was Mr. Vega who asked me my name, and when I told him it was Percy Hope, he said, 'that's it, we'll name our town Hope City.'"

Mr. Jones' forehead furrowed, and he asked, "Magnus Vega said that?"

Liam pointed his finger out the window as if to show where the naming event took place, and said, "He certainly did. Does that mean you'll call your place the Hope General Store?"

Mr. Jones stroked his beard and pursed his lips. "Perhaps I will," he replied and offered a huge smile.

CHAPTER FOURTEEN—THE GOLD DIGGER SALOON

It was nearly eight o'clock, and only a handful of men were playing cards. Suzie's dolls were all standing upright on the shelf behind the bar, and Henry was giving his whiskey glasses a last-minute polish.

Suzie had this idea of using girl dolls, one for each of the five hostesses, to let customers know which girls were available. When a girl was upstairs with one of the guests, the doll was laid down, showing she was working. Upon her return, the doll was stood upright again, indicating her immediate availability.

Worried about the whereabouts of my customers, I stepped out onto the front porch of the saloon and examined the wooden boards spread out onto the road, which allowed people to approach without stepping into boot-sucking mud. I pulled out a cigar and snipped off its end. I reached into my jacket pocket for my lighter, and just as I was about to flick it open, it jumped from my hand and landed on the porch boards, where it took a few bounces and fell off its edge.

"Shit!"

Just as I was about to step off the porch to retrieve it, a voice came from behind me and said, "Allow me, Mr. Vega."

I turned and saw Simon Wible. "Mr. Wible, good evening. Will you be joining us tonight for our grand opening?"

"That's why I'm here," he said, reaching down to pick up my lighter, and handing it to me.

"Excellent," I said, "why don't I introduce you to a few people who will make sure you're properly attended to."

Mr. Wible nodded, and we entered the saloon.

He looked around, placed his hands on his hips, and nodded. "Very impressive, Mr. Vega. You've spared no expense."

"Thank you, Mr. Wible. Make yourself at home. Drinks are on me and please allow Suzie to make sure your evening is most enjoyable."

Mr. Wible's eyes opened wide the moment he saw Suzie. She sauntered over, swaying her ample hips, and offering a smile that caused him to steady himself by grabbing hold of the back of a chair. It was at that moment I knew the man's weak spot, and I chuckled, knowing that I might need to exploit it at some point.

Much to my relief, not long after I finished with Mr. Wible, people started to arrive. It was as if some imaginary bell went off, signaling the grand opening of the Gold Digger Saloon. Within minutes, the tables were full of card players, the bar was lined up with shot glasses of whiskey, and Cameron, our piano player, was banging out the popular tune, *Honey On My Lips*.

Even though Sunrise was more established than the recently named Hope, it was still a young town. It had only been two years since the first prospectors arrived. But in that time, a city was raised out of the wilderness.

As for myself, I came to Sunrise a year ago. I heard about the gold discovery while still in Dawson City, working at the Miller House. It was the largest hotel and casino in the Klondike. Its owner, Thomas Miller, was a dynamic, enterprising man. Although he taught me the intricacies of the hotel, gambling, and whoring business, he was a straight shooter who never partook in any of his offerings. "Stay away from the tables, booze and harlots, otherwise you'll end up like them bums, begging for handouts down by the wharf," he warned me. A lesson that I took to heart, even to this day.

Mr. Miller operated his gambling business more like a real estate venture. He set up various gambling areas in his hotel and rented them out for outrageous sums. In a large room downstairs from the main floor, he provided three tables for faro, two tables for monte, and one for a roulette wheel. For exclusive control of this room, which offered sporting men an opportunity to run their own games, he charged ten-thousand dollars a month. Smaller rooms went for thirty-five hundred per month.

There was a celebrated man, appropriately named Jack Gamble, who leased the entire second floor for the season for sixty-thousand dollars. Just before I left for Sunrise, I heard that the Miller House had, on any given day, over a half-million dollars stacked upon its gaming tables.

But with all of that, the most valuable lesson I learned by working there was the beauty of the whiskey business. Mr. Miller set up a whiskey still in the basement of his hotel, which substantially reduced his costs. He also sold his brew to the other saloons in Dawson City, and if anyone tried to compete with him by building their own stills, Mr. Miller used his army of goons to destroy their facility and pummeled anyone involved in its production.

Later that night, with the last few drunkards stumbling out onto the street, I stood out on the front porch, smoking a cigar. I was surprised to feel a soft hand caressing the back of my neck. I quickly turned and saw Suzie.

"Did I frighten you?"

"No, I didn't hear you coming."

"It seemed like it was a good night," she said, standing alongside me, looking out onto the desolate street.

"You can't always expect large crowds to mean a good night. It all comes down to the winnings for the house, and tonight, there weren't many high-rollers. But they'll come."

"The girls had customers, but I guess they could have done more. But come on, Magnus," she said, putting both hands around my neck, and pulling me in so close that I smelled cigar smoke on her dress, "it's only the first night."

I exhaled and gently pushed her away. "Listen, I need to get some sleep, tomorrow the Company is training a new crew, and I want to see if I can pick up a few recruits."

"Are you still short of men?"

"I'm always looking for muscle. It's the second-best way to motivate people."

"Let me guess what's first," she said, leaning forward and pushing her cleavage into my face.

"No, it's not your tits, though they are great. The best way to get anything done around here is with gold, baby, just gold."

CHAPTER FIFTEEN—RESURRECTION CREEK

We stood along the banks of Resurrection Creek, a narrow, winding, fast-moving river that emptied into Turnagain Arm. Our Company instructor, Hank Stanton, had issued each of us a pan, a handheld pickax, a full-size one, and a shovel. Our small class included myself and Liam, along with two other men, who barely spoke English, and were muttering between themselves, trying to understand Mr. Stanton's instructions.

"Gold panning is a simple, but slow process. You need patience, and determination to succeed," he said, removing his hat, and running his fingers through his long, unkempt hair.

He pointed to the bend in the river and said, "We look for an area where the sediment is placed by the river. We call this a placer deposit."

Mr. Stanton, holding a canvas bag over his shoulder, gave us a nod, showing we should follow him through the shallow part of the river to the spot. He removed a pickax from the bag and used it to loosen the gravel and soil from the riverbed. Mr. Stanton then grabbed a shovel and scooped out a small amount and emptied it into his metal pan.

"Now, let's add some water, swirl and shake," he said, showing the technique. "Gold is heavy, and will sink to the bottom of the pan, with a little encouragement."

What I saw looked easy. If this was all it took to find gold, it wouldn't take us long to make our fortunes, and head back home, by summer's end.

"What you're looking for is *color*," he said, manipulating the remaining dark, small remnants in the bottom of the pan. "Ah, what have we here?" he said, pushing away some gravel and black sand.

We all edged in closer for a look.

"I'll be dammed," he said, wide-eyed, and pulled out, between two fingers, a small nugget of gold.

I looked over to Liam, whose jaw was open so wide, I was sure one of the hundreds of mosquitoes feasting upon us would fly down his throat.

Mr. Stanton passed the nugget to me. I felt its dense weight, even though it was only about a quarter of the size of the fingernail on my pinky. I passed it to Liam, who put it in between his upper and lower set of back teeth and bit down.

The two foreign-born men, whose language was unfamiliar to me, examined the nugget among themselves, before passing it back to Mr. Stanton.

"We call this," he said, gesturing to the waterway, "Resurrection Creek. It's been estimated that over thirty-thousand ounces of gold have been discovered here so far. With the price of gold about twenty dollars per troy ounce, that's over six-hundred thousand dollars pulled out of the creek."

To say that I wasn't excited at hearing these words would have been a lie. I came to Alaska to seek my fortune, but I didn't think it would be so easy, especially after hearing the tales of the poor souls trying to make their way to the Klondike. So many died just trying to get there, and here was Mr. Stanton, within just a few minutes of panning, discovering a one-ounce nugget.

"But you men won't be panning much. With the strength of the rivers, you'll be more productive working the sluice boxes."

"What's a sluice box?" Liam whispered in my ear.

"Well, if it isn't the town's namesake, Percy Hope and his buddy Liam Kampen. Did my friend Hank Stanton fool you boys?" a voice came from behind us.

I turned and saw two men sitting high upon their horses. It was Mr. Vega and Mr. Smith.

"Why don't you mind your own business, Magnus?" Mr. Stanton shot back.

"Nonsense," Mr. Vega said, dismounting his horse. "You boys are being scammed, as he does to all the new recruits. Hank here deftly slips a nugget into the pan, and voila, to everyone's surprise, he's discovered gold."

I, along with Liam and the two foreigners, looked over to Mr. Stanton.

"Get the hell away from us, Magnus, before I—"

"Before you what?" he interrupted before Mr. Stanton could finish his threat.

Mr. Stanton grabbed the pickax and shovel and gestured for us to follow him. "Come on, I'll get you men situated upstream at the sluice boxes."

"Just one minute," Mr. Vega said, holding up his palm, and looking at me and Liam. "Any of you men interested in working for me? I'm paying twenty dollars a week."

"You pay prospectors twenty dollars a week?" Liam asked.

"No, of course not," Magnus said, shaking his head. "What I need done involves particular assignments for strong and capable, young men."

"Can you explain what these 'assignments' are, Mr. Vega?" I asked with my hands on my hips.

He removed his hat, ran his fingers through his hair, and said, "Let's just say, Percy, my interests are making sure things run smoothly along the Arm, and I need strong, young men like you and your friend to ensure they do."

"What do you think?" Liam whispered.

"I don't know, it sounds shady to me," I murmured. "Plus, we signed an agreement with the company."

"It's only for a few days, and we'll be paid twenty dollars. That's nothing to sneeze at."

"I'll tell you now," Mr. Stanton interrupted, "if any of you go with Mr. Vega, don't bother coming back."

I remembered Mr. Whitmore's words onboard the *Bertha*, that Magnus Vega was the cruelest man he had ever known, and for the first time since meeting him, I had a sense Mr. Whitmore was right. I looked over to Liam and said, "We're in no position to take chances. I'm staying put."

Liam exhaled, obviously distressed. "All right, Percy, I'll pass too."

The other two foreigners knew enough English to understand that earning twenty dollars each for a week's work was a good deal. They offered their farewells to Mr. Stanton and went off with Mr. Vega and Mr. Smith.

"You boys made the right decision," said Mr. Stanton, as we headed back to the Company mining storehouse. "After lunch, I'll get you set up on the sluice box upstream. But what was Magnus saying about your name?"

I shrugged and said, "Since I was the first person who stepped onto the shore, he said that he would name the town after me."

"He can't do that, can he?" asked Liam.

"It seems that Magnus Vega has taken control of the entire shoreline along Turnagain Arm. So, if he wants to call this mishmash of people and buildings Hope, I suppose he can. Congratulations, Percy."

I didn't know what to say except, "Thank you," and wondered what my father would think now of his great idea of changing my name, which was intended specifically to help me blend in, rather than to bring attention to myself.

Mr. Stanton, Liam and I sat down upon a log left behind by the carpenters building a nearby cabin to eat our lunch provided by the Company. "Excuse me, Mr. Stanton," I said, holding some sort of beef-filled sandwich. "Did you slip that nugget into the pan, like Mr. Vega claimed?"

Mr. Stanton smiled and patted my knee. "You know what they say, Percy—second-hand gold is as good as new," he said, and reached into his pocket and pulled out the nugget and handed it to me.

I rubbed the nugget between my two fingers, and thought about Mr. Stanton's attempt to deceive us. Perhaps Magnus Vega wasn't the only dubious fellow we should be leery of. I smiled and passed the nugget back to Mr. Stanton.

He waved me off. "You boys keep it; consider it your good-luck charm. But remember this," he said holding up a finger, "lady luck never gives, she only lends."

CHAPTER SIXTEEN—ELLA CARSON

It was obvious that when the creeks ran strong, the sluice-box, with its long, sloping trough, and grooves in the bottom, into which water from the creek was directed, pushing the gold to separate from the gravel, would be far more efficient than the pan.

But it also required back-breaking work—feeding the boxes with buckets of gravel, picked loose with our long axes from the riverbeds and along the embankments.

When Liam and I finally finished for the day, with nothing to show for our efforts, except for a few open blisters, sore backs, and a litany of doubts about Mr. Stanton's so-called expertise, we hobbled into the chow hall on Main Street. Like this formally no-named town, the chow hall was merely a description of its purpose, rather than its business name.

We stood in line holding a wooden bowl, given to us after we paid our thirty-five cents for the meal. The men in front of us looked like I felt, exhausted and worn out. Though I shouldn't complain, considering this was our first day, and many of the men looked like they'd been working the creeks for months, if not years.

"What kind of slop do you think they're serving?" Liam asked, as men shuffled by on their way to the community tables, clutching bowls filled with something that made the meals on the boat look gourmet in comparison.

I puckered my face, and said, "Who would pay for this?"

"Would you like your money back?" a mysterious female voice challenged me.

I tilted my head to look through the few men standing in line in front of us chatting away, waiting to be served. She was like a singular blossoming sunflower among a desolate, dreary landscape—a tall, young woman with long blonde hair, and sparkling blue eyes, that pierced a beeline into mine. Her beauty left me stunned, unable to answer her question.

Moments later, Liam and I were standing before her.

"Well, what's it going to be, boys? Do you want your food, or would you prefer your money back?" she asked, holding out a ladle, with sloppy clumps of the concoction falling off its edge, and plopping back into a large simmering pot.

"Sorry," I said, trying to offer my apology without stammering, "it just looks like the food we ate on the boat. We only arrived yesterday. But yes, we would like to try it."

"What's your name?" she said, filling my bowl.

"I'm Percy, and this is Liam."

Liam stuck his nose into his serving and nodded. "It smells better than it looks." He dipped his wooden spoon and tasted what clung to it. "Well, I'll be; that's damn good."

"Of course, it is," she said, with a glowing smile. "My name's Ella Carson. It's good to meet you boys. Why don't you take a seat," she said, gesturing to the wooden tables and benches lined up, "and I'll join you in a minute."

"Ella Carson? Any relation to Rolf Carson?" I asked.

"Rolf's my brother. Now go eat, I'll be over soon."

"She's beautiful," I whispered to Liam.

"Forget about her, Percy. She'll never go out with guys like us."

"Why the hell not?" I demanded.

Liam lifted his hands and flipped open his palms. "Just look at her, and look at us. She'll be interested in one of those men who strike it rich. Why do you think she's here, in this shit hole?"

"Hey, don't call Hope a shit hole, and you don't know why she's here. Maybe she came with her brother for another reason. Let's ask her, here she comes."

I couldn't help but stare at her as she sauntered over. She swayed, liked the willow tree branches in my parents' backyard, when the summer breeze blew in its cool breath off the Pacific coast. Her mesmerizing approach was abruptly shattered by her body being violently jerked out of my field of view. I quickly got to my feet, and saw an older man with a bushy mustache, grabbing Ella's wrist.

"Come, sweetie, and give ol' Mack a kiss," he said, pushing his craggy-face close to hers.

"Let go of me, Mack," Ella said, trying to break away from the belligerent man's iron grip.

My first reaction was to defend Ella. I stood up and approached. The man appeared to be at least twenty years older than me, and about thirty pounds heavier, even though we were the same height. I took my boxing stance, and demanded with a stern voice, "Let go of her now!"

The tables, filled with at least twenty men, and a few more on the chow line, ceased their conversations, and turned to the disturbance in the middle of the dining hall.

Mack released his grip on Ella and stood before me dumbstruck. "Well, well, what do we have here?"

"You are not to touch her again," I said, wondering if my thumping heartbeat was as audible as it felt.

"What the fuck are you going to do about it?" he asked, laughing and turning to enjoin his cohorts in supporting him.

"I'm not afraid of you," I snarled.

"Percy, what are you doing?" Ella implored.

I noticed Liam's presence alongside me, knowing he would come to my defense if needed. I rolled my shoulders, trying to loosen the muscles in my back, as I felt them tightening up. Then it happened. Mack lunged at me, his fists whirling in a windmill motion.

I blocked his first assault and stood my ground, waiting for his next attempt. Mack was breathing heavily, and his eyes were bulging in anger. He would attack again, and he did.

Mack threw a wild punch that I blocked. His momentum caused him to stumble, allowing me to connect with a left jab into the side of his face.

This knocked him down to the floor, his head settling under one of the long wooden benches.

He lay there a moment, while I stood over him, hoping that this was the end. Unfortunately, he pushed himself back up to his knees. I reached over to grab his arm and helped him back to his feet. Either he would fight back, rejecting my helping hand, or give in knowing I defeated him. Luckily, he chose the latter.

I gave the room a good look about, just in case someone wanted to defend Mack. But no one did. In fact, a few of the men slapped me on the back, one telling me, "Nice boxing kid."

After Mack stumbled out of the chow hall, I sat back down with Liam. I took a gulp of water and smiled at my friend. He reached across the table and patted my arm. From behind me, two gentle hands squeezed my shoulder, followed by soft lips kissing my cheek. I turned and saw Ella.

"Thank you for defending me, Percy. But that wasn't too smart. You don't know these men like I do. They don't enjoy being humiliated," she said, taking a seat next to me.

"Perhaps, but I couldn't let him hurt a woman. It's not right."

"Tell me about yourselves. Where are you boys—," but before she could finish her question, a loud, boisterous voice interrupted, "Where's Percy Hope?"

I turned around and saw Mr. Vega standing with one hand on his hip and the other pointing at me. "There you are. Come with me, Percy, we're

73

having an official naming ceremony for our new town—Hope City. What better way to celebrate, then to have its namesake at the announcement?"

I looked at Ella, who said wide-eyed, "Well, Percy Hope, it looks like you will be the talk of the town."

CHAPTER SEVENTEEN—THE ANNOUNCEMENT

The front porch of Mr. Jones' General Store was decorated with red, white, and blue bunting. A trio of musicians was set up to one side, playing some dandy tune that had its intended effect of gathering the townspeople to the front of the store.

Liam, Ella, and I stood among the assembly. I felt a hand squeeze my shoulder, and I turned to see Rolf.

"I see you boys met my sister."

I nodded. "Yes, in the chow hall."

Ella's eyes opened wide, and she said, "You should have seen Percy defend me against that drunkard Mack Burns. He knocked him to the ground with one punch."

"Is that so, Percy? Where did you learn how to box?"

"My father sent me to a boxing club in the city."

"I'm impressed," Rolf said. "That's a skill that's useful in these parts."

Then, as if on cue, the music stopped, and out from the double doors appeared Mr. Jones, the proprietor of the general store, along with Mr. Vega, who held out his hands to silence the rather large crowd, now huddled six deep, along the railing of the store's front porch.

"Ladies and gentlemen," he began, "just yesterday morning, two young men sailed here on the Bertha, from San Francisco. I was on the banks of Resurrection Creek to greet them as they disembarked. But just moments before they stepped ashore, I said to my head of security, Stan Smith, that the next person who places a foot into our humble community, will have our nameless town named after him."

A stir of conversations washed across the crowd. Mr. Vega held up his hands, and like a conductor bringing an orchestra to attention, instantly silenced them.

"Before I announce the name of our city for the first time, let me introduce the young man who will be, as long as people live upon this rocky shoreline, immortalized as its namesake."

He waved at me, summoning me to the porch. I felt hands gently pushing me forward. I looked over to Liam, who was jerking his head, encouraging me to go. Thoughts of my real name eventually being exposed flooded my mind. For some reason, I feared that this wouldn't end well, but regardless, I allowed the moment to move me up the steps and onto the porch, in between Mr. Vega and Mr. Jones.

Mr. Vega wrapped an arm around me, and pulled me in close to him, and said, "Ladies and Gentlemen, allow me to introduce Percy Hope to the people of Hope City, Alaska."

Thunderous applause and cheers erupted. I tried to smile, but nothing seemed natural.

Things were happening to me that were beyond my control. But at this point, only Liam and I knew it was a charade, and I feared that the longer it carried on, the worse the outcome would be. Lying in general was simply not in my nature, as I always believed that playing tricks with the truth never ended well.

After twenty minutes of shaking hands, and thanking people for something I had nothing to do with, Mr. Jones approached me, and said, "Well, Percy, how would you like a job working evenings, at the Hope General Store? You're a celebrity now, plus you have experience in the business. I'll pay you fifty cents per hour. That's top wage in these parts."

I nodded, and said, "That's a generous offer, Mr. Jones, but please allow me a few days to consider it. After all, I just got here yesterday."

He said he understood and suggested that I visit with him in a few days and let him know my plans. But I had to admit, there was something comforting about working in a place where I knew my way around, unlike prospecting, which was mysterious, unpredictable and physically exhausting.

I found my way back to the chow hall, where Liam, Ella, and Rolf were waiting for me. As I entered, Liam was in the middle of one of his orations of the wonders of cooking with a cast-iron skillet.

"The key is never to wash it with soap," he said.

"You cook with a dirty skillet?" Rolf asked.

Liam nodded. "In a way, yes. While it's still warm, I scrub it with a mixture of salt and cooking oil, then I wipe it clean, and rub it again with a touch more oil. Plus, the next time I use it, I burn off any remaining residue before I start cooking again. My dirty skillet, along with good ingredients, is all I need to dazzle."

"He's a great cook," I said, supporting Liam.

"Perhaps you can show me a few things?" Ella asked, showing more interest in Liam than I liked.

"I brought my own well-seasoned skillet from home." Liam jumped to his feet and took a step toward the front door.

"Not now, Liam. It's getting too late to cook, plus I've already cleaned up the kitchen. But we'll do something soon," Ella said.

Rolf stood up, stretched his muscular arms, and said, "I think I'll turn in for the night. You boys ready?"

I nodded, and gingerly touched the still raw blisters on my hands, and said, "I'm exhausted, and tomorrow Mr. Stanton is sending us back up the creek to work the sluice boxes again."

"You boys should wear gloves," Rolf commented, noticing the trouble with my hands. "Mr. Stanton likes his students to feel the sting the first few days out. Come on, I'll find you boys gloves for tomorrow."

I turned to Ella, smiled, and said, "Good night."

She responded with a tilt of her head, and coyly said, "Good night, Percy Hope."

Liam stepped in between us and added, "Good night, Ella."

"Good night, Liam," she replied, with a disarming, dimple-laden smile.

CHAPTER EIGHTEEN—MAGNUS DISRUPTS

"Go ahead, Patrick, tell Mr. Vega what you saw," Stan said to Patrick Kelly, one of my guys who I sent to observe Mr. Wible's on-site demonstration of the new hydraulic mining equipment.

Even though I'd seen Patrick dozens of times before, I couldn't help but cringe each time I glimpsed into his mouthful of rotten teeth, all because of the scurvy. It had frightened me enough into paying an exorbitant sum for deliveries of California oranges shipped to me each month.

"Come, Patrick, sit down and tell me what you saw," I said, gesturing to the chairs in front of my desk, and added, "Close the door, Stan."

Patrick scratched at his beard, leaned in, and rested his elbows on his knees. "It's remarkable, boss. Mr. Wible took us up onto the other side of Sixmile Creek, where he showed us a run of iron pipes that directed water into a hose made of something he called crinoline." As he said this, he looked at me quizzically hoping I understood. I nodded and told him to continue.

"On the end of the hose was a large nozzle, supported by a metal frame that allowed a man to direct it like a cannon. But instead of shooting a cannonball, it shot a high-powered stream of water through its nozzle onto the face of the embankment."

He scratched at his beard as if it helped him recall the events, and said, "In just a few minutes the hillside disintegrated right before my eyes. It just washed away the gravel and dirt, and I swear even some boulders rolled down the embankment. The runoff was directed downstream through something they called a settling-trough. Mr. Wible said that hydraulic mining would be the cheapest method of recovering gold by reducing his labor costs, and I'm no businessman, Mr. Vega, but I'm thinkin' he's right."

I nodded in agreement, and said, "I think so too, Patrick."

Patrick offered me his broadest toothless smile.

I rubbed my lips with the tips of my fingers, thinking of the fortune to be made controlling the hydraulic mining equipment sales in Sunrise and in Hope. "Thank you, Patrick," I said, flipping him a nugget for his efforts.

He snatched it out of the air, like a dog going for a treat, and smiled. "Thank you, boss," he said, still seated.

"You can go now, Patrick."

He rose, put on his hat, and exited my office, closing the door behind him.

"It looks like Mr. Wible will blast his way to riches," said Stan.

I rose from my chair and looked out through my window on to the frenetic activity on Front Street. "We need to find out where he's getting these hydraulic pipes, hoses, and fittings from."

"What do you have in mind?" Stan asked.

"I think I need to have a chat with Cap and see what he knows about these goods being shipped in."

I tried most afternoons to stroll along the water's edge of Sixmile Creek to clear my head. I enjoyed watching the men panning, shoveling, and washing gravel through wooden sluice boxes, hoping for that lucky break where one's life would change forever. Yet, at the same time, I scoffed at their desperate attempts at hitting the jackpot; I knew my time was better spent focusing on my reliably profitable business enterprises.

I was greeted warmly, and with deference, from those who knew me. After all, I controlled nearly all the whiskey production in Sunrise, and these men loved their whiskey. It was true that they also loved their whiskey in Hope, but Reverend O'Hara had declared their parish as dry. Meaning that if you wanted to drink, you had to find your way to Sunrise. Most could do this; the problem was getting those drunkards back home.

Perhaps now, with the town having an official name, I could convince people, for the sake of their economic wellbeing, that Hope should permit the opening of a drinking and gambling establishment. But changing people's minds would be challenging, especially with the reverend's influence.

In order to overrule the reverend, there would need to be a vocal majority, led by a popular local figure, and for sure, that person couldn't be me, since it would smell of self-serving.

Nearby, I watched a few youthful men panning, and it reminded me of Percy. Then it occurred to me that Percy Hope would be the perfect face to organize such an effort; after all, he was the talk of the town, thanks to me. However, I imagined it would take considerable convincing to persuade him to use his wholesome, good-boy image to be my representative, and perhaps even my business partner, in Hope City.

CHAPTER NINETEEN—GOING TO CHURCH

We could have blocked the sunlight streaming through the south-facing dormer windows with boards that Rolf had brought up, but that had the effect of heating the attic space into a sweltering inferno. Instead, for the sake of ventilation, we forced ourselves to get used to the Alaskan summer nights, where the sun-set briefly for a few hours.

Falling asleep was not a problem, as we were exhausted from our days of picking, digging, and shoveling, and by the time we finished bathing in the wooden bathtubs set up in the backyard, we quickly passed out.

But as much as we tried, when the morning came, both Liam and I struggled to stay asleep, and consequently we were the early risers in the house. This was normally fine, since we could eat breakfast at the chow hall, and see Ella before our laborious day began. So far, I couldn't tell who she favored more, Liam or me. Though I had to admit, Liam's cooking skills offered him more opportunities to connect with her.

But today was Saturday, and we had the day off. Sleeping late would have been a luxury, but the sun and church had other plans.

Liam and I dressed, and climbed down the attic ladder to the top floor, trying to be light on our feet, so as not to wake up the non-religious prospectors happily snoring away. We took the stairs to the ground floor, and just as I turned the front door lever to exit, a voice spoke to us.

"Where you boys off to?"

I turned and saw Rolf standing there, wearing a brown cotton shirt and gray linen pants pulled tight around his waist.

"Good morning, Rolf. We're going for breakfast, then to church. Would you like to join us?" I said.

"I'll join you for breakfast, but I told you I'm not Catholic. I'll be going to services tomorrow at my church."

"Oh yeah, I remember. You follow the Viking Gods, like Odin and Thor," Liam said, noticeably excited.

"Let's go outside and talk, so we don't wake anyone up," he said, gesturing to the door.

Once we were on our way to the chow hall on Main Street, Liam asked Rolf, "What's the name of your religion again?"

"Asatru. Long before Christianity, our ancestors, the Norsemen, practiced Asatru. The word translates into *belief in the Gods,* which means we believe in many deities—a difference from your religion. Also, unlike Christianity, we do not accept the idea of *original sin*, which is the notion we're all tainted from birth, and therefore as Asatrus, we don't need saving."

"Okay," Liam interjected, "but what Gods do you pray to?"

Rolf put his hand around Liam's shoulder and said, "Why don't you come and see tomorrow? You'll be my guest."

84

"I think I will," Liam said.

While they were talking, I was secretly wishing that I could join them. The last thing I wanted, considering I was raised as a Jew, was to go to a Catholic Church. But the Company expected its newcomers to attend religious services, and I had already presented myself as Percy Hope, an observant Catholic.

I noticed Ella as soon as the chow hall came into view. Her long golden hair, was freshly brushed and glittered in the sunlight. She stood on the front porch conversing with a man sporting a priest's collar.

"Good morning, Ella," I said, interrupting their conversation.

"Oh, Percy, let me introduce you to Reverend O'Hara."

I extended my hand. "It's nice to meet you, Reverend."

"Are you the Percy Hope the entire town is talking about?" he asked, shaking my hand with vigor.

I nodded, feeling my face blush.

"Excellent, Percy. I hope you'll be joining us for morning services. I'd love to introduce you to our congregation," he said and turned to Ella. "Wouldn't that be nice?"

"Yes, Reverend, that would be wonderful."

"Ella, you don't go to the Asatru church with your brother?" I asked.

"Oh no, Percy. I'm Catholic," she said, and leaned in to whisper into my ear, "not a heathen."

"I heard that," Rolf said.

"Well, it's true. The thing you call a religion is a farce. You should be ashamed."

The reverend held up his hands, and said, "Let's not argue about the merits of one's personal religion, even if it is rather unusual."

Rolf offered his farewell, and Ella, the reverend, Liam, and I walked down Main Street to the church. Along the way, people recognized me, and called out my name.

"You're famous, Percy," said Ella.

I offered an awkward smile to the townspeople, who had now grown into a good size group, and were following behind us through the church's front doors. I didn't mind being the center of attention, especially since it impressed Ella. But I wished it had been for something well deserved, not the lie I was perpetrating.

When we entered the unmarked building, I realized that this structure was not only for praying, but more of an all-purpose space. There were no crosses, or other religious artifacts to identify it as a Catholic church. A hodgepodge of unmatched chairs and benches were arranged facing toward a wooden table where I assumed the reverend would be conducting his service.

Reverend O'Hara gestured to Ella, Liam, and me to take our seats in the front row. I glanced behind me, and it was obvious that I was the talk of the town. Men and women were chatting among themselves, while pointing and gawking at me, as if I were a visitor from another planet.

When I turned back around to face front, the reverend was standing a few feet away from me. In the short time it took for me to peruse the congregation, he had donned a long, white robe, with a large, gold cross hanging from a gold chain around his neck. He stood serenely, his eyes closed, and his hands pressed together in prayer position.

His austere presence silenced the worshippers. I rubbed the back of my neck and squirmed a bit at the stillness. Finally, he opened his eyes, smiled and looked at me. I fidgeted some more. He flicked his fingers, summoning me to stand by his side. I looked over at Ella, who was nodding, offering her encouragement to join him.

I rose and stood next to the reverend, who was several inches taller, and probably thirty or forty pounds heavier than me. He wrapped his beefy arm around me and pulled me in tight. I looked out onto the congregation, which looked to be at least forty to fifty people in attendance. I saw Mr. Jones, the owner of the newly named Hope General Store, who was smiling like a proud father whose son was about to receive some award.

"This young man, whom some of you may already know," the reverend began, "has come to us from the great city of San Francisco, for the same reason most of you have trekked tremendous distances. But his life took a sudden turn the moment he stepped off the Bertha and onto our shore."

A murmur of conversation washed across the assembly.

"This young man," the reverend said, raising his voice, to overcome the incessant chatter, "was selected, albeit by a most dishonorable individual, to provide a name to our young city." He released his arm and turned to face me. "You, Percy Hope, have been brought to our community, not by chance. For it's apparent that the Almighty has sent you to us for a purpose."

The reverend's provocative words caused the parishioners to become restless. I rubbed the back of my neck, wondering, *Where is he going with this?*

He looked out to the dozens of faces staring back, and said, "Is it not true that we all share a desire to obtain goodness in our lives?"

Heads nodded in agreement.

"And that goodness we seek is something we have yet to possess. It hangs out there, just beyond our reach," the reverend said, stretching and grasping at some imaginary object in front of him.

"But in the end, it all comes down to the choices we make in our lives. The good choices fulfill our desires, while the bad ones set us adrift, aimlessly into a sea of despair . . ." he paused, waving his outstretched arm, emulating the rippling waters.

"But what can we reach for from the toolbox of our lives, to help us make the right choices, so we can attain this goodness?"

Mr. Jones stood up and pointed at me and shouted, "We reach for hope."

The congregation was now openly talking among themselves, no longer trying to subdue their excitement. I twisted in my seat to gawk at Mr. Jones.

The reverend held up his arms and waited for the hullabaloo to quiet. Then he began again, "Mr. Jones is one-hundred percent correct. Hope is the fuel that powers our journey of attaining the goodness we seek."

People were now rising from the seats and moving forward toward me. The chairs and benches were being shoved aside. Within moments, they surrounded me. Hands were reaching out, desperately grasping for a momentary touch.

I jumped to my feet, and tried to back away from the congregation swarming me. But there was no escape, I clenched my teeth, and held out my arms.

The reverend lifted his arms into the air and proclaimed, "Our Church of Hope is grateful to our Lord and Savior, for delivering this young man into our lives."

Suddenly I felt a hand clasp onto my wrist and pull me through the throng. Once we broke free of the pack, I saw it was Ella. She led me outside onto the street.

I rubbed the back of my neck, and said with a gasp, "What in the world just happened in there?"

Ella shook her head. "I think Reverend O'Hara has turned you into a religious symbol."

I wagged a finger at her, and said, "Let's face it, Ella. The only reason people come to this place is to strike it rich. Your reverend may have had the intention of elevating me as some sort of holy messenger, but to these people, I think I've become their lucky charm."

Then I thought about what Mr. Stanton had said, 'Lady luck never gives, she only lends,' and wondered if there would be a price to pay for being that lucky first person to step onto these shores of the newly named Hope City.

CHAPTER TWENTY—MAGNUS AT WORK

There was no doubt that the people of Hope embraced its name. On my way, I passed the newly named Church of Hope, the Hope General Store, the Hope Post Office, and the Hope Café—which was my destination.

Before I dismounted my horse, I stopped in front of the café and looked around from the elevated vantage point. There was certainly commerce in this town, but unlike Sunrise, I was not getting my fair share. The Alaska Commercial Company had its grip on the grubstake business, which from my perspective didn't offer a great return on investment. The Company took care of its prospectors by providing free housing, lunch, mining instruction, and equipment, as part of its grubstake deal. But even with their seventy-five percent take, I couldn't see it as a worthy risk for the exorbitant amount of expenses it incurred. It was nothing like the high margins of whiskey, whores, and cards, along with getting a piece of the action from certain local profitable businesses.

I dismounted, tied my horse up to the hitching post, and entered. The café was empty. I took a table near the window, with a nice view of Resurrection Creek. As usual, the creek was populated with dozens of souls, desperately panning for their next meal.

There was no doubt that both the people of Hope and Sunrise fell into two categories, those who struck it rich, which I could count on my two hands, and still have a few fingers left over, and everyone else—which was now approaching nearly a thousand.

Among the second group, there were the desperate ones. Those who had abandoned their dreams of discovering gold altogether, and resigned themselves to working for wages at one of the local businesses. At least they could provide for themselves, while those too proud, too stupid, or too stubborn, stuck to a belief that their next pan would find the nugget that would change their lives forever. These pitiful souls, while they desperately struggled for that momentous discovery, lived in makeshift tents along the creek, competing with the bears for food scraps from the town's garbage dump.

"What can I get for you, Mr. Vega?" asked Ella, with a pad and pencil in her lovely hands.

If I hadn't been so busy with my ladies in Sunrise, I would have pursued Ella romantically, though I doubted as a teenage girl she would had shown any interest in dating a man at least fifteen years her senior.

"Good afternoon, Ella, and as I told you dozens of times, please call me Magnus."

"All right, Magnus. What can I get for you?"

"I see you gave your establishment a name. The Hope Café—I like it."

"Thank you," she said, with a hint of coldness in her voice. It was obvious she held a level of disdain towards me, which was not surprising, as I was a legitimate threat to any business I found to be lucrative.

"Have you heard about my new place in Sunrise, the Gold Digger Saloon?"

She nodded. "I've heard about it."

"We've been open a week. Why don't you and your friends stop by? I'll be happy to buy you a drink."

"I don't drink, but thank you for the offer."

I looked around at the empty tables. "How's business?"

She shrugged. "It's early; the prospectors usually start coming in after six."

I leaned forward, resting my elbows on the table, and said, "I hear that Percy Hope eats here frequently."

She nodded. "Yes, Percy likes my beef and potato stew."

"Sounds perfect, I'll have the same."

"It comes with sourdough bread, is that all right?"

"Sure," I said with a smile, as she turned away and sauntered back into the kitchen.

It was at the beginning of last summer when Ella and her brother Rolf arrived. They had stepped onto Front Street in Sunrise for the first time when I approached them. I immediately thought they were worthy recruits for one of my enterprises.

Rolf was tall and muscular, and no doubt would have served me well as part of my security team. But Ella was the real gem. Any man would have given up their last bit of gold dust for ten minutes with her. But they thanked me for my offers, though I knew it wasn't sincere, and had since found their own ways.

Ella eventually met Reverend O'Hara and was quickly gone from Sunrise. Her brother went with her and I believe he was there mostly to protect his lovely sister from people like me. Even though Ella was the one with the smarts and did all right watching out for herself.

"Here you go," Ella said, placing the bowl of stew in front of me.

"When did you start offering table service? I remember the chow hall being a self-service joint," I said, pointing to the line of wooden tables where Ella used to line up the bowls and trays of food.

"Not anymore. Now that we're the Hope Café, our customers expect it. Plus, I've been learning a few new dishes from Liam Kampen. He's Percy's friend from San Francisco and an excellent cook."

"Is that right?" I said and took a taste of the stew. "This is remarkable. You said that Liam taught you this?

"Yes, and don't you think of stealing him for that whorehouse of yours."

I held up my hands and smiled. "Come on now, Ella, who do you think I am?"

She smirked and walked away. My gaze followed her swaying hips as she disappeared into the kitchen.

"This is delicious, Ella," I said, when she reappeared.

Ella offered a forced smile and a nod. "Thank you."

I dipped a piece of the sourdough bread into the bowl of the stew and said, "If you see Percy, please tell him that I'll be back soon. I need to speak with him."

Ella nodded and retreated again.

I finished my stew, and left Ella a dollar for the fifty-cent meal.

Mr. Jones was standing on the front porch, with a clipboard in hand, checking in a delivery, when I approached.

"Good evening, Mr. Jones," I said, climbing the three steps.

Mr. Jones turned around and nodded. "Good evening, Mr. Vega, what can I do for you?"

"You got any Cubans?"

"Don't I wish," he said, lifting his eyeglasses and propping them onto his head. "But I just received a shipment of nice Maduros from Mexico."

"That will do," I said, following him into the store.

He walked behind the counter and pulled a beautiful wooden humidor box off the shelf.

"This is something you should have," he said, patting the cover of the humidor. "Even up here in Alaska, the summers can rot one of these in a few days."

He handed me the cigar, and I held it under my nose. I'd smelled better, but this, along with a few other comforts, had to be temporarily sacrificed while I made my fortune, because when I returned home to

Chicago, I would enjoy an abundance of Cuban cigars, Scotch whiskeys, and French foods, all to my heart's content. It would also serve to prove to my father that I wasn't that *good-for-nothing son* he often complained about any longer.

I took a long, slow puff of the cigar, allowing it to linger a bit before I exhaled. "There's something I want to talk to you about," I said, tapping the first ashes into an ornate, silver-plated ashtray set upon the countertop.

"What's that, Mr. Vega?" he asked, the pucker to his face expressing his anxiety.

"Have you heard of hydraulic mining?"

He shrugged. "Can't say that I have."

"Well, you know Mr. Wible?"

"Everyone does."

"He's come up with this idea of blasting water at high pressure through a hose into the hillside, smashing the earth into pieces, and washing the gravel runoff into super long sluices."

Mr. Jones looked at me with scrunched up eyes, and a sideways shift of his mouth, obviously confused.

I exhaled and pursed my lips, trying not to let my lack of patience interfere with my purpose. "It's a method to significantly reduce labor, and all you need are pipes, hoses, and a few other devices. I think Mr. Wible is having them shipped in from the states."

"And you're telling me this because . . ." he asked.

I shook my head. "Don't you get it, Mr. Jones? What if I can supply you with these items? You'll make a fortune."

"Where will you get these pipes and hoses from?"

I smiled, knowing I'd hooked my fish. I took a long drag on the cigar, tilted my head back, blew the smoke into the wood rafters, and said, "You need not worry yourself about that. I'll supply you with everything you'll need, and you'll pay me fifty percent of whatever you sell."

He looked at me and swallowed hard knowing that he couldn't deny me, since he was already in debt to me for several hundred dollars. After all, I could, if I wanted to, take over his store, but then I would need a skilled merchant to operate it, and Mr. Jones was at least good at doing that.

CHAPTER TWENTY-ONE—ELLA

Ever since church this past Saturday, word had spread throughout Hope that according to the reverend, I was some transcendent figure, and consequently had become the center of nearly everyone's attention. Men and women boldly approached, patting my back, and some even hugging me without asking. But most times, people just asked to shake my hand, and when I engaged, they cradled my hand between both of theirs, and caressed like it was something holy.

I did my best not to insult anyone by jerking my hand away, though I desperately wanted to and proclaim to the people of Hope my true identity. *My name is Samuel Rothman, I'm a Jew from San Francisco.*

The overt attention became such a nuisance that Ella needed to set up a table for me in the café's kitchen, so Liam and I could eat in peace. Even Rolf needed to barricade the door of the bunkhouse at night to keep people from barging in and seeking me out while I slept.

Today's meal was the first one that Ella spent time alone with me, since Liam was off at some Asatru event with Rolf.

"I need to tell you, Ella," I began, rubbing the back of my neck, "that the reverend has put me in an awkward situation."

"What do you mean, Percy? Everyone loves you. Isn't that good?" she asked, slipping a lock of her long blonde hair behind her ear.

I had a desire to confess my real name at that moment, but I wondered if she would have been upset with me for not sharing my secret with her sooner. So, I smiled and said, "Yes, it's good people like me, but what will happen when I don't bring them the luck they're seeking?"

She leaned over the table, kissed me on my cheek, and said, "Maybe you will, Percy. You brought me luck. Before you and Liam came, this place was just the chow hall. Now it's the Hope Café and we've never been busier."

This was true. In the week since our arrival, a noticeable transformation had taken place. When Liam and I disembarked the *LJ Perry*, this place was an indistinguishable conglomeration of wooden buildings, rising out of a sea of mud. But in just the past few days, new signage was swinging along posts on Main Street advertising the café, the general store, the Catholic church, and the post office, all with the prefix of the town's new name. Even the muddy roads had dried up, providing easier access for pedestrians and wagons traversing the streets.

But the real person to thank was Magnus Vega. After all, it was his idea to name the town. I was just the lucky random person he selected. What if Liam had stepped off the boat before me? Then this place would have been called Kampen City, which I had to admit didn't have the same vitality for those seeking their fortunes as the word hope implied.

In the meantime, while the attention of the townspeople was bothersome, I wasn't complaining about the interest Ella was offering. The way her light-blue eyes focused upon me left me short of breath. She was unlike any of the girls I pursued in high school, who all seemed like children now in comparison with her.

As we finished up our meal, and I was about to step out of the kitchen and into the dining hall, where I knew I would be enthusiastically greeted, Ella grabbed me by my wrist and said, "Reverend O'Hara has invited us to his house for supper this Saturday after services. Will you come with me?"

I took a breath and exhaled slowly. "That would be nice," I said, forcing a smile.

She looked at me with suspicion. "You don't have to go if you don't want to."

"No, I want to go," I blurted.

"It's better you leave through the back door," she said, leading me through the small, cramped kitchen.

We stood in silence at the door, looking at each other for a timeless moment, until Ella broke the spell by leaning in, and kissing me on my lips. I stood still, while a river of warmth washed through my body. If she hadn't gently pushed me through the door, I would still have been standing there, gawking at her. "Good night, Percy," she said.

"Good night, Ella," I answered, and stepped outside into the night as brightly lit as midday.

CHAPTER TWENTY-TWO—THE INVITATION

I made it a point to always pay Mr. Jones for products I bought, even though I could have easily walked out of the store with a box of Maduros, or anything else I wanted. But business was business, and I didn't want him to think I was taking advantage of our relationship, especially since I needed the Hope General Store to become a reliable outlet for the sale of the hydraulic equipment that I was about to acquire from Mr. Wible.

Just as I stepped out of the store, and onto the porch, Percy Hope was standing directly in front of me. "Percy, I was just about to go looking for you at the café."

"Hello, Mr. Vega. I can't talk right now," he said, pointing past me. "I'm working for Mr. Jones."

I held out my hands and said, "Since when?"

"Today's my first day. I'll be working until closing. Did you know that my father owns a general store in San Francisco?"

"I didn't know that. You are the ambitious one, Percy. I like that."

"Thank you, Mr. Vega. Now if you'll excuse me, I need to get to work. I don't want to be late on my first day."

I pressed my hand on Percy's chest, stopping him from walking by me. "Mr. Jones will allow you a few minutes to speak with me."

"All right, what can I do for you?"

"I understand that you've become somewhat of a celebrity in this town."

Percy shrugged. "Yes, thanks to you and the reverend. Though I would prefer to go unnoticed."

"I think I can make more of that claim than the reverend. Without me, Percy, you would be just another dreamer."

"Dreamer?" he asked.

I gestured around me. "You think these people here have a real chance of striking it rich, or is it just some fantastic fantasy? Whatever gold was here is nearly gone. The Resurrection and Sixmile Creeks have been picked clean. People will soon blast into the hillside with hydraulics."

"Hydraulics?" Percy asked, his forehead furrowed and nose scrunched up, showing his confusion.

"I'll explain later. My point is, there's an easier way to get rich, and it's not by behaving like one of these pitiful prospectors, desperately searching for the next big discovery. But instead, the road to long-lasting wealth is to be the provider of what I like to call *support services* to these poor souls, grasping for their share of glory."

"Support services?" he asked, confused.

"I would like for you to come for a visit to Sunrise, where I could explain what I mean. Tonight, after work, I'll have a wagon waiting to take you over to my new place, the Gold Digger Saloon. You'll love it. Oh, and bring your friend Liam."

Percy nodded and pursed his lips. "Maybe I will, Mr. Vega. I'll ask Liam. Now please, allow me to get to work. I don't want to get fired before I even start."

CHAPTER TWENTY-THREE—THE ASATRUS

"Percy, I need to talk to you," Liam said, barging in through the front door.

"Not now, Liam, I'm working."

Percy lowered his voice. "Something strange happened tonight at the Asatru church. I'm scared."

"All right, Liam. The store closes in twenty minutes. Wait for me on the porch. We'll talk then."

Liam nodded, and I noticed how pale he looked. Whatever had frightened him had drawn any of the color from his face.

When the time came to close, Mr. Jones trained me on the closing procedures of the store for the night. As I shut the front door and turned the key, I saw Liam sitting on the top step of the porch. He stood up, and pointed to a man sitting upon the driving seat of a horse-drawn wagon, and said, "Percy, this man says he's waiting for you."

"Come on, Liam," I said, gesturing to the wagon, "we're going to Sunrise. You can tell me what happened at church, on the way."

"Why are we going to Sunrise?" he asked, shaking his head.

"We've been invited by Mr. Vega to visit his new place, the Gold Digger Saloon."

"Are you serious?"

"Why do you think the wagon is here? Come, let's go."

Liam shrugged and climbed aboard. I followed him, and we sat across from one another on two long and narrow wooden benches. The driver, seated upon his elevated perch, turned and asked, "Are you boys ready?"

I nodded, and he snapped his whip onto the horse's rump and we were off.

This would be the first time since our arrival that we ventured the eight miles to Sunrise, but both Liam and I had heard the gossip from fellow prospectors about the goings-on at the notorious town, while we toiled away for gold in the creek.

"I hear the Gold Digger Saloon has the best-looking girls in Sunrise," Liam said, and raised his eyebrows, seeming to suddenly forget his torment from earlier this evening.

"We need to behave ourselves, Liam. We're guests of Mr. Vega and I don't want to upset him."

"Are you serious? Why else would he invite us to his place where drinking, gambling, and women are for the taking?"

"I know, I know. But let's tread carefully. I have a feeling that Mr. Vega wants something from us, and I don't want to be foolish. So, tell me what made you so upset?"

Liam nodded and furrowed his brow, suddenly remembering his previous anguish. He glanced up at the driver and switched sides, sitting alongside me on the bench and said, "I'm not supposed to speak of what happens in the church, so you must promise not to say a word of this to anyone."

I opened my palms and nodded. "Of course."

Liam rubbed his mouth before he spoke. "The Asatrus believe that Thor was the most powerful God. He ruled over thunder and lightning, wind and rain, sunshine and crops. He would sit upon his throne, with his hammer in hand, while Odin, the God of war, sat next to him, dressed in his full armor. On Thor's other side sat Frey, the God of peace and fertility who displayed an enormous erect phallus."

"An erect phallus?" I repeated, surprised at the description.

Liam nodded. His forehead puckered. "The priests offered sacrifices. For disease or famine, they made an offering to Thor. If they were going to war, then they would kill for Odin, and for weddings, the bride and groom would sacrifice to Frey."

"I've heard of these Norse Gods. We studied them in school. But I've never heard this version," I said.

Liam continued, "Every ninth year there is something called *the blot of nine*, which is a ceremonial feast. At this feast, they offer a sacrifice to the Gods, of nine males of assorted species." He paused, grabbed my wrist, squeezed it hard, and said, "And one of these species is human."

I grimaced and said, "What are you talking about?"

"They'll hang a moose calf, and a dog, or anything that's male, but the ninth one is a human. They string up the nine dead bodies from nine branches of a tree."

"And you saw this? Who did they hang?"

"It hasn't happened yet. They say that, according to the Asatru calendar, that this will take place on the ninth day of the ninth month in the ninth year. That's the ninth day of September, this year."

"That's the craziest thing I've ever heard. You can't go back, Liam."

"I wish that were so. I took some sort of pledge that binds me to them for life. Once you're in this crazy religion, there's no escape."

"Why in the world would you take such a pledge?"

"I don't know why, I just did. Percy, I'm frightened."

"Do you want me to talk to Ella about it? Maybe she can convince her brother to let you out."

Liam shook his head. "No, you mustn't say a word, not even to Ella. I'm afraid they might use me as their ninth, their human sacrifice."

This all sounded too far-fetched to be true. I exhaled, put an arm around Liam, and said, "Maybe they're just trying to scare you into becoming some sort of fanatic or something."

"I don't know. I just don't know," he said, staring down the road as we headed toward Sunrise.

CHAPTER TWENTY-FOUR—BOYS' NIGHT OUT

By the time we had almost reached our destination, Liam had calmed down. I tried to relieve some of his anxiety by making the case that what he heard at the Asatru church couldn't possibly be true. "Come on, Liam, this is 1898. Maybe the Vikings did those types of things thousands of years ago, but not these days," I implored.

He sighed and said, "I suppose you're right."

But I think the real reason he pushed it aside was his anticipation in approaching the sinful city of Sunrise.

It first appeared as a few twinkling flames, flickering through gaps in the foliage as the wagon neared. But when we cleared the forest, and the road opened up, we saw it for the first time. The wagon made its way slowly down the main road, where a sign swinging off a wooden post identified it was Front Street. Sunrise looked like any small rural town, with its post office, bank, general store and doctor's office, as well as a hotel and darkened alleyways crammed in between.

But what was apparent from the first impression, was that Sunrise was more developed than Hope, and unlike its sister city, whose residents would have mostly turned in for the night by this late hour, this town looked like it was still midday. Dozens of men, along with a handful of women, dressed in their evening clothes, made their way along connected wooden walkways, elevated from the clouds of dust circulating inches above the surface of Front Street.

Liam pointed ahead to where a crowd had spilled out onto the street, blocking our wagon from any further progress. We had arrived at the Gold Digger Saloon.

The driver twisted in his seat to look at us and said, with a grin, "This is it, boys. Mr. Vega is waiting inside for you."

We thanked him, climbed down from the wagon, and up the three steps to the crowded front porch of the saloon where dozens of men were gathered, drinking and smoking and carrying on boisterous, loud conversations.

Liam and I maneuvered our way through and beyond the propped open, swinging saloon doors. For a moment I froze, gawking at the splendor of the extravagant debauchery being played out before my eyes.

A layer of heavy cigar smoke hung over the large room, like storm clouds do when they swallow mountains. Piano music blended in with patron's indistinguishable voices, filling the hall. There were dozens of tables filling the space, where men were engaged in card play. Scattered casually across the wooden tabletops were the bets and winnings, comprising of coins and nuggets that glittered in reflection from the large candelabras overhead, which swung by ropes snaking through pulleys and tied off around a large metal cleat bolted to the wall.

An elbow poked at me, and I turned to see Liam pointing. I followed the direction of his finger and saw a young woman, with a painted face, highlighting her cheeks and eyes, and sitting upon a man's lap. Her brown curls were propped on the top of her head, but she had allowed several strands to fall casually down upon her fair complexion, framing out her mesmerizing brown eyes. She wore a pure white cotton outfit that featured an assortment of ruffles where the garment ended along the neckline, around her wrists, and down her long thin legs to her knees. From her knees to her toes, she wore black stockings, upon which was woven a pattern of diamonds.

If I hadn't been suddenly slapped on my back, I might have stared at this seductive woman for the entire evening.

"Percy, Liam, you've made it," said Mr. Vega, who was now directing us, with his heavy hand on my back, through the crowded saloon.

Without the attention of Mr. Vega, Liam and I would have remained unnoticed among the inebriated throng of sweat-encrusted men. The stench reminded me of the steerage facilities on the *Bertha*, except for the momentary sweet fragrance of the perfumed working girls who passed us by.

"Come and sit," Mr. Vega said, gesturing to a semi-circle upholstered banquette, built into a wooden alcove in the saloon's rear.

Liam and I slid into the booth, while Mr. Vega, and his head of security, Mr. Smith sat on opposite ends, locking us in.

"Let's get you boys something to drink," Mr. Vega said, raising his hand and summoning over a man from behind the jam-packed, long wooden bar that hugged the entire side-wall of the saloon.

"Here you go, Mr. Vega," said the pencil-thin man with a sallow complexion and rotting teeth.

Placed on the table before us, was a tall, amber-colored, label-less bottle, and four small crystal shot glasses.

"Thank you, Henry," Mr. Vega said and reached for the bottle. "Let me know what you think of my whiskey. We make it ourselves."

"I'm afraid, Mr. Vega, that I cannot critique your whiskey since I have never tasted it before," I said.

"Me neither," Liam added.

Mr. Vega tilted his head back and released a hearty laugh that turned his cheeks beet-red. "That's wonderful," he roared, returning his focus to Liam and me. He leaned over, with his palms splayed out upon the table before us and said, "Can I assume that neither of you boys has been with a woman before?"

I offered a nervous chuckle and shook my head.

Mr. Vega raised his glass, and said, "Well, boys, tonight will be one of those moments in your lives, that will be forever etched into your memory. That is, of course, if you can remember any of it when you wake up tomorrow morning."

I looked over to Liam, whose eyes were bugging out. No doubt this was the moment he had been waiting for. I too felt the warmth flowing through my veins and figured that tonight might be one of those nights we would reminisce about as old men.

"Who do we have here?" said a woman with luxurious long red hair that swirled in curls, softly falling upon her broad shoulders. She leaned over, placing both hands on the table which allowed her blouse to slightly fall open, exposing the skin on the top part of her large breasts.

"Come and sit with us, Suzie. We're about to toast to our new friends, Liam Kampen and Percy Hope," Mr. Vega said proudly. "Stan, get up and let Suzie sit with us."

Mr. Smith shrugged and rose, allowing Suzie to slip into the booth next to me.

"So, you're Percy Hope," she said, pushing her body against mine.

I squirmed a bit, moving over to give her more room.

"Oh, Percy, don't be shy," she said, putting an arm around me.

She smelled like the lavender-scented soap my father sold in his store.

"I've heard of you, Percy. You're the boy the town of Hope was named after. Isn't that so?"

I smiled and nodded. "Yes, thanks to Mr. Vega, I'm that guy. Though all the attention has become somewhat of a nuisance."

"Nonsense," shouted Mr. Vega. "Let's celebrate." He held up a shot glass filled to its brim to his lips, and in one jerking motion, tilted his head back and drained the whiskey down his throat. Once emptied, he slapped the glass back down on the table. Suzie did the same, while Liam and I watched in awe.

I picked up the glass and brought it to my mouth. There was a funky smell to it, almost like eggs.

112

"It smells awful, so you need to do it fast," advised Suzie.

I took a breath, closed my eyes, and quickly downed the brew. As it coated my throat, a warmth emanated from deep inside me. I felt beads of sweat forming on my forehead and a pleasurable relaxation of my anxieties.

"Let's do a few more, and I'll get you boys upstairs," said Suzie.

I looked over to Liam whose nose was as red as an apple, and was smiling like a Cheshire cat, which was a saying from one of my favorite books, Alice in Wonderland. Which in a way, after that first drink, I felt like Alice going *down the rabbit hole* into a world I knew nothing about.

CHAPTER TWENTY-FIVE—THE PROPOSITION

I walked into the Gold Digger Saloon, just as Percy and Liam were drinking their coffees.

"Ah, gentlemen, how did you enjoy your evenings?" I asked.

Percy's head was hanging as if he was examining something swimming in his cup, while Liam looked more lively, and expressed his enthusiasm. "It was the best night of my life."

I sat down and twisted my neck to make eye-contact with Percy. "And what about you, Mr. Hope?"

He looked at me, confused upon hearing his name, but smiled and said, "I'd like to go home?"

"Sure thing. I'll get my driver to give you boys a ride back to Hope. But before you go, there's something I want to talk to you about."

Percy straightened his spine, sat up tall, and said, "What would that be?"

"What do you think of my little enterprise here?"

Percy made a circular motion in the air with his finger, and said, "You mean the saloon?"

"Yes, I mean the saloon, Percy. Are you impressed?"

He shrugged. "Yes, I'm impressed. You must do very well."

"How does six-hundred dollars sound?"

Liam put down his cup, and said, "You make six hundred dollars a month?"

I laughed. "No, Liam, that's six hundred dollars in one night, every night."

"That is impressive, Mr. Vega," Percy said, pushing his chair back as if he was ready to rise to his feet.

I clamped my hand onto Percy's arm and said, "Just one minute. I have something I want to discuss with you."

He settled back down and nodded.

"As you know, Hope is a dry town, which means they allow none of *this*," I said, gesturing to the interior of the saloon's main hall.

Percy nodded again.

"That's a shame, because, as you can see, such an establishment can generate tremendous income."

Percy looked over at Liam, and said, "I suppose so."

"But Reverend O'Hara's rule over Hope has prevented people from enjoying in harmless fun. However, with your arrival, Percy, I sense an opportunity to change people's minds."

Percy pointed at himself. "Me? What can I do?"

"I'm sure you're aware of what the people of Hope think of you."

"They think I'm their four-leaf clover."

"And what could be more persuasive to these people who have traveled great distances to strike it rich?"

"I'm sorry, Mr. Vega. Maybe it's because I have a throbbing headache, but I'm not sure what you're asking of me," said Percy, holding a hand to his forehead.

"Okay, I'll say it plainly. I want you, Percy, with the help of your buddy Liam, to convince the people of your town into allowing the opening of the Hope Saloon. You and I will be business partners. I'll give you a twenty percent stake in the ownership. I'll take all the risks by putting up the money and providing the expertise. All you have to do is convince the townspeople of Hope to allow us to open the saloon and help me with the day-to-day operations."

Percy exhaled and grimaced. "Would you mind, Mr. Vega, if we discussed this another day when I have my wits about me?"

"Of course, Percy. We'll catch up the next time I'm in Hope. In the meantime, think about my offer."

CHAPTER TWENTY-SIX—THE HIGHLAND FLING

When I could finally open my eyes, I was drenched in sweat. Normally I would wake up the moment the sun directed its beam into our attic space through our south-facing dormer windows. But this morning I had slept hours beyond that time, and the headache I went to sleep with, remained with me upon my awakening.

I looked over at Liam, who was snoring and sweating too. "Liam, are you awake?" I asked, trying to shake him. But he just moaned, turned over and returned to his dreams.

I went downstairs, out to the backyard, and poured some fresh water into the wooden bathtubs. Normally I would heat the water, but a cool bath was in order. Once the tub was filled, I lay down with my head tilted back, resting upon its top edge. Disjointed fragments of memories from last night flashed through my cloudy mind.

"Percy, why didn't you wake me up?" Liam demanded, walking out through the bunkhouse back door.

I groaned, lifted my head up, looked at Liam, and said, "I tried, you wouldn't budge."

"What the hell happened last night?" he said, pumping water from the well into a wooden bucket.

"Whiskey and women, Liam. That's what happened," I said, closing my eyes, and thinking of Greta. The girl who took my virginity.

"I wish I could remember more. Like the name of that girl. I would like to see her again," Liam said, slipping into the tub next to mine.

"Her name was Ingrid, you idiot. You were shouting her name all night. We heard you through the walls."

"Oh, sorry about that," Liam replied with a chuckle.

"Can we not talk for a while, Liam? My head's pounding, and I only have thirty minutes to get ready for church. After that, I've been invited by Ella to accompany her to the reverend's home for supper."

"Are you going to talk to the reverend about what Mr. Vega said, about being a partner in a Hope saloon?"

"Shh, Liam. We don't need anyone overhearing you, and I don't know what to do about that. It all sounds crazy."

"It sounds good to me. After all, Percy, why did we come to Alaska in the first place?"

"To find gold," I reminded him.

"That's right, and as the saying goes, *there's more than one way to skin a cat.*"

I shook my head, and said, "What are you talking about?"

"The end game for everyone in this town is to strike it rich. Mr. Vega has realized that it's easier to do that by taking the prospector's money a bit at a time, by giving them what they want. Take note, my friend. When this is all over, and they strip the gold clean from these creeks, most of these people will go home with nothing to show for their hard work. Why should we be like them? This idea of a saloon could make us a fortune.

118

You heard what Mr. Vega said, that he makes six-hundred dollars in one night. A twenty percent share is one-hundred and twenty dollars. We could go home with three-thousand dollars apiece."

"I'm impressed, Liam. When did you become an accountant?"

"Maybe it was the whiskey," he said, and paused for a moment, "or perhaps it was Ingrid. I've always wanted a muse."

*

I nodded off several times during the reverend's service. If it wasn't for Ella's sharp elbow into my ribs, I would have fallen off my chair.

"What's wrong with you?" she barked at me as the service concluded.

"I didn't get much sleep last night."

"Is that all?" Ella asked, with a tone of suspicion.

"Yes, that's all," I said, sounding defensive, and wondered if she could smell the whiskey on my breath, even though I brushed extra long with baking soda.

She looked at me with a puckered forehead but didn't press me. "The reverend is expecting us at his home for supper in an hour. Will you be all right to go?"

"Yes, I'll be fine. Let me run back to the bunkhouse and then I'll swing by the café in forty-five minutes, and we'll walk over together."

After my farewell to Ella, I spotted Mr. Jones, who was walking back from church.

"Good day, Mr. Jones," I said, trotting a few steps to catch up to him.

"Ah, Percy. It's good to see you."

"You as well, sir. I was wondering if you could help me out," I said, squeezing his elbow and pulling him aside from the other churchgoers.

"What is it, Percy?"

"Last night Mr. Vega invited me and Liam to his saloon in Sunrise."

Mr. Jones' eyeballs bugged out of their sockets and he said, "Oh my, Percy. That place is the devil's den. What happened?"

I shrugged and offered a pained smile and said, "I'm afraid I drank too much, and now I have a throbbing headache. On top of that, I'm expected at the reverend's home for supper within the hour."

Mr. Jones smiled and nodded. "Come with me, my boy. I have just the thing for a hangover."

"Thank you, sir," I said and followed him through the back entrance of the Hope General Store.

He led me up the stairs and into his kitchen. "Please sit, Percy. I'll prepare a special concoction that my grandfather taught me. He called it the *Highland Fling*, named after some Scottish dance popular in the thirties."

"Thank you, Mr. Jones."

He threw a log into the belly of his stove and pulled a tin off his shelf. "All it is, is a bit of cornstarch, mixed with a cup of buttermilk. I'll heat it up, and season it with salt and pepper," he said, preparing his remedy. When it was ready, he handed it to me in a goblet.

I put it to my nose and took a sniff.

120

"Now, don't sip it. You must guzzle it down. In a little while you'll feel good as new, I promise."

I hoped he was right. The last thing I wanted was for the reverend to catch wind of what I was up to last night. I realized that I had crossed a line, and that, if discovered, could have me disgraced. But I was wondering if that was something I really cared about.

I thanked Mr. Jones for his remedy and walked over to the café to meet Ella. On my way, I considered going into partnership with Mr. Vega. It was probably true what Liam said about how running the Hope Saloon could be financially rewarding. I promised Father that I would bring home a fortune, and he would not care where it came from.

CHAPTER TWENTY-SEVEN—HYDRAULICS

"Magnus, you stole my equipment," Simon Wible said, pointing a finger at me.

I was sitting at my booth in the saloon's rear when he approached. It was a few hours before the evening rush, so the place was empty, except for a few of the regulars drinking at the bar.

I gestured to Mr. Wible to take a seat. "Please join me, let's talk," I said, with a smile.

He stood frozen for a moment, the glint in his eyes betraying his anger. The color in his face had a bluish tint like he had been holding his breath for too long.

Suddenly Suzie approached and placed a hand on his back. "Hello, Simon, it's good to see you," she said, leaning in to place a gentle kiss upon his bearded cheek.

Like pulling the plug from a bathtub, the tension visibly drained from Mr. Wible. He released his pent-up breath and exhaled. "Oh, hello, Suzie. It's good to see you too."

"You seem tense. Would you like to come upstairs? I can help you relax."

"No, that's all right, Suzie. I need to speak with Mr. Vega. Perhaps another time," he said, with an appreciative smile.

She shrugged, and with a slight tilt of her head, she responded, "Very well," and walked away.

Mr. Wible slid into the booth and placed his elbows on the table. "Now, you listen to me, Vega. A shipment of mine was commandeered right off the *LJ Perry*, and as I understand it, you're the one responsible."

"That's true, I am responsible," I said, matter-of-factly.

"You admit to it?" he said, his wide-open eyes revealing his surprise.

"Why would I lie to you?"

"I don't understand," he said, rubbing the back of his neck. "Can you tell me why?"

"I wanted to get your attention, and here you are," I said, opening my palms in front of me.

"All right, now that you've got it, can I have my merchandise back, please?"

"Yes. I'm not a thief."

He shook his head and said, "You need to look up the definition of a thief in the dictionary."

"That's clever, Mr. Wible. But please allow me to share with you my reasoning behind interrupting your delivery, and then perhaps you'll understand my motives."

"Interrupting? Is that what you call it?"

"Yes, I intend to return the shipment to you." I paused briefly and then said, "At least most of it."

Mr. Wible froze for a moment, while the blush in his cheeks returned, and he said, "Most of it? What the fuck are you talking about?"

"There's no need for obscenities. Allow me to explain."

"I'm telling you, Vega, if you don't return every item to me, I'll—"

"You'll do what?" I interrupted.

"Do you think you're untouchable? I have friends who know how to break things," he said, gesturing to the interior of the saloon.

"Let's not go there. Please allow me to offer my proposal. If you don't like it, I'll return your entire shipment, and we'll leave it at that."

Mr. Wible exhaled and said, "I guess I have no choice. What is it?"

"The reason I appropriated your shipment, was to prove to you I could. Once people recognize the value of what you're importing, they will want a piece. Let's face it, hydraulic gold mining will be the last hurrah for the desperate people in these parts and desperate people have a tendency to do unfortunate things—like steal."

I stopped for a moment and asked Henry to bring us a bottle of whiskey and two glasses. I poured out two shots and downed mine before I continued. Mr. Wible left his untouched.

"I can guarantee uninterrupted delivery of your merchandise from the steamships out in Cook Inlet, to its transfer to Cap's steamer, and finally into your possession upon these shores. In exchange, I would expect a portion of the hydraulic inventory. It's a small price to pay for peace of mind. Because who knows, maybe the next time your goods go missing, it might be someone less reasonable than me."

"And what sort of *portion* are you expecting?"

I smiled, and said, "I would like twenty percent across the board."

Mr. Wible said nothing for nearly a minute. I watched his eyes twitch, and I imagined he was thinking through the various options. "Tell me, what will you do with twenty percent of my hydraulic mining equipment?"

"I'll sell it at the Hope General Store. Mr. Jones and I have a partnership."

He nodded and slapped his palms hard on the table, causing me to jump. "You've got a deal, Vega, but on three conditions. Number one," he said, holding up his index finger, "I will dictate the prices that we sell the goods for."

I shrugged. This was something I didn't even consider. But I agreed with the concept.

"Number two," he continued, with two fingers in the air, "no one can buy the equipment without a proper claim. We need to maintain a sense of order out there."

I nodded and said, "Makes sense."

"And number three," he said, with three fingers boldly displayed before me, "I don't want those thieves at the Company getting their hands on this equipment. Because if they do, that will be the end of the monopoly on these goods and decimate the margins."

"I have no problem with any of that," I said.

"If you can live up to it, then we have a deal, Mr. Vega."

I refilled my glass and held it out for a toast. "I can abide by those conditions, Mr. Wible. Can we drink to it?"

Mr. Wible held up his glass, and said, "Oh, I almost forgot, there is one more thing."

"What would that be?"

Mr. Wible smiled, and said, "I want a regular, weekly visit with Suzie, on the house."

"I think that can be arranged," I said and summoned Suzie over. "Let's toast to our partnership."

We both guzzled our shots, and I sent Mr. Wible upstairs with Suzie to seal the deal.

CHAPTER TWENTY-EIGHT—SUPPER WITH THE REVEREND

"What was up with you this morning at church? You looked like death washed over you," Ella whispered to me at the dining table, while we waited for the reverend to join us.

I shook my head, with my eyes closed, then turned to her and said, "I apologize. I didn't sleep well. It's stifling in that attic. If a room doesn't open up soon, we must find a new place."

"What does my brother say?"

I shrugged. "Rolf's surprised that no one has vacated, he keeps saying that a room will be available soon. But that's what he's been telling Liam and me since we arrived three weeks ago."

A sudden crash sounded from the kitchen. Just as I was about to stand to see what was amiss, the reverend walked into the dining room. "No need to worry. Just a small accident. Mrs. Hayes dropped the teakettle."

"Is she all right?" Ella asked.

"She's fine, no harm done. Let's sit and talk while she finishes preparing supper," the reverend said, pulling out the wooden chair at the head of the table.

"You have a nice home, Reverend," I said, looking at the assortment of paintings on the walls, the various knick-knacks displayed on shelves, and comfortable-looking furniture decorating the adjacent living room.

"Thank you, Percy. I tried to bring as much as I could from home, which was quite a chore shipping it up from Ohio."

"Ohio? That's far away," I said.

The reverend nodded, unfolded his cloth napkin, and placed it upon his lap. "It is, Percy. But when I learned about this mad stampede of men, charging into the wilderness seeking their fortunes, I took it as a calling to provide our fellow Catholics with a dose of religion, as a way to temper the overwhelming temptations of the seven deadly sins."

I must have looked confused, because the reverend said, "You are familiar with the seven deadly sins, aren't you, Percy?"

As a Jew, I learned the ten commandments in Sunday school, but I had no clue what the seven deadly sins were.

Luckily, Ella picked up on my lack of knowledge and jumped in. "Well, Reverend, they are greed, pride, envy, gluttony, lust, anger, and sloth."

"Excellent, Ella. You're a good Catholic," the reverend said, rising from his chair, to reach for the water pitcher sitting on the sideboard.

"Thank you," she said, and while the reverend was turned away, Ella gave me an apprehensive look, which hinted that this was something she would want to delve into later.

"Well, Percy, I want to expand upon what I spoke of at last week's sermon. I'm sure you remember," he said pouring water into my glass.

"I do, sir. And I have to tell you, since then I can't walk the streets of Hope without people wanting to engage with me. It's become intolerable. I even need to hide out in the café's kitchen to eat my meal in peace."

The reverend clapped his hands together, and said with enthusiasm, "Excellent, that's exactly the response I was hoping for."

I looked over at Ella, who offered me a shrug.

"If you don't mind me saying, sir, but this pedestal you're putting me on, I'm afraid will only end in disappointment."

The reverend cocked his head. "Why would you say that?" he asked.

"I'm only seventeen years old, what do I know about giving people hope, as you suggested?"

"Do you know what our Lord and Savior was doing at your age?" he asked, folding his arms across his chest.

I shook my head.

"It's true that between the ages of twelve and twenty-nine there's limited knowledge of his life. Some say he was working as a carpenter in Galilee. While others say he traveled great distances and learned many things. There are accounts of his visits as a young man around your age, to India, where he exhorted the Hindus to stop worshiping idols"—he paused, and wagged a finger at me—"so don't tell me you're only seventeen years old. I have always believed, Percy, that when a young, impressive person like yourself comes into our lives, it's a time for the elders to relearn what's important and meaningful, instead of indoctrinating the young person into our outdated, and stale ways."

I looked over to Ella, then back to the reverend, and said, "Are you comparing me to Jesus Christ?"

The reverend burst into laughter. "Of course not, Percy. But what I am telling you, is that you're not too young to make an impression upon people, for their betterment," he said, flipping out his palms. "Isn't that what a good Catholic is supposed to do?"

I nodded because that seemed obvious to anyone regardless of their religion.

The reverend pointed his index finger into the air, and said, "The people of this community need someone to admire as a beacon of goodness, and I believe that you, Percy Hope, could be that person. You coming here, and subsequently having the town bear your name, is no accident. Most people who come to Hope have wild dreams of striking it rich. I'm sure that's why you and your friend Liam made the journey."

"That's true," I said.

"It's also true that there are many temptations, especially in the sinful city of Sunrise, and people need a tangible reminder of someone good and wholesome, so we can stay true to our calling of serving God. Because once we submit to even one of the seven deadly sins, the others fall easily, and before we know it, we have become Magnus Vega. Our devil in residence."

I smiled at Ella, wondering what she would think of me if I had the courage to confess that my name was Samuel Rothman, a Jew from San Francisco, and that last night I lost my virginity to Greta at the Gold

Digger Saloon. Plus, that I was offered a partnership from the devil himself, Magnus Vega, to open a saloon in Hope, where most likely all seven deadly sins would be committed, multiple times each day. Instead, I remained uncomfortably silent.

CHAPTER TWENTY-NINE—BAKERSFIELD OUTFITTERS

The moment I heard that Mr. Wible was working the hydraulics, I grabbed my hat and took off in a full run along the banks of Sixmile Creek. "It's just around the bend," I said breathlessly to Stan, who was trying to keep up.

As it came into view, I stopped short, causing Stan to slam into me. "Will you look at that," I said pointing.

This was the first time I had witnessed the magnificent, destructive power of hydraulic mining. Standing behind the sleek-looking water cannon perched upon a rock outcropping was a man gripping its handles and aiming it at the embankment on the opposite side of Sixmile Creek. A powerful stream of high-pressured water struck the earth, and like Thor's hammer, violently scattered the rocks, gravel, and dirt. A task that would have taken a team of several men many hours, or more likely days to achieve, was done in mere minutes.

But that was not the extent of the ingenuity. A long, wooden settling trough, similar in design to the much smaller sluice box, with grooves along its bottom, into which water was directed, was strategically placed to catch the runoff, separating the gold from the gravel.

Stan and I stood by watching until Mr. Wible spotted us and directed his man handling the water cannon to cease operations.

"Ah, Mr. Vega and Mr. Smith, thank you for coming. Let's see if our efforts have anything to show," he said, leading us to the far end of the settling trough.

I had to admit that the excitement was intoxicating. I needed to remind myself about my promise that I would not get caught up within the *stampeder's* frenzy. But it was easy to understand why all these men, and thousands more in the Klondike, had left their homes, and risked their lives, for the chance of discovering gold.

Mr. Wible kneeled down and reached into the collection tray of the settling trough and scooped out the accumulated material with his hand. He stood up, held out his palm, and with the fingers from his other hand, he gently pushed away the gravel and stopped when he saw the color.

"Well, what do we have here?" he said, picking up a small gold nugget between two fingers. He kneeled back down and dipped it into the creek to wash it off. "Looks like we have an ounce or two. Not bad for twenty minutes of work."

"Not bad at all," I said, as he handed me the nugget.

"Impressive is it not, Mr. Vega?" he said, stepping up onto the bank.

"Seeing it actually work is amazing."

"Listen, Mr. Vega, I need to run. We're stocking the shelves today, and I want to make sure Bakersfield Outfitters can open by tomorrow."

"Bakersfield Outfitters?" I asked, confused.

"Oh, it's my store in Sunrise. Don't worry, you'll have your inventory for your store in Hope, as we agreed."

"Wait a second, what do you mean, you're opening a store?"

Mr. Wible took a step toward me, looked into my eyes and said, "Don't become troublesome, Vega. I'm only putting up with you for the sake of peace. But I am prepared to fight you." He paused and pointed to his team of men working across the creek. "You can ask any of them what I am capable of—do not test me."

I looked over to Stan, whose face reflected what I felt—shock. I wasn't used to being on the receiving end of gut-twisting threats. I quickly recalculated my position and realized that making a fuss now wasn't wise. "All right, Mr. Wible, no need to get angry. I was just surprised to hear that you were planning to open an outfitting store."

"Why else would I be bringing in all these goods? Maybe you're not as clever as I thought you were," he said, flicking his wrist dismissively and walking away.

I took a step toward Mr. Wible, and just as I was to raise my hand and call out, Stan grabbed it, and said under his breath, "Not now, Magnus."

He was right, this was not the time. But his deceit would not go unpunished. Somehow, I would show him I too was a force to be reckoned with.

"Mr. Wible is formidable, and it's better not to act impulsively," Stan said, surprising me with his wisdom.

I exhaled, letting my pent-up anger dissipate into the cool summer day. "Let's go to Hope and find Percy. Perhaps we'll have more luck with him."

CHAPTER THIRTY—ELATION

Liam and I spent most of the morning working a new spot on Resurrection Creek, the furthest we had gone from its mouth, where it emptied into Turnagain Arm.

"Come on, Percy, I've had enough. My hands are frozen, and my back's killing me," Liam said, using his shovel's handle to prop himself up.

"All right, last one," I said, burying my shovel into the gravel, and scraping it along the bedrock.

"This is all a big waste of time," Percy complained. "This entire area is mined out. People are saying the new place to go is Nome. Maybe we should check it out? We're already in Alaska. How far can it be from here?"

"Nome? How about six hundred miles through the wilderness," I said, since I had overheard people discussing it at the café just the day before.

"I don't know, Percy, this is getting crazy. We're wasting our summer up here. Maybe we should just go home."

I dumped the gravel into the bucket and walked it down to the creek's edge with my shovel. I scooped out a shovel full and dropped it into my pan. The moment I tilted the pan, something heavy slid off and plopped into the ankle-deep water beneath me. I flung the pan aside and reached for it. The moment I touched it; I knew what it was. I pulled my hand out of the icy water and looked at a golden nugget settled within my palm. I closed my fingers and lifted my hand up and down, feeling the nugget's density.

I turned, and held my hand out, and cradling the treasure muttered, "Oh my God, Liam."

"Oh my God, Samuel," Liam said. Each one of his eyes was nearly as big as the nugget.

"You mean Percy."

"No, at this moment I mean Samuel Rothman. It's time to be real. Can I hold it?" he asked, reaching out.

I looked at my nugget once more. I tilted my head at various angles and took notice of how the sun made it sparkle.

"Hand it to me," Liam said, breaking the spell.

"Sorry, here," I said, handing it to him.

"It's heavy. What do you think it weighs?"

"I don't know, but it's big," I said, as Liam gave it back to me.

"My body's tingling. Even my hands are shaking," I said, showing Liam my left trembling hand, while my right tightly clutched the nugget. "It's better than that night at the saloon."

"You mean, it's better than sex?"

I nodded. "Yes, Liam, I think it is."

*

Liam and I ran back home like small children, jumping from stone to stone, laughing all the way. Just as we stepped onto Main Street, there was

Ella, standing like a guard in front of the café. She stared at me with her arms folded across her chest, without her charming, dimpled smile. I figured she wanted to address that moment with the reverend, when I failed to name the seven deadly sins.

"I'll catch up with you later," I said to Liam.

Liam gave me *the eyes,* showing he knew what was coming, and took off for the bunkhouse.

I stepped up and onto the porch, next to Ella, and meekly said, "Hi."

"Come inside, I want to ask you something," she said, and turned to enter.

I followed behind her into the empty café—dinner was still a few hours away. We sat at a table toward the back.

"There's something I want to ask you, Percy, and I want you to tell me the truth."

Whatever I felt a few moments earlier was replaced with the exact opposite—the feeling of dread. I said, "Okay, Ella."

She squinted her eyes and cocked her head slightly and asked, "Are you Catholic?"

"What are you talking about?"

"Because you didn't know the seven deadly sins," she said, lifting her eyebrows.

I held up my hands. "Sure, I do," I said, as I had since memorized them. "They are greed, pride, envy, gluttony, lust, anger, and sloth."

She narrowed her eyes once more, expressing her suspicion. "Then why did you hesitate when the reverend asked you?"

I shrugged. "Because he makes me nervous."

"Well, the reverend can be intimidating, I'll grant you that. But there's something about you, Percy Hope, that seems off. I just can't figure it out. At least not yet."

"Well, I have great news," I said, reaching out and taking her arm.

She smirked. "What great news?"

"Liam and I just got back," I said, gesturing toward Main Street, "from up a way on Resurrection Creek, and I discovered this." I reached into the pouch tied to my waist, and pulled out the nugget, and handed it to Ella.

She took it and gawked at it for a long moment before she looked up, and said, "Oh my, Percy, this is a fortune. Congratulations."

"I'm guessing it's close to forty ounces."

She cupped it in her palm, feeling its heft. "Could be more. You should bring it to the Company mining office and register it. You'll get your twenty-five percent on the spot."

"Will you come with me?"

"All right, let's go now. I need to get back for the dinner rush."

Thirty minutes later, after the weighing, examining and testing, I was issued three-hundred dollars, my share of the twelve-hundred-dollar value for the sixty-ounce nugget.

I held the fifteen twenty-dollar banknotes in my hand, and with Ella by my side, made an impulsive decision. I carefully folded the canvas pouch, holding my fortune, and as we swiftly exited the Company mining office, I said to Ella, "Come with me, I have an idea."

"Where we going, Percy?"

"To see the reverend."

Sitting at the same table where we had supper several days before, I opened the pouch and removed the money, and placed the bills neatly in front of me. I looked at Ella, whose face was filled with bewilderment, and then to the reverend, who offered a similar perplexed expression.

"Reverend," I began. "I would like to donate this money to the Church of Hope so it can construct a proper house of worship," I said, pushing the cash toward him.

An audible gasp came from Ella. "Percy, are you sure?"

I nodded, and said, "I would like to see this money do something for the good people of Hope."

"I don't know what to say, Percy," said the reverend, with tears welling up in his eyes.

"There's nothing to say, only something to do. Let's find a trustworthy builder and get started."

The reverend wagged a finger at me, and said, "I knew there was something special about you, Percy Hope."

I looked over to Ella, who was also crying. She reached over, grasped my hand and silently mouthed the words, "I love you."

CHAPTER THIRTY-ONE—THE HYDRAULIC GIANT

I waited for Percy to finish with the customer and held the door open for him as he exited with his purchase. I locked the door and walked over to Percy, who was recording details into the journal that Mr. Jones used to keep track of the daily purchases.

"Is it true what I heard, Percy?"

Percy looked up at me, slightly tilted his head, and said, "What did you hear, Mr. Vega?"

I sighed. He knew damn well what I was referring to. Everyone in Hope and Sunrise had heard about the discovery and Percy's outrageous donation of his grubstake share to finance a new building for the Church of Hope. Percy had, in one fell swoop, elevated his status from the town's resident good luck charm, to some divine-like deity. But I was here to remind him that his fortune lived with me, as I still held the ace card, and could use it, at the most inopportune time.

"That you are quite the philanthropist."

"Oh, that," he said, trying to make light of his remarkable donation. "Giving is a wonderful thing, Mr. Vega, you should try it."

I smiled and said, "Perhaps I will, Percy. Maybe I'll give the devout followers of the Church of Hope some of the dirty details about your *sinful* behavior at the saloon."

Percy shrugged. "Go ahead, I'll deny it. No one will believe you over me. I'll tell them you're making the whole thing up."

I jerked my head back. Perhaps he was right to call my bluff, but I wasn't ready to test my threat just yet. Instead, I said, "I never thought of you as the fool. I offered to make you a partner, and instead, you burn bridges with me."

"I don't want you as an enemy, Mr. Vega. But I think it would be best if you kept your salacious business enterprises away from the good people of Hope."

I heard heavy footfalls on the wooden staircase and saw the shadow of Mr. Jones approaching. I took a step toward Percy, pointed a finger inches from his face, and said loud enough for Percy's ears only, "Never forget that I made you, and I can just as easily break you."

Percy returned my words with a scowl.

Then Mr. Jones broke the spell.

"What are you doing, Mr. Vega?"

I gently patted Percy's cheek, and turned to face Mr. Jones, and said, "Nothing that concerns you."

"Percy's welfare concerns me," he said, surprising me with his out-of-character boldness.

"Does it, now?" I said, glaring.

"Do you know what Percy did for the people of Hope?"

I held up my palm as a gesture for him to stop. "Yes, I know all about the sixty-ounce nugget, and how Saint Percy the Benevolent donated his share to the church."

"He's quite a boy, Mr. Vega. You must agree."

"Oh, I do. He's the special one," I said, walking over to the new display of the hydraulic mining equipment, set up in front of the store.

Mr. Jones followed and stood beside me.

"Tell me, how are sales?" I asked, with my arms folded across my chest.

"They were going great until we sold out of the Hydro-Giant. You know that's the long cannon-like piece that directs the water flow."

"I gather you sold the floor model?"

He nodded. "A few days ago, two fellas from Seattle staked a claim up on Resurrection Creek. We only had six units to begin with. Now I can't sell the pipes, or the hoses, because they're useless without the Giant."

"Let me see what I can do," I said, rubbing my forehead.

*

When I got back to Sunrise later that day, I sat down at my desk and reviewed the first manifest of the shipment my team expropriated, and there it was—six Hydro-Giants. The records showed that Mr. Jones reordered the Giants twice, but the two subsequent shipments from Cap showed a delivery of zero of these crucial devices.

I tapped my finger on my desk, wondering if Mr. Wible had intentionally decided not to allocate me any of the Giants. This would be a swift and effective way to prevent me from selling the hydraulic equipment. Perhaps it was time to pay him a visit and show him the consequences of his deceit.

CHAPTER THIRTY-TWO—LOVE STORY

It wasn't until the next day that I was able to pull Ella away from the café. Those three big words she mouthed to me at the Reverend's home—*I love you*—had occupied my mind since then. Even Liam noticed my absent-mindedness earlier when we were placer mining.

"What's going on with you today? You seem distant," he asked, knee deep in the creek.

"Oh, it's nothing, Liam," I said, offering him a smile, while I dumped a load of gravel into my pan.

*

I got to the café thirty minutes before closing and ask Ella if she was able to get off early.

She nodded and held up a finger. "Liam, can you handle closing up tonight? I'm going out with Percy."

Liam stuck his head out from the kitchen's pass-through window, took a moment to look at me and Ella, and nodded. "Sure, no problem," he said curtly.

"Thank you," she said, and removed her apron.

She took my hand and we bounded out of the café, and onto Main Street.

"I thought we could take a walk along the Arm," I said, pointing to a trail I knew.

We strolled awhile along the grassy shoreline, making our way around washed up pieces of weathered driftwood, and steep, rocky outcroppings. We eventually reached a wide beach inlaid with round, smooth stones, each one standing on its edge and packed tight against one another, as if someone took the time to arrange them in this pattern.

I picked up one of the flat stones and tossed it side-arm, watching it skip five times before it sank into the chilling, blackish waters of Turnagain Arm.

"I've been meaning to ask you, Ella," I began, trying to summon the courage, "about what you said to me yesterday."

She smiled and took the stone from my hand, and tossed it aside. "I assume you're referring to when I said that I love you?"

My cheeks blushed by her ease at saying those words. I swallowed, took a breath and nodded.

"It's true, Percy. I love you," she said, bending down to grab a stone and flinging it into the water.

"I love you too," I muttered softly with her back toward me.

"What was that? I can't hear you," she asked playfully.

Once the words passed my lips, I gathered my courage, grabbed her arm and pulled her close to me. I gazed into her blue eyes and said, strongly this time, "I love you, Ella."

We spent the next hour kissing and lounging under the sun reflecting off the ripples of the Arm, as playful and carefree as two children living in the moment. There, at the water's edge, I could convince myself that I had found my true love, for I had never before felt so happy. But on our walk back to town, my mind began to swirl. What if Ella learned of my deception? How much suffering would she have to endure when she found out the truth of who I really was? If I truly loved her, how could I cause her such pain?

CHAPTER THIRTY-THREE—DOWN THE RABBIT HOLE

It took several days of agonizing meetings by the building committee, of which I was a member, to decide who would build the Church of Hope. According to the parameters we had set forth, the most qualified name by far was Erik Andersson, a Swede.

There was little debate over the man's skills. Unlike the other candidates, he had built most of the newer structures in Hope, and a few in Sunrise, and even constructed a sailboat that glided effortlessly across Turnagain Arm. His portfolio of quality workmanship was visible for all to see. No one could deny that Mr. Andersson was the man for the job.

The only hesitation was that the Swede was not Catholic. In fact, he was a devout congregant of the blasphemous Asatru church that Rolf and Liam attended.

However, I found Mr. Andersson to be a pleasant man, and I expressed my opinion to the committee to overlook his religious affiliation. "A building is just a shell, it's what we do on the inside that makes it a Catholic church," I said, with a hand over my heart, while at the same time I was thinking about the hypocrisy of these words coming from my lips. After all, I was a Jew masquerading as a Catholic, while at the same time, the Asatru church, according to Liam, was practicing human sacrifice.

Ella, who was also on the committee, vouched for him. "Mr. Andersson and I are from the same country, but we first met here, in Hope, and I can tell you," she said, taking a moment to look the others seated at the table, "he's a trustworthy man."

That, and along with the fact the reverend also supported him, convinced the seven-person committee, by a vote of five to two, to proceed with Mr. Andersson.

*

During this time, my emotions toward Ella shifted as quickly as the tides lapping upon the shore. I relived, over and over, the day we had spent sharing our love for one another, and my fear of what would happen to our romance if things went too far.

Ella quickly realized that something was wrong. "You seem nervous," she said to me one evening, as I avoided eye contact.

"I'm not nervous," I said, too hastily, and rubbed my damp palms together.

She squinted her beautiful blue eyes at me. "I don't get you, Percy. The other day, we seemed so close. But now you're not the same person. Did I do something wrong?"

I desperately wanted to tell her I loved her more than anything. When I considered her response to my growing list of deceptions, I thought perhaps she would understand the reason for my name change, but I knew my pretending to be a Catholic would certainly be devastating. So, rather than risk hurting Ella, I made the agonizing decision with my head, rather than my heart, not to pursue her, and to reject any of her advances.

I should have had the courage to confess, but, as with my previous secrets, I allowed my cowardice to rule me and I said, "No you didn't do anything wrong."

She stared at me for a moment, without saying a word, then she nodded. "All right, Percy, I think I understand," she said, and turned away, leaving me to wonder if I had lost the woman of my dreams.

*

A rhythm to my daily life was taking shape since that day of my big discovery. I would rise at six, and along with Liam, we would go to the café for breakfast. Along the way, the residents of Hope made it a point to greet me with warm regards and demonstrative expressions of their gratitude. My reputation had grown exponentially since my donation to build the church.

It was also becoming obvious that being the center of attention wherever I went, was annoying Liam. When people approached me, as if I was some holy messenger, Liam stood by mostly unnoticed, and ignored. He complained that it was like he was invisible when we walked together, and I couldn't deny his claim.

We spent our days working the sluice boxes up Resurrection Creek. Neither of us discovered anything more than dustings of gold flakes, which were of little value. It had become obvious that the action was where the hydraulics were now plowing into the embankments along the creeks, and the tributaries feeding them.

During our breaks we walked over to watch the violence of the water cannon tearing into the earth, exposing the bedrock within minutes. When we asked Mr. Stanton if it was possible to be part of this new method of mining, he said that the Company could not come to an agreement with Mr. Wible since he controlled the monopoly of hydraulic equipment along the Arm.

Once the workday was over, Liam and I bathed in the wooden bathtubs in the bunkhouse's backyard, and dressed for dinner. Eventually Rolf assigned us a proper room when two prospectors from Texas headed back home with just enough money for their passage.

Upon our arrival at the café, I decided not to sit at my secluded table in the kitchen in order to eat my dinner in peace. After my sudden shift in behavior toward Ella, I felt it to be more appropriate to eat in the dining hall with everyone else.

Ella served me my meals cordially, without any expression of disdain for how I shut her down. I wondered though if she felt the same heartache that was gnawing away at me, or if she was able to let it go.

It didn't take long for me to figure that she could move on without me, and that message came loud and clear through her sudden interest in Liam. At first, I noticed a gentle touch that Liam would place on Ella's arm as they stopped to speak to each other, or the smile she would offer Liam as they parted.

I tried my best to subdue my frustration that it was Liam on the receiving end of Ella's affection, rather than me. But I suppose I deserved it, and Liam had nothing to hide.

While I waited for my meal of Liam's popular beef stew one afternoon, Ella approached, and asked, "Is all right if I ask you something?"

I shrugged and said, "Sure, why not?"

"I don't want to bother you while you're eating, that's all."

"You're not bothering me," I said, feeling blood rush to my ears.

She nodded and sat down. "Did you hear what happened at the building site today?" she asked, rubbing her fingertips upon her forehead.

I shook my head, and said, "No, what happened?"

"Mr. Vega stopped by this afternoon and forced Mr. Andersson to halt any further construction."

I furrowed my brow and insisted, "He can't do that."

She leaned over the table and said, "Apparently he can. He said that he had purchased the lot next to the church and that our building was encroaching upon his property."

"Is that true?" I asked, leaning back and folding my arms across my chest.

"It's hard to say. He provided a deed of sale, but the property lines are questionable."

"What did the reverend say?"

"He said we need to work this out amicably with Mr. Vega."

I shook my head. "I'm afraid that amicable and Magnus Vega are two things that don't mix well—like oil and water."

"What do you think we should do?" she asked.

"I suppose I must speak to him."

"That's good, because Mr. Vega told the reverend that the only person who could resolve this issue was you," she said, pointing at me.

"He said that?"

"Yes, he wants you to visit him at his saloon tonight to discuss it."

I hadn't been back to Sunrise since that fateful evening exactly two weeks ago. But I couldn't allow this to linger too long, because Mr. Andersson would undoubtedly find other work, and would leave us searching for a new builder to complete the church.

I wasn't looking forward to dealing with Mr. Vega as I knew what he was capable of. But the more I thought about it, the more I had a feeling that this property line controversy was a ruse and nothing more than a good way to get my attention.

"You know, Ella," I said, with a sly smile, "what if I went to the Company's office? Maybe they would have some information as to the property lots in town?"

Ella smiled and said, "That's a good idea."

"Ella, I need you," Liam interrupted, poking his head out from around the corner.

"One second, Liam," she said, with a noticeable change of sweetness to her tone. "I have to go. But see what you can find out."

She stood up, and just as she turned away, she stopped and looked back at me, and said, "Thank you, Percy. I don't know what we would do without you."

I nodded my acknowledgment, and as she headed back to the kitchen, I couldn't help but sigh and stare at her.

"Hey," a voice called out. I looked up and saw Liam, still standing where he'd just been.

"Oh, hi, Liam," I said.

He gave me a curious look, then turned to Ella.

As I sat there, a strange and sad emptiness washed over me. It was impossible to deny my emotions, nor the irony of my behavior. I wanted nothing more than to be with Ella, but as long as I was living dishonestly, my love for her forced me to keep me distance from her.

Meanwhile, as a result, Ella and Liam seemed to be growing closer, while I sat on the sidelines glancing out the window onto busy Main Street, where the people of Hope were going about their early evening activities. I took a breath and thought about how just a short time ago I was just another teenager, living carefree in San Francisco, working in my father's store. I swallowed hard and wondered how these strange things could have happened to me so quickly.

It had been three weeks since I was dropped onto this small plot of land, an oasis from the normal world, nestled within the elbow of

Turnagain Arm, and encompassed by majestic, snow-capped mountains. I wished I had the courage to free myself from the lies that consumed me. But the longer they lingered, the further Ella drifted away from me, and the more comfortable she became in Liam's arms.

CHAPTER THIRTY-FOUR—PINKERTON

I knew that dealing with Mr. Wible would prove to be more formidable than the usual array of the locals I did business with. He was not unnerved by the strong-arm tactics I typically used to get my way.

For example, Mr. Jones learned quickly about the consequences of his defiance. When I first approached him at the beginning of last summer, he had shunned my offers.

"Why do I need you to protect my shipments? They've been arriving without incident since I opened last year," he argued.

After two of his deliveries went missing, Mr. Jones floundered for cash because of a lack of merchandise to sell. Consequently, the next time I paid him a visit; he was much more amenable to my offer of protecting his shipments. To show my gratitude, I generously lent him two-hundred dollars to carry him forward until the next order arrived.

But Mr. Wible had already proven that he was far more cunning than Mr. Jones. I enjoyed the prospect of stepping up my game, especially with the stakes much higher than the mundane household items and groceries sold at a general store.

"What do you want, Vega?" Mr. Wible barked out at me when I entered his newly opened Bakersfield Outfitters.

The first thing I saw was the Hydro-Giant on display in the middle of the store. I pointed at it and said, "I've come inquiring about these. Mr. Jones has sold the six we started with and he needs more. He can't sell the pipes and hoses without it."

"That's all you're getting," he said dismissively, turned his back on me and walked toward the rear of his well-stocked store.

I took a brief look around. He had everything one would need for prospecting. Neatly displayed upon the wooden shelves were items such as axes, handsaws, hatchets, knives, prospector picks, gold-dust bags, pans, and sluice boxes. Featured in the center of the store was an impressive display of the hydraulic supplies of hoses, pipes, fittings, and—the Giant.

"I'm here to convince you otherwise," I said.

Mr. Wible stopped, turned around and walked towards me, which caused me to take an involuntary step backwards. But as he got closer, I realized he was passing me by and heading for the front door. I turned and saw a tall, mustachioed man wearing a black Fedora hat and an expensive-looking suit entering the store.

"Ah, you must be Detective Siringo," Mr. Wible said, greeting the man.

"Indeed, and you must be Mr. Wible," the distinguished-looking man said, extending his hand.

"Please, let's go to my office in the back, we have many things to discuss. Then we'll walk over to the house and get you situated."

157

They walked past me and as if suddenly remembering I was standing there, Mr. Wible stopped and turned around. "Oh, and this is Mr. Magnus Vega, the man I telegraphed you about," he said gesturing to me. "Mr. Vega, allow me to introduce Detective Charles Siringo of the Pinkerton Detective Agency. He's here to help us organize and institute a system of law and order for Sunrise City."

"Pinkerton?" was all I could mutter.

"That's right, Mr. Vega," Detective Siringo said with a smile, showing off his full set of white teeth.

I looked over to Mr. Wible who reached over, patted my back and said, "I'm sure Detective Siringo will seek you out for a conversation shortly. But for now, if you would excuse us, I'm sure my guest would like to relax after his long journey."

I nodded and exited Bakersfield Outfitters with my head hung low, trying to figure out what I would do next. Until today, there were no official police or systems of justice in Sunrise. The only semblance of order was in Hope, and that came through the iron hand of the reverend.

It was true that the Pinkerton's were hired guns, so to speak, but their reputation for keeping the peace in lawless towns like ours was legendary. It wouldn't be long before effective law enforcement was in place. This would require that I reevaluate my methods, what with these new, daunting challenges now facing me.

*

Friday was the busiest night at the saloon, and with my fortunes suddenly put into jeopardy by the appearance of Detective Siringo, I wanted everything to run smoothly. But just as I dismounted my horse, and tied him to the post in front of the saloon, I remembered a saying my mother told me. She liked to complain that *when it rains, it pours*, meaning that when something bad happens, other bad things usually happen at the same time. And wouldn't you know it, just as I pushed my way through the saloon doors, I heard a commotion.

As I stepped in, I saw Stan Smith flail a wide swinging punch at Percy Hope's face. Percy deftly took a step backward, avoiding Stan's fist, and jabbed a right into his exposed ribs. Stan cringed and doubled over.

I caught a quick glance of Suzie, whose eyes were locked in on the fighters, her mouth agape. Meanwhile, Stan threw another punch, landing one on Percy's upper right arm, stunning him. Percy yelled something, like he was summoning his strength from some sacred power, causing Stan to hesitate, and within the blink of an eye, Percy attacked. He fired precision punches to the torso and landed a decisive one to his chin, forcing Stan backwards, where he tripped over a nearby chair, causing him to tumble.

He lay awhile on the floor, where the fresh layer of sawdust that was just spread out this morning was now coating his perspiring skin.

Percy reached down and offered Stan a hand to help him back to his feet. Stan smacked it away and staggered back to a standing position. He slouched over, propping himself up by placing his hands on his bent knees.

"That's enough," I shouted, not wanting to see Stan humiliated any further.

Percy dropped his hands and stood down. Stan nodded in defeat, and Henry brought a chair over for him.

I pulled up a chair for Percy and gestured for him to sit.

"Let's give them some air," I said, dismissing Suzie and her entourage.

"Come on, girls, let the boys work things out," she said, ushering them upstairs.

"Wow, Percy, that was quite something," said Greta, who was Percy's girl the last time he was here.

Percy nodded to Greta as she hustled up the staircase to her room.

I exhaled and said, "Okay, can you tell me what this was about?"

Stan shrugged and pointed at Percy. "We got into an argument over the property lines of the new church, and its encroachment onto your property."

Percy stood up, walked over to another table, and picked up a leather satchel. "It's all in here," he said, reaching inside and handed over an official-looking document.

"What's this?" I said, looking.

"This is proof from the Alaska Commercial Company, showing the property lot lines between the church and your property, Mr. Vega. Your claim is unwarranted, sir. I've come to tell you because this Monday Mr. Andersson will be back at work."

"And I told him to go fuck himself," Stan interjected.

I shook my head. "Stan, you must control your temper."

"I am partly to blame because I engaged with Mr. Smith. We argued and ended up throwing punches."

I patted Stan on his back, and said, "It looks like you met your match." I turned to Percy, and asked, "Tell me, Percy, who taught you how to box?"

"A boxing club back home."

"You're constantly surprising me," I said, looking at the document. From what I could tell, it was accurate. But I didn't want the church to be built, because once that happened, I would never turn Hope away from the church. I wanted to keep the pressure on, regardless of what the deed proclaimed.

"You can plainly see that the two lots are clearly marked, and the church is being built well within its parameters. May I consider this issue resolved, so we can resume building?"

"Do you think I care about a piece of paper?" I said, lowering my voice for effect.

"It's not just a piece of paper. It's a legal document," Percy replied.

"Here's what I think of your document," I said, reaching for my lighter. I flicked it and the blue flame wavered on the edge before the paper caught on fire. I held on to it for a moment and then let it float down to the sawdust-covered floor, where it continued to burn, and eventually smolder out.

Percy shrugged. "That means nothing," he said, rising to his feet. "This is a warning, Mr. Vega, do not interfere with the building of our church." He walked toward the doors but paused when he got there, turned, and said, "The reverend wants you to know that nearly half of our congregants are residents of Sunrise, and there've been discussions of turning it into a dry town, in which case all of this"—he waved his hand—"will be gone."

I watched Percy walk out through the saloon doors, and as the doors swung closed, it felt like a slap in my face. I stood up and climbed the staircase leading up to my rooms. Halfway up the steps I stopped, looked at Stan whose arms and half his face were covered with a coating of sawdust, and barked, "Get yourself cleaned up, you look like a breaded chicken breast right before it goes into the oven."

CHAPTER THIRTY-FIVE—CONFUSION

I waited for Mr. Andersson to finish speaking with two of his carpenters before I approached.

"It's good to have you back, Mr. Andersson," I said.

"It's good to be back, Percy, but please call me Erik," he said, strapping his leather tool belt around his waist. Then he continued, "I understand that you came to blows with Vega's henchman over the dispute."

I shrugged. "Yeah, it's nothing I'm proud of and did little good. Mr. Vega made a mockery of the document by burning it."

"Well, it's legally binding, so there's little he can do to stop us, and Stan Smith deserved to be knocked on his ass." He laughed and patted me on my back.

"I suppose so, and hopefully you won't have any further disruptions," I said as one of Erik's carpenters approached.

"Have you met Tommy?" Erik asked, gesturing to a man with arms that looked as thick as a normal man's thigh.

I reached out and shook his hand and felt his iron grip up to my elbow. "Hello, Tommy."

Tommy nodded without a word, or any noticeable change in his solemn expression.

"Tommy is the son of Chief Ephanasy of the Knik tribe."

"Knik?" I said, unfamiliar with the name.

"The Kniks are natives of these parts. One tribe lives in a settlement just west of Hope."

"It's an honor to meet you."

The chief's son nodded and said, "You can call me Tommy, but my real name is Wahska."

"Okay, Tommy," I said, with the sudden urge to confess my real name. But I offered my farewells and headed off to church.

On my way to services I caught up with Ella, and gestured to the worksite behind me, and said, "Good morning, Ella, it looks like things are back to normal."

Ella wagged a finger at me, and said, "It's the Sabbath. Mr. Andersson should not be working today."

"It's our Sabbath, not his. The Asatrus consider Sunday their holy day," I reminded Ella.

"All the same, it's not respectable to be building a Catholic church on a Saturday. But that's not what I want to speak to you about."

"What is it, Ella? Is everything okay?"

Ella looked around, tugged at my elbow, and said, "Not here."

It was impossible for Ella to share her thoughts with me immediately, because we were constantly interrupted by fellow congregants on their way to church, wishing me a good Sabbath, and even by the agnostics, who offered warm greetings, as they went about their early morning chores.

Frustrated, Ella gestured for us to slip into an alleyway in between the general store and the post office.

"What is it, Ella?" I asked, concerned at her stealthy behavior.

She pursed her lips, and said, "Liam told me some disturbing things about the Asatru church last night."

"Let me guess, he told you about the sacrifices?"

"You know about them? Why didn't you say something?" she asked, rubbing her cheek.

I shrugged. "He swore me to secrecy. Don't forget I live with Rolf too, and it frightened Liam that there would be repercussions if he spoke about it to outsiders."

"Did you know that there's a ceremony planned for tonight? Apparently, it's the seventh day of the seventh month, and there will be a sacrifice of seven male animals, hung upon seven branches."

"No, I didn't. He told me about the ninth day of the ninth month where they do the same thing, but what frightened Liam was what they sacrificed on the ninth branch."

Ella's normally pale skin turned translucent as the blood rushed from her face. "Oh my God, Percy," she said, grabbing my arm to steady herself. "Don't tell me they sacrifice a human?"

I nodded. "But that isn't for another eight weeks. I thought there would be time to deal with it."

"But there isn't. Don't you understand? There's a ceremony tonight!"

I shrugged. "So what, they're only sacrificing animals. What's the harm?"

Ella shook her head. "What kind of Catholic are you, Percy? Each creature on this earth reflects our Creator. The presence of God's wisdom, goodness and beauty is captured within each bird, fish, and four-legged animal. Percy, this is an act of desecration against the holy spirit, and must be stopped."

"Stopped?" I said, surprised at her boldness. "How do you propose we do that?"

She nodded quickly and said, "Tonight, we'll take the footpath along the Arm. Liam told me they meet just before Sixmile Creek. He said there's a beachhead that's encompassed by a naturally formed jetty that offers privacy, and I think I know where it is."

"Then what? Do we just pop in and declare it as some sacrilegious desecration, or whatever you called it? What would that do except put us in danger?"

"I realize that. We just need to see for ourselves, you know, be an eyewitness. Then we can go back and report what we saw to the reverend. He'll know what to do."

"Why don't we just tell him now. I'm sure he's heard rumors about their strange behaviors."

"Rumors are one thing. Hearing it first-hand from me and you is entirely different."

*

After church services, Ella and I agreed to rendezvous behind the café later in the evening for our espionage adventure. I suggested that it might be a good idea for me to spend some time beforehand with Liam, and try to uncover any insights into tonight's ceremony that might be helpful.

Liam and I had spoken about trying our hand at salmon fishing. This seemed like a good excuse to get some time alone with him and see what he would share.

We tried our luck at Resurrection Creek. Rolf lent us two fishing rods and silver fishing lures, along with a quick lesson in the basics on how to catch the *pinks*.

"You cast out as far as you can, then just as the hook hits the water, start cranking the casting reel. Jerk the rod, reel a bit, then jerk it again, reel it and keep repeating until you return the lure to the rod when you'll cast it out again, unless you're lucky and you've hooked a pink."

Apparently good fortune wasn't on our side, but within a few hours of practice, we learned how to cast, and not look like two clueless city-boys.

While our fishing was unproductive, our conversations provided some useful insights.

"So once more you're the talk of the town, Percy," Liam said.

"Oh, are you talking about yesterday at the saloon?"

"Yeah, I heard you got into a fight with Mr. Smith," he said, flicking his wrist, and casting out about thirty feet out into the fast-moving creek.

I shrugged and said, "I just got lucky. He's a big guy, and I hope he's not looking for a rematch."

"Come on, you knocked him on his ass once, you can do it again," Liam said, smiling but keeping his eyes glued to the line.

"I don't know about that," I said, casting my line out.

"You're a good fighter with quick hands. He's a slow, old, fat man."

I laughed and shifted the conversation. "How are things at the café?"

"Good. It's better than wasting my time prospecting. I can't believe we came all this way searching for gold, and I find more joy in cooking."

"I know, me too. I look forward to my hours at the general store. I guess I could have stayed home and worked for Father."

Liam turned to me and said, "I still can't believe you donated all of your proceeds to the building of the church. What will you tell your parents?"

"That I did a *mitzvah*?"

"A what?"

"A *mitzvah*. It's a Jewish word for doing a good deed."

"A good deed?" he asked with a smirk. "What's the Jewish words for *you're in deep shit*?"

I nodded. Liam was right. The longer I put up this charade of lying about my name and religion, the deeper the hole I was digging for myself.

"It will be tricky figuring a way of getting out of this unscathed. But what about you and this Norse God stuff you're involved with? From what you told me, there's some crazy stuff going on there."

Liam puckered his mouth and shook his head, reacting like I'd triggered something emotional.

168

"I can't talk about it," he said, barely moving his lips.

I reached over and grabbed Liam's forearm and squeezed it. "If you're in danger, you need to tell me."

"And what will you do about it?" he asked, glaring at me.

"I don't know," I sputtered. "But we're supposed to look out for each other."

"Don't worry about me, and while you're at it, stop your gawking at Ella," he said, handing me the fishing rod and walking away.

"Liam, what are you doing? Come back, let's talk."

But he kept walking.

CHAPTER THIRTY-SIX—LAW & ORDER

Every chair was taken, while other residents sat side-by-side on the bar top with their legs dangling off. Along the staircase, people found spots on the steps, squeezing their faces in between the spindles of the railing. Suzie and her girls were lined up along the balcony, gawking at the spectacle below. There were dozens of men standing or leaning their backs against the walls of the saloon. There was even a crowd gathered on the front porch, trying to listen to the proceedings through the two front windows propped open.

Detective Siringo had asked if we could conduct the meetings at the saloon, since it was the largest indoor space to accommodate such a large gathering. I agreed, feeling that this display of city-unity in my saloon would provide me some legitimacy among the population of Sunrise.

I wondered how many people we squeezed into my twelve-hundred-foot square saloon. Certainly, more than any of the busiest nights since we'd opened. It was also loud. I looked over to Mr. Wible, who was trying to quiet the crowd by raising his hands and pleading for attention, which was mostly ignored. That was until Detective Siringo fired two rounds from his Colt 45 skywards, which startled everyone into silence, except for me, as I was mortified that he had just shot two holes into the roof of my saloon.

"Are you fucking kidding," I blurted out over the sudden silence.

Mr. Wible glared at me and shook his head before he began. "Thank you all for coming. As you may have heard, tonight we have a special visitor. He is a detective with the Pinkerton Detective Agency and is here to help our city of Sunrise organize and implement a system of law and order. Please give your full attention to Detective Charles Siringo."

A polite, but brief round of applause followed the introduction.

Detective Siringo held up his palm to acknowledge the welcome and reached into his jacket pocket and pulled out a document. "In any growing city with a population approaching one thousand residents, it is mandatory that a system of law and order be implemented."

A wave of conversations washed across the saloon.

"Let the detective speak. He's come a long way, please show him respect," Mr. Wible called out.

The crowd hushed.

The detective nodded to Mr. Wible, and continued, "The American form of law and order is well known. I've worked with several cities across Colorado, Nevada, and California in setting up institutions of justice. We will do it exactly the same way here."

People's heads nodded, showing their collective approval.

"In a nutshell, this is how it will work. To write the laws and determine the taxes, the residents of Sunrise will elect a Mayor who will name four trustees. To enforce these laws and collect the taxes, the voters will elect a Sheriff, and the Sheriff will appoint two deputies. And lastly, to interpret the laws and apply equal justice, an election will appoint a Judge, who will appoint a clerk of the court."

"When will we be voting?" someone yelled out, followed by more chatter.

Detective Siringo raised his hands, and waited for silence to continue, "I have designated the first Tuesday in August as our day of elections."

"Who can run for these positions?" asked a man standing near the front door.

"Anyone can run as long as they are over twenty-one years of age, and a resident of Sunrise. During the next seven days, we'll be accepting nominations. To be nominated, the potential candidate must record a minimum of two-hundred signatures from fellow residents who are eligible to vote. On Tuesday, August the second, at nine in the morning, we will open the polls for voting. The winners will be announced after the polls close at nine o'clock that night, and the ballots counted."

"This sounds all good and well, Detective," said a large, barrel-chested man, pushing his way to the front by zig-zagging through an amalgamation of people sitting at the tables. "But government needs more than a mayor, a sheriff and a judge. We'll need a city hall to keep records, a sheriff's office to jail prisoners and a courtroom to try them. How do you plan to get that accomplished, and who will pay for it?"

"May I ask your name, sir?" asked Mr. Wible.

"I'm Herman Cole, Attorney at Law from the great State of Oregon," he said, with his baritone voice that matched his over-sized physique.

172

Mr. Wible, a large man himself, almost looked small in stature next to Mr. Cole. But he stood tall and said, "Well, Mr. Cole, we plan on building these facilities over the next few weeks. As for who will pay for it, I'll be giving the city a loan, which will be paid back once enough taxes are collected."

A burst of yelps and applause followed Mr. Wible's announcement. He held up his hands to quiet the audience and continued addressing Mr. Cole. "Obviously a man with your credentials should be nominated for an office. You could probably get most of your signatures here tonight."

"If I can muster the signatures, I'll run for judge," he said to a rousing cheer.

I couldn't deny the sense of excitement that was buzzing throughout the room. It was like a contagion, and I caught its effect too.

Mr. Wible leaned in close to me and said, "Are you ready to make a few bucks tonight?"

I shrugged and said, "Always."

With that, Mr. Wible stretched both arms into the air. "Gentlemen and Ladies," he said and glanced up to Suzie, who offered her most alluring smile, "let's celebrate the making of Sunrise into a city with law and order, and may we all discover the fortunes we seek." A roar went up that rattled the crystal chandeliers hanging from the rafters.

Within moments, the saloon returned to its true purpose. Cards and poker chips were spread across the tables, Henry poured shots of whiskey as quickly as he was able, Cameron banged out popular tunes on the piano, and Suzie and her girls got busy.

Tonight would be a big night, but gnawing at the back of my mind was the notion that my free-wheeling methods of doing business would need to change. Operating within the law would create significant challenges, and I had only a few weeks to figure out how to take advantage of them, instead of being buried by them.

CHAPTER THIRTY-SEVEN—THE SACRIFICE

Pointing, Ella whispered, "I think I can see the campfire."

I blinked, trying to shake the raindrops from my eyes, and saw in between the thick summer foliage, glimpses of a flickering orange flame.

"Let's see if we can get closer," Ella said, gesturing to a rocky outcropping along the shore.

"I can see them," I said, also pointing.

"Come on," Ella said, taking my hand.

Cautiously, we moved as one through the thick brush. With each step, the sounds of indistinguishable voices rose from a low murmur into nearly audible conversations. Ella squeezed my hand, signaling for me to stop.

We crouched down to our knees on the rain-soaked forest floor, giving us a keen, unobstructed view of the Asatru congregants as they stood in a circle encompassing a large tree with branches forming a canopy over the beachhead. The campfire illuminated the strange, flickering images of the ceremony in progress.

Ella gestured, and whispered, "There are Rolf and Liam."

"I see them, and there's Erik Andersson."

All three were standing next to each other and looking up into the tree. I tried to follow their gaze and could make out nothing more than shadowy figures hanging from ropes. "What's that swinging from the tree branches?" I whispered to Ella.

"Those must be the sacrificial animals," she said, placing her hand over her mouth. "Percy, I think I'm going to be sick."

I put my arm around her shoulder and pulled her in tight. "If you need to puke, I'll hold you."

Ella closed her eyes for a minute, then opened them and said, "No, it's passed. I'm all right."

"Do you want to get closer?"

Ella nodded.

We crawled along the rain-soaked forest floor and through the ground cover of Devil's Club, a plant that sported sharp spines on its large leaves and sturdy stems. I tried to push them aside, clearing a path for Ella, but regardless, we were both stung and scratched up by the vicious plant.

When we got within several feet of the circle of Asatru men, the full scene of the atrocities was visible. As Ella thought, there were seven ropes with seven animals hanging off seven branches of an impressively large tree. After a few moments of trying to make out what it was I was witnessing, I saw swinging from the ropes: a dog, a moose calf, a cat, a fox, a grouse, a squirrel, and a seagull. Each one was bleeding out onto the black gravel beneath them.

Rolf then stepped forward, positioning himself beneath each animal. He lifted a long blade and sliced into the bellies of each beast, allowing its blood to drain onto him. When his head was awash in the mingled blood of all seven creatures, he held both arms up to the heavens and said a prayer.

"Thunder rolls and lightning strikes, my hammer flies across the sky.

Gods of weather, chariots of storm, masters of rain and torrents,

Son of the strength of Mother Earth,

I ask you to grant me that strength for myself.

You whose tree is the mighty oak,

O', Thor, grant me unending sturdiness.

Let me not break beneath the blows of misfortune.

You who are the guardian of the common man,

You who care for the farmers and workers,

Look upon me here in this place where I am only one of many and

protect my steps.

Make me resilient and mighty as your own arm,

Make me unbreakable, you who are a friend of Man.

I ask for one small part of the vigor of the right arm of Thor,

That I might brave the tempest and stand firm in the gales.

Thunder rolls, lightning strikes, and my hammer flies across the sky."

Rolf finished and stood motionless. He gazed upwards, causing me to look too. But all I saw were black rain clouds emptying themselves upon the earth below. Rolf reached out with one arm, stretching out his hand like he was ready to grasp something. *Perhaps it's Thor's hammer*, I imagined.

It was quite a sight. Like a statue of a Norse God, Rolf stood frozen in place, his shirt washed in the blood of the seven male animals, clinging to his mighty and muscular frame.

Then slowly, like a beating drum, the chanting began:

"Thor, Thor, Hahrd-hoo-gahd-ur, Thor, Thor, Ah-sah-Thor."

It was repeated over and over again, until Rolf released his pose, and collapsed into the puddle of purple blood beneath his feet.

"Rolf," Ella shouted, stood up and ran to her brother.

"Ella, stop!" I yelled, reaching for her. But she was already beyond the cover of the foliage and no longer hidden. "Damn it," I said, and chased after her.

It took a second for the circle of men to take notice of Ella. Liam stepped toward her and said, "Ella, what are you doing here?"

When I emerged, Rolf had stood up and was approaching his sister. I ran toward her but was stopped by someone clutching my wrist. I turned and saw it was Erik Andersson. "Let go of me," I demanded.

"Why are you here?" he asked.

Ella pointed up to the swinging dead animals, still dripping in blood, and screamed, "What kind of sick religion is this? This is the work of the devil."

Rolf tried to wipe the blood off his hands and reached out to his sister. "Ella, you can't be here."

I struggled in vain to release myself from Erik's iron grip.

"Why have you come, Sam? You've ruined everything," Liam said, standing inches from my face.

"We were worried about you, and Rolf," I said, realizing Liam had called out my real name. I prayed that no one else noticed, especially Ella, who had collapsed and lay curled up on the beach, sobbing.

With great force, I ripped my wrist free from Erik and went to her. But Liam put a hand against my chest, stopping me. "I'll go," he said.

Liam approached Ella, gently rubbed her back, and whispered, "Ella, I'm sorry."

Ella glanced up with a look of disgust and swatted Liam's hand away. "Don't you dare touch me." She stood up and walked toward me and said, "Let's go."

I followed Ella through the dreaded Devil's Club and along the footpath back to Hope. Neither of us said a word during the three hours until we reached the café when Ella turned to me and said, "Can you tell me why Liam called you Sam?"

CHAPTER THIRTY-EIGHT—SUZIE & SIMON

"Wake up, Magnus," Suzie said, shaking me.

"Why?" was the only word I could muster.

"Because Henry's knocking."

"What time is it?" I asked, trying to shake the cobwebs from my brain.

"I don't know. Just go get the door. I can't stand the banging. He's relentless."

"Yeah, I told him to wake me up at ten," I said, swinging my legs off the edge of the bed.

"Hey, boss, open up. I got your coffee," came Henry's muffled voice from the hallway.

"One second," I shouted, stood up and took a step toward the door.

"You're answering the door like that?" asked Suzie still tucked under the blanket.

I scratched my belly and looked down at my nakedness and shrugged. Lying on the floor was Suzie's silk nightgown. I bent over, picked it up and slipped it on. "Better?" I asked Suzie.

"Not really," she snickered.

I opened the door, and Henry's eyes nearly popped from their sockets. "Morning, boss," he said, and glanced over to Suzie. "Where would you like it?" he asked, jerking his head to the silver tray he was carrying with a coffee pot, two ceramic cups, and a sugar bowl with two small silver spoons, all lying upon a linen napkin.

"On the porch," I said, pulling the front of the skimpy gown, trying to cover my privates.

"Sure thing, boss," he said, stepping quickly away.

Once Henry was gone, I took off the nightgown and tossed it to Suzie. I quickly found my trousers and an old, wrinkled linen shirt to put on, and stepped out onto the deck. The morning was full of sunshine and unusually warm.

"Good morning, sweetie," Suzie said, joining me on my wooden porch overlooking Front Street.

I turned my head to look at her, and said, "Would you like some coffee?"

"Sure, I'd love some."

"That was some night," I said, glimpsing her long, naked leg slipping through the front of her nightgown, as she sat down across from me.

"What do you think will happen to us once we have this so-called law and order in Sunrise?"

I shrugged, stood up and walked over to the railing and looked down upon the activity on Front Street below. "The only way to know is by making sure we control the people who get elected."

"What do you mean? Are you going to run for an office?" she said, taking a sip of coffee.

I shrugged. "Maybe I should run for mayor."

Suzie pointed a finger at me and said, "That would be great. Me and the girls will campaign for you."

I grimaced and shook my head. "That's probably not a good idea, though I appreciate the offer."

"You're probably right," she said, joining me by the railing. "It looks like Mr. Cole will be a shoo-in for Judge. I think he's gathered more than enough signatures last night for the nomination."

I frowned, thinking about him. "He seems incorruptible, though you never know."

Suzie pointed below to Stan Smith heading our way. "Maybe Stan can run for sheriff."

I shook my head and said, "Nah, he hasn't the smarts. Even if he got elected, he would cause more problems than he would solve. We must find someone else."

"I'd better wake the girls. Last night was busy, and I'm sure it will take them a while to freshen themselves up for the day," she said, kissing me on my lips.

"I'll meet you downstairs after I take my bath."

I watched Suzie saunter back into the bedroom—a sight I never tired of—and thought about the time when we first met two years ago. We were both employed at the Miller House in Dawson City. Suzie was one of the working girls under the auspices of Madame Lily, while I was saloon manager.

We found ourselves spending our free time together, which was one day a week, when the saloon was closed. Eventually, we became a couple, and I imagined that after I made my fortune, Suzie would return home with me to Chicago, where we would make a life as a regular couple. Occasionally, people would ask if it bothered me that she spread her legs for a living. I would just shrug and say, "That's what she does best."

When I learned of the discovery of gold in Sunrise, we left the Klondike and see if we could make it on our own. We had both saved money, which included a collection of a few good-sized golden nuggets that Suzie earned or swiped from her inebriated or passed out customers.

Between my accumulated knowledge of what I learned of the saloon business from Mr. Miller, and Suzie's education of the whoring life under the tutelage of Madame Lily, we were confident of our chances of success in the burgeoning city of Sunrise, Alaska.

After I bathed and dressed, I proceeded downstairs to the saloon. My plan was to head over to Bakersfield's and probe my idea of running for mayor with Mr. Wible. Just as I was about to step outside through the saloon doors, I glanced off to my left and stopped short.

"Mr. Wible, I was just about to walk over to see you at the store," I exclaimed.

"No need," he said, exhaling a puff from his cigar, "please join me."

I nodded, and we sat down at one of the card tables. "That was quite an event last night."

He smiled and leaned back in his chair. "It was. In fact, that's why I came to talk to you," he said and took another puff on his cigar, before he continued. "What would you think about running for mayor?"

"Me?" I said, trying to act surprised.

"Isn't that what you want?"

I had always thought of myself as someone who was incalculable and used this as an asset to have my way. But Mr. Wible had already proven to be one step ahead of me with his clever maneuvers regarding the hydraulics. Now he foresaw my desire to run for mayor.

"I was thinking about it," I confessed with a shrug.

"Good, and I want you to know that I'll support you."

"You will?"

He nodded and gestured for me to lean in. "You'll run for mayor, and I'll make sure you win. I can also tell you that Mr. Cole will be the city's Judge and Detective Siringo will be Sheriff."

"How do you know that?"

Mr. Wible smiled while pinching the cigar between his yellowed teeth and said, "Such is the nature of democracy in a city filled with sinners. The people of Sunrise are here for one reason and one reason only, to strike it rich. Eventually, they'll all go back to whence they came, with most of them having nothing to show for their efforts."

I nodded.

"This city has a year at most, before it will disappear into the dustbin of history. Until then, I will blast the hell out of these hillsides and pull as much gold out as I can. But to do this, I'll need law and order to keep the good people of Sunrise in their place, and that's where you, Detective Siringo, and Mr. Cole will come in."

"How so?"

"Think of yourself as a shepherd, and the residents of Sunrise, as your flock. Your responsibility as mayor will be to keep them in order, and out of my way. In exchange, I'll pay you a five percent share of my net."

"But what about my saloon?" I asked.

"Nothing changes, it will remain as is."

I nodded and said, "All right, Mr. Wible, you can count me in."

He patted my back and said, "There's one more thing. From what I understand, the reverend over in Hope is preaching against the sins of Sunrise."

"You're talking about Reverend O'Hara."

Mr. Wible nodded. "I am, and he's a powerful voice that must be silenced before we find his influence seeping into Sunrise. I can tell you from experience, once the word of God infiltrates into our community, we can say goodbye to these grand plans."

"What do you have in mind?"

Mr. Wible stood up and smiled. "Nothing sinister, but I'll leave that up to you, Mr. Mayor. Just let me know when it's done," he said and walked out of the saloon.

CHAPTER THIRTY-NINE—SAMUEL ROTHMAN

When I awoke the next morning, Liam was not in his bed. I dressed quickly and ran downstairs to ask if anyone had seen him. After questioning several of the bunk-house residents before they headed off to the creeks and rivers for the day, I learned that Liam had not come home last night, and neither had Rolf.

Their absence gave me welcome relief, knowing that my inevitable confrontation with them regarding the previous evening's debacle, would be postponed at least for a while. But in the meantime, I was expected at the café to meet with Ella and provide an answer to her question as to why Liam called me Sam. This anxiety churned my stomach, and forced an extended visit to the outhouse.

Once I emptied my loose bowels, I headed down Main Street to the Hope Café. Along the way, I was greeted in the usual warm fashion by the townspeople. But with my mind preoccupied, I could barely drum up my forced go-to smile for them.

When I stepped into the café and saw Ella sitting at a table with Rolf and Liam, my stomach churned once more.

"Come, Percy, and sit with us," Ella said, gesturing to the empty chair. "Or should we be calling you Sam?"

I looked over to Liam, whose puckered face needed no words to express his displeasure with me. "It's time to speak the truth," he said.

Any effort to continue my charade seemed futile. "All right," I said, taking a seat, ready to confess. "As you have learned," I began by looking at Liam, "my name's not Percy Hope. I used that name as an alias, at the request of my parents, to protect myself."

"To protect you from what?" asked Ella, her wrinkled forehead expressing her concern.

"From people who have unflattering opinions of Jews," I said, looking at Ella, eager to gauge her reaction at the remark.

"You're a Jew?" she said, pointing at me.

"I am, and my name is Samuel Rothman."

"But why did you pretend to be Catholic?" asked Rolf.

"It sort of just happened after Mr. Vega named the town after me, and then the reverend proclaimed me as some sort of a holy messenger. I couldn't muster the courage to tell the truth."

"So, you lied?" Ella said, with a grimace.

I bit my lip and nodded.

"And that's why you didn't know the seven deadly sins," she said wagging a finger.

I nodded again.

Ella closed her eyes for a moment. When she opened them, she tilted her head and said, "I knew there was something about you that wasn't quite right. It's not easy living a lie, is it, Sam?"

I took a breath, and looked down at my hands folded on the table and shook my head. "No, Ella, you're right. It's not easy." I straightened back up and added, "But you must know that none of this was ever my intention."

"I believe you. I can see how you got yourself into this mess. Certainly your father had concerns for your welfare, and I can't blame you for that."

"Thank you, Ella," I said softly.

"But I can't guarantee anyone else would be so forgiving." Ella put her hand to her forehead and asked, "What's the reverend going to say once he finds out you're a fraud?"

I shrugged and said, "Does he have to find out?"

Ella took a breath and looked at Liam, Rolf and back to me. She leaned in, and whispered, "Lucky for you, it's just the three of us who know."

I looked around at the empty tables in the café.

Ella turned to Liam and her brother and pointed a finger at them. "This doesn't diminish that disgusting display of satanic behavior we witnessed last night. Do you know what would happen if I told the reverend about all of this?" She paused, waiting for someone to answer.

While we all sat dumbstruck, she continued, "The two of you would be banished from Hope."

I took a deep breath and slowly exhaled, realizing my fate was resting in Ella's hands.

"This is what we will do," she began by looking at Liam and Rolf. "The two of you are going to renounce your affiliation with the Asatru religion and confess your sins. Hopefully, the reverend will find it in his heart to offer you absolution."

Liam reached out and gently touched Ella's hand. "I'll do as you say, but I'm also asking for your forgiveness."

Ella shook her head and said, "Liam, it is not my place to offer you redemption. You have tempted fate by foolishly getting involved in this devil's worship. You should concern yourself with finding your way back to our Lord and Savior through prayer and devotion to the church, before worrying about me."

Liam hung his head shamefully, and muttered, "I will try."

Ella stuck a finger into Rolf's chest and said, "The same goes for you, Brother."

"Okay, Ella, I promise."

She then looked at me. "As for you, Samuel Rothman," she said, and leaned over the table to emphasize her words, "we will keep your true identity and religion a secret. If this was ever to become public knowledge, who knows how the townspeople would react. They think of you as modern-day messiah. If they learned of your deception, I'm afraid of what would happen to you."

I swallowed hard, and said, "Okay, Ella."

"And you two better keep your mouths shut."

Rolf and Liam nodded.

"All of us, including me," Ella said tapping her finger on the tabletop, "are now in this together."

CHAPTER FORTY—ELECTION DAY

I waited in line to vote at the newly completed Sunrise Municipal Building, where, by the end of the day, law and order would find a home. The election itself was a foregone conclusion of who would preside over the courtroom, the sheriff's office, and the city hall facilities. This was because Mr. Wible had cleverly identified a dozen influential residents of Sunrise and bribed them to encourage their friends and family on who to vote for.

People approached me while waiting in line, already calling me Mr. Mayor, even though it was another six hours before the polls would close. I nodded to Mr. Cole and Detective Siringo who passed me by after they voted, and imagined that they were also feeling the anticipation of being elected Sunrise's first judge and sheriff, respectively.

However, during these last few weeks, it wasn't a sure thing that I would be elected Mayor of Sunrise. Mr. Wible almost pulled his endorsement, because of my reluctance to *take care of the reverend problem*. The true reason for my hesitancy was my fear for my eternal soul ending up in hell as punishment for harming a man of God, even though I hadn't entered a church since I was a boy.

Fortunately, I convinced Mr. Wible to maintain his endorsement until after the elections, promising him that I would make sure that Reverend O'Hara's influence in Sunrise would no longer be an issue.

After hours of contemplation, I eventually came up with an idea that would remove the reverend permanently, without causing him any physical harm. After all, Mr. Wible said not to do anything *sinister* to the reverend.

My inspiration was triggered when I was in Hope and stopped by the building site of the new church. That was when I saw, working alongside Erik Andersson, Chief Ephanasy's son Tommy of the Knik Indian tribe. But the seed of this idea was first planted after I met Chief Ephanasy when he paid me a visit a week earlier at the saloon. It was lunchtime when he barged in, nearly knocking the saloon doors off its hinges.

"Where's Magnus Vega?" he demanded.

The few patrons slouched over at the bar, turned around at the disturbance. Someone pointed to me where I was seated in my booth, reviewing the previous day's receipts. At the commotion, I looked up to see a short, but sturdy man, wearing what looked like a confederate hat from the civil war, come barreling toward me. Around his neck hung a beaded bib woven in rows of red and white that swung to and fro, in rhythm with his heavy footfalls.

He stopped at the edge of the table and pointed a stubby finger at me and said, "Are you Magnus Vega?"

I nodded, and replied, "And who are you, sir?"

"I am Chief Ephanasy of the Knik tribe."

"What can I do for you, Chief?" I said, and summoned Stan over, worried that this agitated native man might pull a knife on me.

191

Stan, already aware of the danger, was approaching.

"This place serves whiskey?" he said, waving his arm around.

"Would you like a drink? It's on the house. Henry, bring a bottle over for the chief," I shouted.

"Right away," Henry replied.

"I don't want a damn drink!" he said, slapping both hands on the table.

"Okay, Chief, calm down. Please take a seat and tell me what's bothering you."

The chief nodded and sat down. "This saloon is causing a problem in my village. You're selling liquor to my people."

"To tell you the truth, Chief, I wasn't even aware that your people were frequenting my establishment."

"Well, they are, and it must stop."

I shook my head, and asked, "Why must it stop?"

The chief leaned in and looked at me with brown eyes that swam in an angry sea of red and said, "Because I do not allow it."

"Perhaps if you could identify them, I would be happy to oblige."

The chief held a finger up and stood. "Wait one second," he said, and walked across the saloon floor and out onto the front porch. Moments later he reentered, followed by seven young men.

"These men here," he said, sweeping his arm out, "will not be allowed in here anymore."

Standing before me were seven braves of the Knik tribe. A tribe I had heard lived in a village to the west of Hope. Perhaps I recalled seeing one or two of these men, but never paid them much mind. However, as they were lined up before me, I recognized a resemblance to the chief's facial features.

"Are all these yours?"

"Do you mean, am I their father?"

I nodded.

"Don't be stupid. Only Tommy is mine," he said, patting the muscular shoulder of one of the men. "The rest are from other families. This is Stephan, Pedro, Alexander, Kusema, Nicholai, and Yeshim," he said, pointing to each man as he said their name.

"All right, Chief," I said and turned to Stan. "These men are not permitted in the saloon from this day forward."

Wagging a stubby finger, the chief said, "I will not provide a warning next time."

"Understood, Chief," I said.

The chief nodded. "Good, then that's it," he said, and marched out of the saloon with his seven braves trailing dutifully behind him.

But that wasn't the end for Tommy. He came back the next day, saying he was fed up with his controlling father and wanted to leave the tribe, and he asked me for a job. I told him when I had an opening, I would consider him.

But when I saw him working on the church with the Swede, an idea popped into my head. Perhaps I could employ the rebellious Tommy by using him to abduct the reverend and force him onto the next steamship back to the States.

Once onboard, he would escort the reverend to Seattle where Tommy would see that he was put on a train back to his home in Ohio, never to be heard from again.

When I called Tommy over and explained that I had a job for him, he was interested in learning more. "Come to Sunrise next week, and we'll discuss the details. You'll find me at the saloon."

CHAPTER FORTY-ONE—LIAM'S SURPRISE

With Rolf as the lone representative of the Asatru's clergy, the congregation had no choice but to disband upon its leader's return to the Catholic church. Even Erik followed Rolf and Liam into the confessional, asking the reverend for forgiveness for his multitude of sins.

This, however, didn't offer the reset that Liam was hoping for. While the church forgave his indiscretions, Ella was not so benevolent. Each time he made advances, trying to resurrect their previous chemistry, she was in no mood to respond.

During our days while placer mining the creek, he would not speak to me for hours, and when he did, he displayed his frustration with me. On the third day, after Ella and Rolf learned of my true identity, I forced Liam into a confrontation to hopefully clear the air and return to our friendship.

"Listen, Liam," I said, standing in ankle-deep water, "do you want to tell me why you're acting this way?"

Liam, kneeling on a rock, focused on the pan in his hands, slowly looked up at me and scowled. "Tell me, Sam, why are we here?" he said, rising to his feet and tossing the pan aside.

"To discover gold," I said with a shrug.

"Exactly, and the only luck we've had so far was that nugget you found, and you donated your share to that church."

"And you have a problem with that?"

He nodded and pursed his lips. "Yeah, I do. You let your infatuation with Ella screw up everything."

"What are you talking about?" I said, even though I understood his point.

Liam said nothing while he picked up his supplies, threw them into his canvas bag and started walking down the river bank back towards Hope.

"Where are you going?" I barked.

Liam stopped, turned around, pointed a finger at me and said, "I'm headed back to the bunkhouse to pack my things. I've taken a job as a cook at the Gold Digger Saloon."

"You're not serious."

Liam took three steps toward me. "I am serious. At least with Magnus Vega, I know where he stands. He's more honest than you."

I shook my head and said, "I'm sorry, Liam. I didn't mean for any of this to happen."

Liam flicked his wrist at me like he was swatting away a mosquito, and quickly turned away, leaving me standing in the frigid waters of Resurrection Creek wondering what had become of my relationship with my best friend.

When I returned to Hope, my intention was to go straight to the café and share the news about Liam with Ella. However, as I passed the site of the new church, Erik called out to me.

"Hi, Percy, have you seen Tommy?"

"No, I haven't," I said, looking up at the Swede working on the nearly completed roof.

"This is the second day in a row he's been a no-show."

"I can ask around, if you like," I offered.

"Don't bother, if he doesn't show up by the end of the day, he's through," he said and returned to his task.

I stood there a moment, taking in Erik's work. It was a sturdy structure, offering a simple design. At the front of the building were two large wooden entry doors centered between two square windows. Above that, and before the angled roofline began, was a second row of three equally sized windows.

According to Erik, the building's south-facing façade array of windows would offer natural light in order to harvest the sun's warmth into a chilly interior, and provide an abundance of illumination upon the sanctuary and altar.

For someone who, as the reverend said to me in confidence, *had danced with the devil*, Erik was building a remarkable spiritual sanctuary for the congregants of the Church of Hope.

I found Ella sweeping the dirt off the front porch of the café. When she saw me, a bright smile lit up her face. She stopped sweeping, and leaned against the broom, waiting for me to climb the three steps to join her.

"You're done early," she said.

"Yeah, I guess so. Do you think we can talk inside?" I asked, holding the door to the café open.

"Of course," she said.

Once inside, we sat at the table by the window overlooking the creek.

"What's on your mind, Percy?"

"You know, Ella, you don't have to call me Percy when we're alone," I reminded her.

She tilted her head a bit and said, "I think it's best. This way I won't make a mistake like Liam did. Anyway, you'll always be Percy to me, even if it's not your real name."

"I'm sorry for deceiving you, Ella. Every day I wanted to confess to you, but I was afraid you would never speak to me again."

"Was that why you turned cold on me?"

I frowned and nodded. "I didn't want to hurt you in case you learned the truth, especially after you said you loved me."

Ella swallowed, and her cheeks reddened.

"The last thing I wanted for us, Ella, was to end up as another sad story."

Tears welled up in her blue eyes, and at that moment, my heart spoke and I said, "I love you, Ella."

Ella rose from her chair, leaned over the table and kissed my lips. When she sat back down, all I could do was stare at her. I had never seen such innocent beauty. Her long blonde hair fell in waves across her white, unblemished skin. Those lips, which had just pressed against mine, were still puckered, waiting for more.

I reached across the table and as I held her hand, a terrible thought crossed my mind, *What if she finds out about my indiscretion with Greta at the Gold Digger Saloon?* That would be unforgivable. *Maybe it would be better if I told her now.*

But before I could offer another shocking confession, she said, "You said you needed to tell me something. What was it?"

I took a breath to gather myself. "Liam has moved to Sunrise and taken a job at the saloon for Mr. Vega as a cook."

"Why would he do that?"

"He's upset with me donating my share of the gold to the church. He thinks I did it because of you."

Ella opened her eyes wide and said, "Because of me?"

I nodded.

"Is it true?"

I shrugged and offered a reserved smile and said, "I wanted to do something that would draw you close to me."

Ella stood up and walked over to me. She reached down and grabbed my hand, encouraging me to stand up. When we were face to face, she said, "I'm happy you did."

I put my arms around Ella's waist and pulled her body against mine. I kissed her and knew that this kiss was sealing my fate with this woman, which I had no problem accepting, whatever the outcome.

CHAPTER FORTY-TWO—SUNRISE CITY HALL

Sitting alongside me were Judge Cole and Sheriff Siringo. As mayor of Sunrise, I had the duty of presiding upon the first annual meeting. The newly completed municipal building included an all-purpose room that could accommodate three-hundred people, which at the moment, seemed a mistake not to have made it larger. Every seat was taken, and those who couldn't get a seat leaned against the walls surrounding the assembly.

"Bang the gavel," Judge Cole suggested, as my plea for silence went unnoticed.

I grabbed the wooden handle, noticing its dense weight in its carved, round knocker end, and with a swift motion smacked it three times onto a wooden block. The effect on the people was sudden. Their chatter stopped, and all eyes turned to the dais.

"Citizens of Sunrise," I began, "please allow me to bring to order the first annual meeting of the City of Sunrise."

I took a breath, as everyone's attention was now focused upon me.

"The purpose of this meeting is to hear from its citizens—your concerns, your wishes and how to make Sunrise a better community for all of us to live and prosper in."

Dozens of hands shot up into the air from people eager to speak.

"But, before we open the floor to your questions and comments, please allow me to introduce our other duly elected officials, who would like to address you."

By the time the meeting was nearly over, I thanked the stars in heaven that all of us had survived the night. But my stomach took a sudden turn when I saw the reverend raise his hand. This, I knew, would not end well. With all the eyes upon the religious man, I had no choice but to recognize him as the next speaker.

The reverend offered me a polite nod and rose from his chair. "I realize that I am not a resident of Sunrise, but over half of my congregation lives here," he said, holding his arms out to his side.

Upon this gesture, over thirty men and women raised their hands.

"These fine, God-fearing people of Sunrise have asked me to speak on their behalf."

Dozens of heads nodded on cue.

The reverend stepped around the knees of people in the row he was seated in, and into the center aisle. And as if he was preaching from a pulpit, he began his oration. "Many of you have heard me pontificate on the seven deadly sins."

Heads bobbed up and down.

"Over the past year and a half, I have heard many confessions from those who have strayed off the path of righteousness and committed one of these sins now and then. But in all my time as a leader of the Catholic

201

Church, I have never witnessed a situation where not one, or even two of God's seven deadly sins were committed, but all seven."

The assembly erupted, many rising to their feet, pointing fingers at me, as if they already knew who was guilty of the reverend's accusations. I banged the gavel over and over, insisting that decorum be restored. Both Judge Cole and Sheriff Siringo were red-faced by the outburst of the unruly crowd and wondering about this *situation* the reverend was referring to.

It wasn't until the reverend held up his arms that the people settled down. He marched to the front of the room and looked at me. He turned to face the assembly, raised his arms and spoke, "I am talking of a place where the unholy union of flesh meets flesh. This is the sin of lust." He held up his right palm to quiet the outrage and continued, "I am speaking of a place where whiskey flows like water. Friends, this is the sin of gluttony. I am speaking of a place where people gamble in pursuit of riches." The reverend closed his eyes and nodded. "We know this as the sin of greed. This place of which I speak is where men sink into the depths of despair, and into Satan's sloth."

The members of the assembly were holding on to each other, as the reverend skillfully wove a tale of horror, while my saloon hung in the balance.

"Good people of Sunrise," he continued, "I speak of a place where fighting is common, what our scriptures call, the sin of wrath. I am speaking of a place where jealousy prevails," he said, waving a pointed finger like a magician's magic wand. "And this is the sin of envy."

He paused, pressing his palms in prayer, and said, "Lastly, I share the sad tale of a man who puts himself upon a pedestal, without regard for others. We all know of this as the sin of pride," he finished with his strong, heavy hand pointing directly at me.

For the first time in my life, I experienced unbridled fear. Hundreds of scowling eyes bore holes into me. I wondered if the reverend himself was committing an eighth deadly sin, by turning an angry mob against me.

Sheriff Siringo leaned close to me and said, "Excuse yourself and go hide out in your saloon. I'll send my deputies over to help protect you if need be."

I did as he said and made a quick exit through the back door. It only took three minutes to step back into the saloon, but in that short time, I imagined a scene of the townspeople coming for me with pitchforks and torches and burning the Gold Digger Saloon into the ground.

*

But they never came, and when I woke the next morning and walked out onto the porch off my bedroom, I could almost convince myself that everything was back to normal—as if last night never happened. But I knew better. So, while I bathed, I considered the possibility of adding one or two more men to my security team, in addition to Stan. I had no doubt that casually walking the streets of Sunrise, without looking over my shoulder, was no longer possible.

After I dressed, I made my way downstairs and saw Stan waiting for me. He jerked his head, directing my attention to the table to where Judge Cole and Sheriff Siringo were seated.

"Good morning, Mr. Mayor," said the judge, his voice so deep the crystals in the chandelier rattled.

I smiled and slid into the booth alongside them, and said, "That was something last night."

Detective Siringo looked at me for a moment with narrowed eyes, before he answered, "Last night after you left, we were able to settle everyone down, and come up with a compromise."

"A compromise?"

"Instead of shutting you down, we convinced the people, at least for now, to allow you to continue to operate under one condition."

"What is that?"

"That your girls cannot live here in the saloon."

I held out my hands. "Where are they supposed to live?"

"A majority agreed that they can work here, but after hours they need to sleep on the other side of Sixmile Creek," said the sheriff.

I looked at Judge Cole and then back to Sheriff Siringo. "I don't understand. There's nothing there."

The sheriff shrugged. "You'll need to build them a place to live and a bridge to cross the creek."

"And when am I supposed to have this done by?"

"By the end of next week, or the reverend said he will see that the Gold Digger Saloon is shut down for good."

"That fucking reverend," I said, pounding my fist on the table. "Mark my words; this is just his first step towards shutting my doors."

The judge nodded. "It may very well be. Reverend O'Hara is very persuasive."

Sheriff Siringo and Judge Cole slid out from the booth and stood looking down at me. The sheriff pointed a finger at me and said, "Get going on this housing thing, right away. I wouldn't test the resolve of the reverend. He's not a man to be trifled with."

"I understand," I said, and just as the judge and sheriff turned to leave, the chief's son Tommy walked into the saloon, and I smiled, because I knew exactly what to do next.

CHAPTER FORTY-THREE—DAVID AND GOLIATH

"Come on," Ella said, reaching down to grab my hand.

"I can't believe how high up we are. I think I can see your café from here," I said pointing.

"Yes, that's Main Street, and there, you can see the trail leading to Sunrise."

I climbed up to where Ella stood, and looked out onto the grand vista that featured a wide view of the where Cook Inlet meets Turnagain Arm.

"It's beautiful," I said, pulling her close and kissing her.

She pushed away upon hearing the roar of a wave that seemed to roll on and on. "There," she pointed and said, "they call that a bore wave. It happens when the high tide comes in. I was once down along the shore, when I saw a big one, it was as tall as you."

"That's incredible."

"Come on, I want to show you something," she said, resuming her hike up the trail.

Drenched in sweat, and my legs turning to rubber, I did my best to keep up. I was relieved when she finally stopped.

"Is this it?" I asked bending over to put my hands on my knees to catch my breath.

"The last time I saw them, it was just over this ridge," she said, and stepped gingerly along a narrow pathway, where a wrong step to the left or right, would send you rolling down the cliffside.

"Ella, where are you going?" I asked, too frightened to follow.

She turned to me. "Come, take my hand," she said reaching for me.

We walked another few steps and then we saw them. In small clusters of three or four, perched upon rocky outcroppings were white-as-snow animals, who had all turned to look at us with their black beady eyes, a few with curved horns crowning their heads.

"Are they goats?" I asked.

"Aren't they adorable?" Ella said.

I nodded. "They sure are."

That night, after a nourishing meal at the café, Ella and I laid down in her bed. We kissed for a long while, but when I tried to go further and explore her body with my hands, she stopped me.

"The church does not permit such things," she insisted.

I was too tired to persuade her and moments later I was asleep.

*

When I awoke the next morning, I unwound myself from her arms, trying not to wake her. I quickly dressed and emerged from her small bedroom tucked off the back of the café onto Main Street. It was early morning, and the town was desolate, except for a three-legged dog wobbling along, searching for food scraps.

I thought about my parents and my failed promise to write once a week. I wondered how to tell Mother and Father that I had fallen in love with a beautiful Catholic woman from Sweden named Ella. That was something I could never explain in a letter, or for that matter that Liam and I were not speaking to each other. Then there were the stories of the town being named after me, the Asatru sacrifice, the Gold Digger Saloon, and the Church of Hope along with the array of colorful characters such as Reverend O'Hara, Magnus Vega, and Russell Jones. My parents would go into shock if they knew what was going on. Instead, I would write and say things were going well, and that I missed them and was looking forward to our passage home in four more weeks.

But as things stood now, I wasn't sure whether I was ready to head back to San Francisco. When I asked Ella about her plans for the winter, she said that she would stay on and keep the café open, even though most people in Hope planned to go south.

As I walked down Main Street, contemplating my future, the reverend appeared.

"Good morning, Percy. I'm surprised to find you here at this time of the morning."

"Good morning, Reverend."

"I'm glad I ran into you. I have something to ask of you."

"How can I be of service?"

"As you can probably imagine, the multitude of sins being committed over at the Gold Digger Saloon is immeasurable. Each day, countless times, men, and some notorious women frolic in that den of iniquity."

"So I've heard," I said, trying to sound oblivious to the goings on in the saloon.

"Last night, at Sunrise's first city hall meeting, I was able to get Mr. Vega to agree to house those ladies of ill repute across the creek, allowing them into town only during working hours."

"Across the creek? But there is no place to live," I said, dumbfounded.

"Mr. Vega will build them housing, along with a suspension footbridge to cross the creek. But this is just the beginning. That place must be shuttered. But to do so, I will need more than the support of our thirty congregants from the Sunrise. The entire community must be outraged and insist upon it."

"That will not be easy. From what I hear, people love the Gold Digger Saloon. Someone told me that Mr. Vega makes over six-hundred dollars a night," I said, trying to sound as if it were hearsay, and not directly from Mr. Vega himself.

"Exactly," the reverend acknowledged. "That's why I need you, Percy, to lead this crusade against those sinners of Sunrise. You will need to drive out the evil that has taken root in their community."

"Me?" I shrugged. "What can I do against an entire city?"

The reverend raised his hand in the air and said, "Like Samson did when he massacred the Philistine army with the jawbone of a donkey."

"Samson was given superhuman strength, what do I have?"

The reverend shook his head and smiled. "You still do not understand, do you?"

"Understand what?"

Reverend O'Hara put both hands upon my shoulders and squeezed tight. "You, Percy Hope, are the one. That is why God has brought you here. I have foreseen your arrival in my dreams. This is undeniably the truth, and if I'm lying, may the Lord strike me down, here and now," he said, looking up into the overcast gray sky.

"Good morning, Reverend," came the sweet voice of an angel.

I turned and saw Ella walking toward us.

"Ah, good morning, Ella. So nice to see you. Percy and I were just talking about my dreams."

"Your dreams?" Ella asked.

"The ones I told you about. Do you remember?"

Ella looked at me and nodded. "Yes, I do."

The reverend asked slowly, "What do you remember, Ella?"

"You dreamed of a visitor that would one day come and build us a church." She paused a moment, before continuing, "And this person would be beloved by the community as a beacon of goodness," she said, never taking her eyes off me.

"That's exactly right, Ella."

Ella continued to look at me, drawing me in. It seemed as if she had weaved an invisible web capturing my mind and, dare I say, my soul. I should have put an end to all of this, and confessed my deadly sin of lust, but I didn't want to break the spell.

The reverend touched my elbow, shaking me loose from Ella's presence. I looked at him, and he took both of my hands, closed his eyes and said, "Like David bested Goliath, you, Percy Hope, shall slay evil, and accept your true calling as the Savior of Sunrise."

CHAPTER FORTY-FOUR—LIAM THE COOK

"Here you go, Mr. Vega," Liam said, serving me a bowl of his now infamous beef stew.

I leaned over and inhaled. The delicious aroma wound its way deep inside me, causing my mouth to water. Having Liam as my cook would be a wonderful addition to the saloon. I dipped my spoon in and scooped out a heap and blew a cooling breath upon the steaming concoction. Liam waited while I gave it a taste.

"Incredible," I said, as the seasoned meat, softened by the stew, slid down my throat.

Liam nodded and turned to walk back to the kitchen.

"One second, Liam. Come and sit," I said, gesturing to a seat.

Liam nodded, removed his apron, and slid in next to me.

"It's good to have you here. But you never told me why you left Hope. Did you have an argument with Percy?"

Liam's hands were folded together on the table, and he took a breath and said, "Let's just say I needed a change of scenery."

"Well, I think the scenery is more interesting here than in Hope," I said with a smile and pointed over to two of the girls sitting at a table nearby chatting, while they waited for the customers.

Liam looked over and grinned. "That's for sure."

"I understand that you're still planning on prospecting during the day."

Liam shrugged. "That's why I came to Alaska. If I wanted to do this," he said pointing to my bowl of stew, "I could have stayed at home, and cooked for my father."

I held up my palms. "I understand. Why don't I introduce you to Mr. Wible? He's running the hydraulics up on Sixmile, and he's expanding over to Resurrection, and is looking for a few enterprising, young men to help manage his operations."

"You don't mind if I work there during the day?"

"Why should I? As long as you're back here to cook at dinnertime."

"That shouldn't be a problem."

"Excellent. Is there anything else I can help you out with?"

"Perhaps you can recommend a room nearby that I could let?" he said, squinting his eyes as if it took courage to ask the question.

"Why not take a room here," I said, and summoned Suzie over. "You remember Suzie?"

Liam blushed and nodded quickly.

"Our new cook needs a room."

Suzie offered her million-dollar smile, took Liam by the hand and said, "Come with me, sweetie, I'll find you a nice one."

When Suzie returned, I asked her about finding Liam a steady girlfriend. "There's nothing like having a warm bed after a long day," I reminded her, with a gentle pat on her ass.

"Don't you worry, boss. I've already spoken with Ingrid. That was Liam's girl that first night he and Percy were here. She was also his first fuck. He'll be in love with her before the week's out," she said.

"Perfect."

"What's not so perfect," Suzie volleyed back, "is moving us girls out of here and into that shit hole you're building across the creek. No one is happy about it, Magnus, and I'm afraid we will lose a few girls the next time a steamship sets sail to the Southlands."

I shrugged. "It's that, or we close. But I'm working on a plan of dealing with the source of the problem. You and the girls will need to make do for now."

Suzie closed her eyes and shook her head.

"I'll make it up to you, don't worry."

"We'll see," she growled and walked away.

*

After lunch, I headed over to check out the progress on the girl's bunkhouse. This new arrangement, while inconvenient for them, had some advantages I hadn't previously considered. Though the girls under Suzie's supervision were generally well behaved, there were the occasional after-hours *female* outbursts, that would disturb my sleep. But with them here during business hours only, I figured that discomfort would disappear, and although I would never share this thought with Suzie; I was looking forward to having my bed all to myself.

We suspended the footbridge with thick steel cables provided by Bakersfield's and tethered into mature trees on both sides of the creek. Heavy metal plates squeezed wooden planks in place along the cables stretching above the fast-moving waters. It was a sturdy bridge and seemed that it should last the summer.

Just a few yards on the other side of the creek, stood the house, still being framed. It was a good spot, with a picturesque view of the creek. There was no reason why the girls couldn't be comfortable here.

There was work being done on the front door by a carpenter whose back was turned to me as I approached. The sound of my footfall on the front porch alerted the man, who turned.

"Hello, Mr. Vega," Tommy said.

"Oh, it's you, Tommy. It's good to see you. How are things going?"

He nodded, slipped his hammer into his tool belt, and held open the door. "Come and look," he said.

I followed him inside. The wood cladding still needed to be nailed into place, but the framing provided an idea of how the space was designed. It was not a large home, but seemed to be spacious enough for the girls.

Once we returned to the porch, I asked him where the other carpenters were. He told me that they had gone into town for lunch, but he kept working. "I eat one meal a day," he said.

"Come, let's sit," I said, pointing to the steps leading off the porch. "There's something I've been meaning to discuss with you."

"What can I do for you?" he asked as he sat next to me.

I leaned forward, pressing my elbows onto my knees and rubbing my hands together and said, "I have something important that I would like you to do, and if you can see it through, I will give you this." I reached into my pocket, and pulled out a twenty-ounce golden nugget, and handed it to Tommy.

He took it from me and held it like he was cradling an eagle's egg.

I whispered, "It's worth four hundred dollars."

He turned his head to look at me and asked, "What do you need me to do?"

CHAPTER FORTY-FIVE—THE SAVIOR OF SUNRISE

"Be careful," Ella said, as I offered my farewell.

"I'm only going to Sunrise," I reminded her.

She squinted her eyes, grabbed both my hands, and whispered, "Remember who you are, Percy, and don't be lured by temptation."

Those words shattered the small amount of confidence I could muster since the reverend deemed me the so-called Savior of Sunrise. A title that I knew I was unworthy of.

I swallowed hard, said goodbye to Ella, and boarded the *LJ Perry* for the twenty-minute boat ride to Sunrise, which was arranged the night before, when Cap was at the café for dinner.

Once the boat left the mouth of Resurrection Creek, I stood alongside Cap as he maneuvered the steamer out into the deeper waters of Turnagain Arm.

With his eyes glued on the shifting tides, Cap said, "She's the prettiest girl I've ever seen. You're a lucky man, Percy."

I nodded. "Thank you, Cap, but I'm not feeling so lucky right now."

"Why is that?"

"Well, you see the reason I'm heading into Sunrise is that the reverend wants me to convince the people there that they are sinners and must redeem their souls before it's too late."

"That's quite a tall task for a young man. But you have a reputation that people admire."

"A reputation?" I asked.

"You're Percy Hope, the man who gave the city its name. A hundred years from now, when you're forgotten, this place will carry on as Hope City. The question is, how long will you be around?"

"What does that mean?" I asked, a defensive edge coming through in my tone.

"You've struck a nerve in the people living along the Arm," he said, pointing to the shoreline off the starboard side. "It's like when a miner finds a quartz vein. He will squeeze that quartz until it releases the gold. You are the quartz, Percy, and these people, from both Hope and Sunrise, will squeeze you until you have given them all the gold you have, then you'll be discarded, like worthless gravel dumped back into the creek."

My mind spun like the water emptying from a bathtub. "What are you saying? That the people of Hope are no better than those of Sunrise?"

Cap shook his head. "You're young, Percy, and will learn that things in life are not so simple. It's human nature to separate good from bad, black from white, but there are good people in Sunrise, who may do bad things. That does not make them evil, as the reverend wants you to believe. No man or woman is so righteous as to say that they have never sinned, or contemplated bad thoughts."

"That's true," I said, thinking about my indiscretions at the Gold Digger Saloon.

"Be cautious, Percy, nobody enjoys being preached to. Take note from the Gospel According to John, *He that is without sin among you, let him first cast a stone at her.*"

By the time I stepped ashore, I had taken Cap's words to heart and dropped this ridiculous church-led crusade against the people of Sunrise. After all, what would a Jewish boy from San Francisco know about the Catholic religion?

But did that mean that I couldn't rebuke those who took advantage of the weak and powerless for their own advancement? Could I not claim a moral high ground over someone like Magnus Vega, whose only interest was lining his pockets with gold, regardless of the consequences to others? Perhaps I could make a difference by standing up for those who lacked the courage, or the will to do so for themselves.

With valise in hand, I walked along Front Street, headed for the Gold Digger Saloon. It was approaching dinnertime, and I knew that I would find Liam cooking there. Regardless of whose fault it was, I wanted to apologize to my best friend. We didn't come all this way to end up not speaking to each other. This would be my first task, before I could figure out a way of dealing with the ignoble Mr. Vega.

CHAPTER FORTY-SIX—ROUND TWO

The house was full. Every card table was spoken for, and the bar was jammed. Henry and the two recently hired bartenders were serving whiskey as fast as they could pour. Cameron's piano playing could hardly be heard over the racket of conversations, and Suzie's dolls on the shelf spent most of the evening on their backs.

Mr. Wible, Judge Cole, and Sheriff Siringo were all in attendance, enjoying the evening and playing cards at the five-dollar blackjack table. But just as I was thinking this could be my first one-thousand-dollar night, Percy Hope walked into the saloon.

"Good evening, Mr. Vega," he said, standing before my booth, with a weathered valise in his hand.

"Percy, are you going somewhere?"

He looked down at his valise, and said, "I decided before the summer was out, to see what life was like in Sunrise."

I nodded. "That's a terrific idea. Do you need a room?"

Percy shrugged, and said, "I suppose I do."

"Excellent, I'll have Suzie find you one," I said, craning my neck looking for her. "Oh, and by the way, your buddy Liam is in the kitchen cooking, if you want to say hello."

Percy looked around, trying to figure out which way to go.

"It's through that door," I said, pointing.

"Can I leave my valise with you?"

"Sure, put it right on the floor next to me. I'll keep an eye on it, and when you come back, I'll have Suzie take you upstairs."

The moment Percy walked into the kitchen, I started to wonder what brought him to Sunrise. Liam had told me he was angry with Percy for his donation to the church. But I didn't believe that was the real reason behind their disagreement. If I had to make a bet, I would say it had something to do with Ella.

Just as I came to that conclusion, a loud crash of pots and pans exploded from the kitchen and out stumbled Percy.

"What the fuck is going on?" I shouted and quickly slid myself out from the booth.

A second later, Stan Smith burst through the door, his face beet red, his hands curled into tight fists. "You fucker," he shouted, charging at Percy.

Percy regained his footing and blocked Stan's assault.

Both men squared off, poised for battle. The customers quickly rose to their feet and formed a misshapen boxing ring around the combatants. By the expressions on both of the opponents' faces, this appeared to be a fight to the finish, unless of course the sheriff stepped in.

Whatever happened in the kitchen, I was sure it didn't take much to ignite Stan. After their last encounter, he had been champing at the bit for a chance to get into a rematch against Percy, and I wasn't about to stop it now. Entertainment like this was good for business.

Stan looked like a bull in the heat of battle against the matador; he arched his back, tilted his head towards his enemy, breathing heavily.

Percy, in comparison, looked poised and ready to defend himself.

"I've had enough of this fucker," Stan blurted out, along with a spray of saliva.

"I did nothing. I just walked into the kitchen, and he went crazy," Percy said loud enough for everyone to hear.

Seemingly out of nowhere, Liam appeared in the middle of the scrum, holding up his hands. "Stop," he shouted.

"Get the fuck out of my way, Liam," bellowed Stan.

I took a step toward Liam, reached out and grabbed his wrist, and pulled him back. "They need to finish this once and for all."

Coins and nuggets changed hands as bets were placed.

"Give me room," bellowed the deep baritone voice of Judge Cole as he stepped into the make-shift ring.

I figured this would be the end of it, but instead he held up his hands, silencing the mob.

"This will be a fair fight. No kicking, biting, or hitting below the waist. The winner will be the last man standing," he said, and backed away.

The spectators roared, and Stan attacked.

He delivered a flurry of fists that impressed with its speed and impact. Percy was stunned and grabbed his rib cage. He appeared injured. Stan focused his attack, driving his fist into Percy's bruised torso, forcing him to drop to one knee. He grimaced in pain and looked unable to get back to his feet.

Judge Cole stepped forward, blocking Stan's advance, allowing Percy a moment. "Come on, Judge, let them fight," I said holding out my arms.

Percy stood and adjusted his stance, protecting his right side. This would put him at a disadvantage since he could not land a right punch without his body weight behind it.

Meanwhile, Stan was bent over with both hands on his knees, trying to catch his breath, as Percy regained his footing and prepared for another assault.

Stan didn't disappoint and attacked with a combination that Percy skillfully evaded. He countered with a feint with his right, followed by a sweeping, powerful left hook that connected squarely under Stan's jaw, causing his head to jerk straight back, along with an audible crack which hushed the crowd.

Stan's body went limp instantly and he collapsed like a rag doll. His head bounced twice on the sawdust covered wooden floor.

Complete silence filled the saloon, until someone yelled, "I think Percy killed him."

I squeezed in closer for a look.

Judge Cole dropped to his knees and gave Stan a shake. There was no response. He put two fingers on his neck and paused for a moment, feeling for a pulse. He shook his head and said, "He's dead."

Those who had bet on Percy solemnly collected on their bets.

A sudden jolt jerked Stan's body, and blood oozed from the corner of his mouth.

Percy bent over and put his hand upon Stan's chest and shook him. "Wake up, Stan. Why don't you wake up?"

A hand squeezed his shoulder. "He's gone, Percy," said Liam.

With his face flush, forehead deeply puckered, and eyes ready to flood with tears, Percy said, "I killed him."

Liam helped Percy get to his feet.

"Percy Hope, you must come with me," said Sheriff Siringo.

"But why? What did I do?" he pleaded.

"What are you doing?" I asked, grasping the sheriff's arm.

He jerked away from me and pointed, creating a pathway through the crowd. "He's under arrest for murder."

"Murder?" Liam shouted. "But it was a fair fight!"

"That will be for the judge and jury to decide. In the meantime, I will lock him up in the city jail," he said, taking him into custody.

CHAPTER FORTY-SEVEN—JAIL

"Congratulations, Percy," Sheriff Siringo said, holding the jail cell door open, "you're our first prisoner."

I stepped past him into the windowless cell. There was an unblemished canvas bunk, and a new wool blanket folded up on one end. A never-before-used wooden bucket was stationed in the corner which I assumed was to move my bowels in.

"Make yourself comfortable," the sheriff said, closing the door. He unclipped the key chain from his belt and turned the lock. He grabbed one of the metal bars, jiggled the door, making sure I was secure, and retreated to his desk. Sheriff Siringo then pulled out a chair and sat down.

I stood up and walked over to the bars and pleaded my case. "You saw what happened, Sheriff. Why would you think that was murder? It was a fair fight, which he started. All I did was walk into the kitchen to say hello to Liam, and Stan exploded at the sight of me."

"Save it for the judge. My job is to enforce the law. You killed a man, did you not?"

I nodded, and said sorrowfully, "I did."

"I'm sure you're aware of how justice works. A jury of your peers will decide your fate, not me. You'll either walk free, or hang from the gallows," he said with a shrug, leaned back in his chair and lifted his feet on top of the desk. "Try to get some sleep. I'll have breakfast brought to you in the morning," he said, and pulled out a book from a satchel.

Looking to make a personal connection with the Sheriff, I asked him, "What are you reading?"

The sheriff looked at the leather binding and read out loud, "Dracula by Bram Stoker. From what I've read so far, it's about an English lawyer who travels to a castle in a country called Transylvania to conclude a real estate deal with a nobleman named Count Dracula."

"Sounds interesting. Perhaps I can borrow it from you when you're finished?"

He thumbed through the pages until he got to the end. "There are over four hundred pages. If you're still around, Percy, I'll lend it to you. Now, why don't you get to sleep? I'll bring you to see Judge Cole in the morning."

I stood there a moment, thinking about what had happened. "Sheriff, have you ever killed a man?"

Sheriff Siringo put down his book and swung his feet off the desk and back to the ground. "In all my twenty-two years carrying these," he said, patting one of his guns lying on the desk, "I've shot and killed a man only once. He was robbing a stagecoach they hired me to escort from Denver to Colorado Springs."

"How did it make you feel?" I asked thinking how I watched Stan's life leave his body even before he hit the floor.

The sheriff shrugged. "Sadness; it's just sadness watching a life pass on to the other side, be it a man or beast."

I nodded. "Thank you, Sheriff," I said, and lay down on my bunk and stared into the void.

Hundreds of questions flooded my mind, causing me to toss and turn through a sleepless night. I had never imagined my boxing lessons back home, would result in me killing someone. Father said he wanted me to learn to fight in order to defend myself, which was certainly the case with Stan, but I couldn't get the image of his lifeless body lying on the barroom floor out of my head. I wished I could redo what happened, but instead I sighed, knowing the only way forward was to find a way to cope with the sadness and to continue to remind myself that I had had the right to defend myself against Stan's unwarranted attack.

Another concern was about who would be on the jury to decide my fate. I imagined that it could include anybody from one of those scurvy-ridden, uneducated prospectors, or possibly a wealthy, prominent member of Sunrise society.

The words, "I've brought the prisoner breakfast," caught my attention.

I bounded from my bunk and saw Liam carrying a tray. "Liam, it's good to see you."

"How are you holding up?" he asked, placing the silver tray filled with toast, oatmeal, and coffee on the sheriff's desk.

The sheriff rose from his chair, unlocked the cell door, and cocked his head. "Go ahead, Liam, you can bring it to him. I'll be outside getting some air."

Liam put the tray down on the bed and opened his arms. We embraced. Tears burst from my eyes and flooded down my cheeks. Liam hugged me tighter. "What am I going to do?" I said in between my heaves.

"You're innocent; everyone who saw it says so. Even Judge Cole was there."

"But you never know what can happen in a courtroom. I once read a story in *The Examiner* about a man who was convicted of a murder he didn't commit. The jury found him guilty just because he looked like a murderer and was hung."

Liam shook his head. "That will not happen."

I sat down, wiped the tears from my face, and took a bite of toast. "This is some mess I'm in," I said, and looked at Liam, tilted my head and frowned. "I'm sorry you and I got into a fight."

Liam shook his head. "No, Sam, it was my fault, not yours."

I patted him on his arm and said, "You're a good friend."

Liam smiled. "So are you. As for the matter at hand, do you want me to contact your parents? I could try to have the Company send them a telegram."

"God, no. Besides, what could they do? By the time they could get here, I would have already been hung for murder, or we would be on our way back home."

Liam looked out through the doorway to where the sheriff was standing, smoking a cigar, and whispered, "What if you escaped? We can hide out until the *Bertha* was ready to set sail and sneak our way onboard."

"No, no, no. That's crazy. We'll get ourselves shot."

Liam rubbed his chin and squinted. "Do you want me to go tell Ella what happened?"

I nodded. "It's better if you told her before someone else does. I'm sure word will reach Hope about what happened before the end of the day."

"I'll head over there now," he said, stood up and left my cell.

"Oh, and, Liam," I called out, "tell the reverend too. If anyone can stop this madness, it's him."

Liam nodded and as he departed, the sheriff came back and said, "Hurry and finish your breakfast, Percy, Judge Cole is ready for your hearing."

CHAPTER FORTY-EIGHT—THE TRIAL

There were not enough seats in the courtroom for everyone who wanted to witness the trial of the People of the City of Sunrise versus Percy Hope, in the murder of Stanley Smith. As mayor, I had the privilege of a front-row seat alongside Sheriff Siringo. The Hope contingent of Ella, Rolf, and Liam were given entrance because of their association with the defendant and were sitting directly behind Percy.

It surprised me to see that Suzie, Ingrid, and Greta had got themselves inside the small courtroom space, which was not designed to accommodate so many spectators. Conspicuously absent was Reverend O'Hara, whom Percy had selected in his hearing the previous day to represent him at his trial, since neither Sunrise nor Hope had any Attorneys at Law, beside Judge Cole.

Percy was seated at a table in front of the judge's desk and had turned around in his chair to talk with Liam and Ella. I assumed, by their downturned mouths and hand gestures, that it had to do with the reverend's whereabouts. Perhaps Tommy had acted on my offer and was onboard the *Bertha* with the reverend sailing for Seattle.

Glorious thoughts of having the reverend gone from Hope caused me to sit tall in my seat, relieved that he would no longer be an obstacle. I even chuckled to myself at the irony of building the Hope Saloon on my property next door to the Church of Hope.

But in the meantime, I pondered which outcome would benefit me more: having Percy acquitted of the murder charge, or being found guilty and hung. The problem with Percy being strung up for all to see was that his legacy would be that of a religious martyr, and if that happened, the people of Hope would never allow my saloon to open.

The best outcome would be for him to be found not guilty, but with a tarnished reputation. I held one last card close to my vest to use against Percy, and that was to make public his salacious romp with Greta, which would change people's minds about his saint-like status.

I got up from my seat and turned to the back of the room and made eye-contact with Suzie. I jerked my head as a cue for her to meet me out in the hallway. Once outside, we quickly devised a plan that she would share with Greta, on how to embarrass Percy at an opportune moment during the trial, should they acquit him.

Judge Cole banged his gavel, calling the proceedings to order. The forty or so people in the room fell silent. "Does anyone know where Reverend O'Hara is?" the judge asked, looking around the room as if he were hiding somewhere.

Ella raised her hand, and said, "I saw Reverend O'Hara last night, your honor, and he told me he planned on being here today to defend Percy."

Judge Cole pulled his watch out from his vest pocket and looked at the time. "I'm afraid we're running late. Percy, do you have someone who can stand in for the reverend?"

Percy twisted in his chair and huddled with Ella and Liam. Liam was nodding with enthusiasm and stood up, and said, "Your honor, I will speak on behalf of the defendant."

"Very well, Mr. Kampen," Judge Cole said, and looked across to the prosecutor's table, where Mr. Wible sat, who had agreed to represent the People of Sunrise. "And are you ready, sir?"

Mr. Wible nodded. "I am, your honor."

After a reading of the account by Judge Cole, he turned to Percy. "Mr. Hope, do you agree with the facts as I have just read them?"

Percy and Liam conferred, and both nodded. "We do, your honor," Percy said.

"And do you have anything to add?" asked the judge.

After a brief tête-à-tête, Liam said, "No, your honor, we have nothing to add."

Judge Cole turned to Mr. Wible. "Do you, sir, agree with the account and do you have anything to add?"

"I agree with the facts, and I do have something to add," Mr. Wible said and pushed back his chair and rose to his feet. He walked over to where Percy and Liam sat and leaned over, pressing his palms flat on the table. "Has it been six weeks since you arrived in Alaska?" he began, looked directly at Percy, then paused, waiting for his reply.

Percy shrugged and nodded.

"During this time, many things have occurred. Mayor Vega has named a city after you," he said, pointing at me. "You've made a significant discovery of gold and donated your share for the building of the Church of Hope. For such a young man, you have made a significant impression upon the community."

This recitation of Percy's accomplishments stirred the spectators into hushed conversations. Judge Cole banged the gavel down three times and demanded silence. "I will clear the courtroom," he warned.

"Yet, here you are, standing accused of breaking one of the Lord's commandments, thou shalt not kill," he said, staring into Percy's bloodshot eyes.

"And you know what, Percy? I agree that the fight between you and the deceased was self-defense, and you should not be charged with murder," he said, and paused again, because of the unbridled conversations echoing within the courtroom.

"Silence," shouted the judge, banging the gavel.

"But what bothers me, Percy, and I'm not sure if it's a crime or not, is your honesty."

Upon this remark, Percy looked at Liam and I swear that I could see the blood drain from his face. I glanced at Ella, who put her hand to her mouth, as if she were expecting something terrible. And then it came.

"During my preparations for the trial, I did some research. Early this morning, I had Cap Lathrop take me out on his steamer, to the *Bertha*, and when I got there, I explained to Captain James about the official nature of my visit and if I could peruse the ship's manifest. He allowed me to do so," he said, pulling his shoulders back and taking a few steps toward the judge's table. He then turned to face the spectators. "And do you know what I found?" he asked in anticipation, raising his bushy eyebrows.

Silence washed over the courtroom. I could feel my heart beating in anticipation of what he was about to say.

"We have all traveled here by steamship, and as you know when we purchase our ticket, we must give our legal name, not an alias. So, when the *Bertha* departed from its point of origin in San Francisco, two teenage boys, Liam Kampen, and Samuel Rothman were entered into the ship's manifest.

"We know this man as Liam Kampen," he said pointing. "But the man sitting next to him, the accused, is not who he says he is. Ladies and Gentlemen, Percy Hope's real name is Samuel Rothman."

Shouts of surprise and outrage bounced off the walls like gunshots.

Mr. Wible held up his hand to silence the gallery. "Upon my return, Cap dropped me off in Hope and I went to the Company's office and sent a telegram to its headquarters in San Francisco. That is how I learned that a Mr. Benjamin Rothman, Samuel's father, purchased the ticket. As the clerk told me, Benjamin owns a popular business in the city, called Rothman's General Store."

The hubbub returned, forcing Judge Cole to once again bang his gavel.

"That is not all," Mr. Wible said, holding up his arms to assist in silencing the chaos. "The clerk knows the family, and this young man, who pretends to be a good and honest Catholic, is actually a Jew."

People rose to their feet and pushed their way forward. Percy jumped up and backed away from the angry crowd as they looked like they wanted a piece of him.

Judge Cole cracked the gavel down hard, demanding order. Once the people settled down, Judge Cole said, "Mr. Wible, we must stick to the facts of the case. What you have stated is upsetting and deceitful, but it's not criminal. Are you saying that Stan Smith's murder was self-defense and that the Case of the City of Sunrise versus Percy Hope, or whatever his name is, should be dismissed?"

"I am, your honor," said Mr. Wible.

Judge Cole looked over to Percy and said, "You're under oath, sir, I will give you one more chance to state your real name for the court."

Percy rose from his chair, took a breath and said, "Thank you, your honor. What Mr. Wible says is true. My real name is Samuel Rothman."

An outburst of chatter filled the courtroom once again.

Judge Cole banged down his gavel, trying to restore order. He beckoned to the defendant, demanding he come closer. I was near enough to hear Judge Cole ask, "Are you really a Jew?"

Samuel nodded.

The judge sent him back to his seat. He looked out to the courtroom and then over to the defendant's table and said, "Using a fictitious name or attending a church not of one's own religion is not a crime, and since the prosecution has agreed that Percy's actions were in self-defense, I have no choice but to dismiss this case."

The courtroom burst into a combination of people hugging and shouting in joy, alongside a few in the gallery yelling obscenities, wanting to see Percy hung. I waved and got Suzie's attention, who said something to Greta. Greta climbed up onto a chair and waved her arms and shouted at the top of her lungs, "Excuse me, I have something to say."

Judge Cole looked over to me and I nodded. He banged his gavel, restoring order and said, "Well, young lady, step forward, and address the court."

Greta pushed her way through the crowd, who were now on their feet and gathered closely together. She made it to the front of the courtroom, spun around to face Samuel and the dozens of faces staring back at her in bewilderment.

"I work over at the Gold Digger Saloon. Some of you may know me," she said with a giggle.

"Come on now, get on with it," encouraged Judge Cole.

"Of course," she said, with a smile and a nervous curtsy. "I was Percy's first. At least that's what he told me. But I guess he's not Percy anymore."

All eyes reflexively looked at Ella, whose posture had stiffened in reaction to the hurtful words. She raised a hand and swiftly slapped

Percy's cheek so hard the spectators reacted with a collective gasp. Ella turned, and like a soldier, marched her way out of the courtroom.

"Thank you, Miss Greta," said Judge Cole, shaking his head, "and with that, the case is dismissed." He banged his gavel one last time. "Samuel Rothman, you're free to go. Good luck, to you, it looks like you will need it."

CHAPTER FORTY-NINE—THE MISSING REVEREND

Upon my release, I left the courthouse and found Liam sitting on a bench in front of the Gold Digger Saloon.

"Congratulations, Sam," Liam said.

I sat down next to him, shook my head and said, "Thank you."

Liam patted my knee. "Are you okay?"

"Yeah. But it will probably take a few days to settle my nerves."

"I'm sure," Liam said. "And what did you think of Greta's public declaration?"

"Right now, I don't know what to think."

Liam nodded. "I understand."

"Have you seen Ella? I was looking for her, hoping to explain."

Liam pointed down Front Street. "Before I could talk to her, she took off on one of the wagons heading back to Hope."

"I suppose that's the end of that. She'll probably never speak to me again."

"But at least you're not guilty of murder."

"I know," I said with a sigh. I turned to look behind me at the saloon. "Well, it looks like this will be our home for a few more weeks until the *Bertha* returns," I said.

Liam frowned and shook his head. "I don't know about that, Sam. Mr. Vega said you should go and get your valise. He would prefer you find another place to live."

"Are you serious? He's kicking me out?"

Liam nodded. "We'll both need to find a place. There's a miner's bunkhouse down by Sixmile Creek that has a few rooms."

"He's throwing you out too?"

Liam shook his head. "No, just you, but where you go, I go. That's the way it will be from now on."

I wrapped my arm around Liam's shoulder and said, "You're a good friend."

Liam smiled.

"Hey, isn't that Erik?" I said, pointing to a man walking toward us.

"Looks like him," Liam said.

As the man got closer, he lifted his arm and waved, "Hi, Percy."

"Hi Erik, actually my name's Sam."

He pinched his eyebrows together. "Sam? What happened to Percy?"

I shrugged. "That was a made-up name, and it's a long story. Just call me Sam from now on," I said, rather dismissively.

"All right, Sam," he said with a shrug, and looked over at Liam. "Are you still Liam, or did you change your name too?"

Liam exhaled, smiled and said, "No, I'm still Liam."

"Why are you in Sunrise?" I asked.

"Ella told me you were here."

"She did? What else did she say?"

"That's it, except she seemed upset. Did it have something to do with the trial? Which I heard turned out okay for you."

"Oh yeah, the charges were dismissed, but Ella's angry with me because of something that happened in here," I said, jerking my thumb behind me at the saloon.

Erik nodded his head, knowingly. "Nothing ever ends up well after walking through those doors."

"Ain't that the truth. Why are you in Sunrise?"

"The reverend has gone missing. I've searched everywhere for him. He's not in Hope, and I've been asking around town, and he's not in Sunrise either."

"He was supposed to be at my trial this morning."

Erik lowered his voice and said, "I think maybe something bad happened to Reverend O'Hara."

"What do you mean?" I asked.

"You remember Tommy, the chief's son, who used to work for me?"

Liam and I nodded.

"This morning, Chief Ephanasy came over to see me while I was working on the church and said Tommy was missing and wondered if I'd seen him. I told him he quit working for me a few days ago."

"What has that got to do with the reverend?" Liam asked.

"Maybe nothing, but it seems like a strange coincidence that both men are missing at the same time."

"Tommy was working on the new bunkhouse that Mr. Vega is building for the girls on the other side of the creek," Liam said.

"Ah, well, maybe he's there. Would you mind showing me the way, and at least we can resolve one of these two missing persons."

*

With no one at the girl's bunkhouse, I had no choice to return to Hope, seeing that the reverend and now Tommy were unaccounted for. What if Tommy, as Erik implied, had something to do with the disappearance of Reverend O'Hara?

As Liam and I rode in the back of Erik's wagon, headed toward Hope, I thought about Greta's shocking announcement to the court, of how I lost my virginity to her. But why would she feel compelled to betray me in such a forum? As this question bounced around in my brain, I came up with the possibility that it was Mr. Vega who put her up to it.

I tapped Liam on the knee as the wagon made a final turn down Main Street and said, "Do you think that Mr. Vega counseled Greta into making that announcement as a way to discredit me?"

Liam squinted, expressing his doubt. "Why would he do that?"

"Think about it. Who would benefit with the reverend gone from Hope?"

Liam shrugged. "I don't know, who?"

"Magnus Vega would. He's been champing at the bit to open a saloon in Hope ever since we met him. You remember the offer he made, to make me a partner if I could change people's minds?"

Percy nodded.

"But Reverend O'Hara, would never allow it. However, with him gone, nothing would stand in his way and Mr. Vega will get what he wants."

Liam put his hand on his cheek and whispered, "What are you saying, Sam? That Magnus Vega is behind the disappearance of the reverend?"

I nodded. "In one fell swoop, he skillfully got rid of the reverend, and publicly disgraced me."

Liam tilted his head, and narrowed his eyes, "Maybe we should go visit Chief Ephanasy and see what he knows about his son Tommy."

CHAPTER FIFTY—THE WARNING

The trial and humiliation of Samuel Rothman, along with the abduction of Reverend O'Hara, left Hope no longer protected from me opening the Hope Saloon. The only problem was that summer was ending in a few weeks, and there wouldn't be enough time to construct a building next to the Church of Hope. But that wouldn't prevent me from repurposing an existing building and having something operational within a matter of days.

After a brief deliberation, I come up with an ideal place that would work—the Hope General Store. In fact, except for its size, its layout was perfectly suited for a conversion into a saloon. The existing counter where Mr. Jones conducted his business, could easily be adapted into a bar. With the merchandise gone from the floor, an arrangement of a dozen card tables was possible, and the three rooms upstairs would make do for the girls and their customers.

While it wasn't on the scale of what I had built in Sunrise, I figured that in just the last four weeks of the season; it was possible to gross several thousand dollars. This would depend upon the cooperation of Mr. Jones, who I was sure would jump at the chance of zeroing out his debt to me in exchange for the temporary use of his building. His sales toward the end of the season were not as brisk as they were when the prospectors first arrived in June.

I planned to visit with Mr. Jones first thing in the morning. But today, I needed to see if the girls' bunkhouse was close to being ready. With Tommy gone and on his way to Seattle with the reverend, I was certain that the construction had slowed.

According to the agreement, which I figured would still be enforced by Judge Cole, a stickler for such things, even though the reverend was no longer around to insist upon it, I needed to have the girls out of the saloon by the end of the week. That left me only three more days to comply with the order.

I told Henry that I would be back in an hour, and just as I was about to walk out onto the porch, Mr. Wible entered.

"Ah, Mr. Mayor, just the man I've come to see. Do you have a minute?"

"Of course, Mr. Wible, please let's sit over here," I said, pointing to a table by the window.

"I'll get right to the point," he said, taking a seat. "I've just come back from a conversation with Judge Cole and Sheriff Siringo. We've heard that Reverend O'Hara has disappeared. He was absent at the trial and apparently no one in Hope has seen him since yesterday."

"Oh, is that right?" I asked, trying to sound surprised.

Mr. Wible leaned back in his chair, folded his arms across his chest and said, "Do you want to tell me what you did with him?"

"Me?" I said, pointing to myself. "I did nothing. Why would you think I did?"

Mr. Wible took a moment to light his cigar, tilted his head back, and exhaled a stream of smoke and said, "Because I'm the one who told you to take care of the reverend problem. That he had a powerful voice that needed to be silenced."

I pointed at him and nodded. "That's right you did."

"But I also said not to do anything sinister, and it appears you haven't heeded my warning."

"It's true that I've been thinking of ways of protecting our city from reverend's influence," I said with a shrug, "but I have yet to figure that out."

"You're exhausting," Mr. Wible said with his cigar pinched between his teeth. "Everyone knows you want the reverend gone from Hope so you can open your saloon. But you can't make people just disappear to have your way. It's illegal and you can go to jail, even if you are the mayor of Sunrise."

"I'm aware that Sunrise has law and order. But you realize that the reverend lives in Hope, which is not part of our jurisdiction?" I said, holding up both my palms. "Regardless, I have no idea of the reverend's whereabouts, I swear."

"You think you're clever, don't you," Mr. Wible said, pushing back his chair and rising to his feet. "This is a warning. Nothing had better have happened to the reverend, or you will be paying the price. That I can promise you," he said and stomped out of the saloon.

CHAPTER FIFTY-ONE—THE KNIK VILLAGE

The footpath to the Knik village began on the other side of Resurrection Creek and ran parallel from the mudflats along the Turnagain Arm coast. It took Liam and me about a twenty-minute, brisk walk to arrive at the small enclave.

During my time in Hope, I had seen the Knik people going about their business, delivering moose meat, and salmon to Ella at the café, or tanned moose-hides to Mr. Jones at the Hope General Store. They seemed to be a self-sufficient group, as I would expect an indigenous people to be. After all, they were here long before the white man discovered gold, and would remain behind after we shook the rivers clean, and blew the embankments to smithereens with the hydraulics.

Unlike the books I read about tribes of the western United States, the Kniks did not live in teepees or wigwams like the Apaches. Instead, they lived in sturdy log-homes, similar to the ones the white people built in Hope and in Sunrise.

I expected that upon entering the Knik village, Liam and I would be approached. But instead, we were mostly ignored. We saw native women tending to large pots poised over fires, a young man who sat upon on a stump, making repairs to a bow, and small children kicking a lopsided moose-hide covered ball that rolled in between two birchbark canoes, beached on the embankment.

"Who are you looking for?" came a voice from behind us. I turned around, and facing me, stood a man around my age, with a round face and dark brown eyes.

"I'm Sam and this is Liam, we're looking for Tommy, the chief's son."

The man shook his head. "I thought your name was Percy Hope. The one the town's named after."

"I am, I mean I was. My real name is Sam. It's confusing, I know. What's your name?"

"My name is Nicholai. Why are you looking for Tommy?"

"Reverend O'Hara has gone missing and we're concerned that Tommy had something to do with it."

"Why would Tommy have anything to do with the reverend?" Nicholai asked, shaking his head.

"He was working for Mr. Vega and we're suspicious that he put Tommy up to something dastardly."

Nicholai held out his arms. "We haven't seen him since the argument he had with his father, Chief Ephanasy."

"And no one is worried about him?" Liam asked.

"Not really. Ever since he was a child, we knew him to disappear from time to time. Tommy finds life in the tribe confining."

"How so?" I asked.

"Our elders taught us that everything in life, everything we do, all of our experiences are part of a circle. The sky is round," he said, pointing upwards, and made large circles with his arm. "Birds make their nests in circles. Seasons come in cycles, returning to where they began, over and over. Our elders meet in the round, and as children, we learn to live within this circle. As long as I can remember, Tommy felt he never belonged within this circle with the rest of us."

I rubbed my chin and asked, "If Tommy wanted to make the reverend disappear, where would he take him?"

Nicholai shrugged. "Probably to one of the villages along the inlet or up Knik Arm."

I looked over at Liam, sighed, looked back at Nicholai and said, "How do we get there?"

Nicholai laughed and wagged his finger between us. "You two?"

"Why not? Can you show us the way?"

"You can't walk there. You must go by water. Do you have a boat?"

I shook my head and pointed to the canoes. "Can we borrow one of yours?"

Nicholai shook his head and beckoned for us to follow him. We walked down to the mudflats and climbed on a rocky outcropping that brought us ten feet above the lapping waters.

"Look," he said, gesturing outwards, "you see those hills across the Arm?"

I nodded.

"Looks like all you have to do is paddle and you'll be there in no time."

Liam looked at me and we both shrugged. "Yes, it doesn't seem far," I said.

"The tides are swift and the currents strong. Without someone who knows these waters, you'll end up swept down into the inlet."

"All right, who can we ask?" Liam said.

Nicholai turned to face us and said, "I'd ask Cap Lathrop. He found Tommy last time and knows the villages up on the other Arm."

We thanked Nicholai and headed back along the pathway toward Hope.

"Hold up," a voice shouted from behind us. It was Nicholai. "It's best I go with you. The tribes along Knik Arm are not as welcoming as we are."

We went directly to Cap's cabin, but he wasn't there.

"Let's go ask Mr. Jones. Maybe he knows where Cap is," I said.

"He could be in Sunrise," Liam reminded us.

Nicholai, Liam, and I walked into the general store and saw Mr. Jones carefully wrapping some glassware.

"Mr. Jones, what's going on?" I asked, looking at the stacks of crates filling up his store.

"Ah, Percy, I'm glad you're here. I could use your help."

"You mean Sam. Why are you packing things up?" I asked.

"Right, Sam, sorry. Haven't you heard? Mr. Vega is turning my store into the Hope Saloon."

"You're joking," I said, sharing a look of surprise with Liam and Nicholai. "The reverend will never allow it."

Mr. Jones shrugged and held his arms out. "Reverend O'Hara has gone missing."

"Yes, we've heard, and Tommy too. We're thinking Tommy has something to do with the reverend's disappearance. Perhaps Mr. Vega is behind this?"

Mr. Jones nodded. "I wouldn't be surprised if he is. That man is the devil. I'm convinced of it."

"Do you know where Cap is?" Liam asked.

"He was just here in a rage. Looks like someone stole the *LJ Perry* last night."

"I bet it was Tommy," Nicholai said. "He used to work for Cap and knows how to operate it."

"Now what do we do?" I said.

"Let's go," Nicholai said, heading toward the door. "I hope you boys can paddle."

Before stepping off the Hope General Store's front porch, I took a moment to look across Main Street at the Hope Café. I could see Ella through the windows, serving customers and wondered if I should go in and tell her our plans to rescue the reverend. She would, of course, be interested in his well-being, but upset with me for the scandal with Greta at the Gold Digger Saloon.

250

I clenched my fists. I knew what I should do; I should have the guts to walk right up to her, tell her about our imminent departure, profess my love for her, and beg her forgiveness for my indiscretion.

Instead, as usual, I dismissed such bold action and ran down the steps to catch up with Liam and Nicholai.

CHAPTER FIFTY-TWO—TWO DEAD SQUATTERS

Cap Lathrop barged into the saloon and banged both fists on the table. "You know where I just came from, Vega?"

I shrugged. "No idea, Cap, why don't you tell me?"

"Standing on the banks of Resurrection Creek watching that horse's ass Tommy, take off with my boat."

"Is that right?"

"Don't you act so fuckin' innocent," he said, leaning over the table, making me realize that I needed someone soon to replace Stan as my head of security.

"Come now, Cap, don't get yourself so excited. You know Tommy, I'm sure he had a good reason and will return soon."

"If I find out you had something to do with this . . ." he paused and looked around. The few customers at the bar, and Suzie and her girls, were all gawking at Cap.

This outburst was not something people saw from the typically dignified Cap Lathrop. Having realized that he lost his temper, he straightened his posture, pulled down on his captain's jacket, pointed a finger at me and said for my ears only, "If the *LJ Perry* is not in dock by the end of the day, I'll be back, and it won't be pretty. I can promise you that."

I watched Cap turn and storm out of the saloon and wondered what he would do if his boat was not returned anytime soon. I assumed Tommy borrowed it to transfer him and the reverend onto the *Bertha*. Once they boarded, unless Tommy made arrangements for the *LJ Perry* to be returned, it could be drifting somewhere in Cook Inlet on its way to the gulf.

Suzie came over and sat down. "We need to talk," she said snapping me out of my worries.

"Sure, what can I do for you?"

"It's about the new bunkhouse."

I redirected my attention to Suzie. "I knew you would like it. Nice and quiet over there."

Suzie shook her head. "It was quiet, until early this morning when two squatters, sleeping in those make-shift tents along the creek, paid us a visit. They barged right in the front door and scared the living crap out of me and the girls."

"Oh shit, what did you do?"

"I was sleeping in my bedroom when Ingrid screamed and woke me up. I slipped on my nightgown and grabbed my shotgun. When I opened my door, Ingrid was being forced down onto the floor, while the other scumbag was pulling his pants down, ready to climb on top of her. I shouted that he should stop, but I doubted he heard me over his drunken stupor. With his pants down to his ankles and his junk hanging out, he dropped to his knees. I screamed again for him to back off, and this time he heard me and looked up, and that's when I shot him."

My eyes and mouth drooped, like I had lost control of all the muscles in my face. "You did what?"

"I filled him with buckshot. He fell backwards from the force. The other one turned and got to his feet and brandished a knife, threatening me. So, I shot him too."

I put my hand to my forehead and looked at Suzie. "Are you telling me that there are two dead men lying in your bunkhouse right now?"

"No, Magnus, they're out behind the bunkhouse, in the bushes waitin' to be buried.

"Holy shit, Suzie. Why did you do that? Couldn't you have just scared them away?"

Suzie leaned in, pointing a finger at me. "You promised to protect us, keep us safe. If I were you, Magnus, I'd get over there right away and get rid of the bodies before the sheriff discovers them, and throws my ass and yours in jail."

CHAPTER FIFTY-THREE—FIRE ISLAND

We needed to wait for the tide to go out before we could push off from the shore. When I turned to look behind me, I saw Chief Ephanasy poised on the bluff. He placed his palm over his heart and smiled offering goodwill for our journey. I smiled and returned the gesture.

I took the bow of the canoe, with Liam seated behind me. Nicholai navigated from the stern, acting as its rudder to guide us through the treacherous currents caused by the fast-changing tides.

He gave us a quick lesson on what he called *rowing with a purpose*. "Reach forward as far as you can, dip your paddle in deep and pull back strong. Lift on the back end of the stroke, twist the paddle blade sideways, so it doesn't catch the wind, and repeat."

Under his directions, the swift tide quickly pulled us from the shore. This was the first time I was this close to the water's surface. When upon on the *Bertha* or the *LJ Perry*, I could never reach out and dip my hand into the chilly sea and inhale its sweetness.

"How long before we get to the village?" I asked.

"Depends once we get into the inlet. The winds and tides run strong there."

We paddled for a while, observing several eagles soaring above us, until Liam broke the silence and asked, "Nicholai, how come your people didn't collect the gold before the prospectors arrived? It seems like it would have been easy pickings."

"Unlike white man's greed, we don't take from the earth for our pleasure. Gold, like any other stone, should lie where it belongs, in the ground."

"You speak English well, Nicholai. How did you learn?" I asked.

"Chief Ephanasy arranged English lessons for our people. Our teacher lives there," he said, pointing off into the mist rising off the water's surface. "The last three summers he would visit us and teach the chief and the young men of our village English. He was with us just a few days ago."

Liam and I looked over and saw a large tree-covered island in the middle of Cook Inlet.

"People live there?" Liam asked.

"Yes, that's Fire Island and Major Lawrence is the only white man. He lives in a fish camp among the Dena'ina tribe."

"A fish camp, what's that?" I asked.

Nicholai shrugged. "Fisherman who live in small huts, catch fish and sell it to the villages along the inlet and up Knik Arm. We will stop there and ask if anyone has seen Tommy and the reverend."

As we approached the island, dilapidated wooden huts, elevated with stilts ten feet off the mudflats, came into view. At least six or more birchbark canoes were beached along the shoreline. Off to the right, high upon a stone bluff, were racks of long horizontal branches supported by wooden legs, where dozens of salmon hung with their mouths wide open, seeming to be drinking in the brilliant blue sky. Large nets with cork buoys were draped upon tree branches.

It wasn't until we pulled up in our canoe, that we saw signs of human life. Nicholai greeted a young Dena'ina native in their native tongue, while the man, wearing knee-high mukluk boots stained in the same gray color as the mudflats, reached for the sturdy frame of the canoe, and pulled us deep onto a grassy part of the shore.

We had just stepped from the canoe when a voice from the sky boomed down upon us. "Nicholai, my young friend, what a pleasant surprise."

We tilted our heads back to look up, and standing on the edge of the bluff was a man sporting a hearty mane of unkempt red hair, along with an equally impressive red beard.

"It's good to see you, Major."

"Who do we have here?" he said, looking at Liam and me.

That was when I saw his long robe, fashioned from animal furs, with a leather strap wrapped around his waist, stressing his wide shoulders and powerful physique.

"These are my friends," Nicolai said smiling, "Sam and Liam. They're from San Francisco."

"What are two city boys doing out here in the wilderness?" he said, as we climbed the zigzagged array of wooden ladders.

When we reached the top, I shook the major's hand. "It's nice to meet you, sir," I began. "Liam and I came up for the summer to try our luck prospecting."

"How's that going?" he said, scratching his long beard, causing a cloud of dust to burst free from its coarseness.

I nodded, and said with pride, "I discovered a sixty-ounce nugget."

"Yeah," Liam chimed in, "and he donated the proceeds to build the new church."

Major Lawrence put one hand over his mouth and pointed at me and said, "Are you Percy Hope?"

I nodded quickly. "I am, I mean I was," I bumbled out, took a breath to calm my nerves, and said, "I used to be Percy Hope, but my real name is Sam Rothman."

"Does it really matter?" the major said, patting me on my back. "I heard about what you did when I was visiting the Knik village last week. What you did was an act of kindness, not common among white folk these days."

I smiled and heard approaching footsteps. We all turned and saw three round faces with long, stringy hair staring back at us.

"These are my friends. Come, I'll introduce you," he said. "We'll sit at the campsite, and you can tell me why you're here."

We followed the major and were joined by several Dena'ina men into a clearing in the woods. Arranged around a smoldering campfire were short stumps that served as stools, stationed in a circle. At the head of the circle was something more than a stump. It was a seat, carved expertly into the trunk of a living tree that soared into the canopy above us.

Major Lawrence sat down upon this throne-like chair, and the Dena'ina men each took a seat in the circular arrangement. The three of us stood watching, until the major barked out orders in the foreign language, and three natives jumped to their feet and fetched more stumps, allowing us to join the circle.

I remembered what Nicholai told us about the significance of the circle to the Knik tribe, and imagined that the Dena'ina people shared similar customs. But what was different here was seeing Major Lawrence, a white, red-bearded man, dressed like a figure from a bible story, seated at the place of honor, like a chief or a king.

CHAPTER FIFTY-FOUR—GOODBYE SUZIE

When I arrived, Mr. Jones was climbing down the ladder, carrying his sign painted with large block letters—HOPE GENERAL STORE.

"Is that the last of it?" I asked, stepping onto the porch.

Mr. Jones sighed. "The place is all yours. I'll be moving into the miner's bunkhouse. Rolf found me a room. Just do me a favor, please make sure the place is in one piece when you're done with it. I would like to open up again next year," he said, putting the sign down and folding up his ladder.

"No, please leave it. I'm waiting for Mr. Oppenheimer from the lumbermill to hang the new sign."

"I guess that's it then," Mr. Jones said, with a pained smile. "Your crew has been here since early this morning. It looks like the Hope Saloon is ready for its grand opening."

I stood with hands on my hips, admiring the accomplishment. There were few, if any, at all, who would believe that I could have pulled this off. After this, the people of Hope would need to think twice about doubting my willpower.

With things under control, I headed back to Sunrise to check on Henry. Hopefully, by now he had dealt with the two dead squatters that

Suzie filled with gunshot the night before. But when I got to the Gold Digger Saloon, Henry was waiting for me out on Front Street.

I could tell by his grave expression that something was amiss. When I approached, he grabbed my arm and leaned in to whisper, "I couldn't find them, boss. I spent the entire morning looking."

"What do you mean you can't find them?"

"I looked, but there were no bodies where Suzie said they'd be."

"Fuck! Where is she?"

"I saw her heading upstairs just a few minutes ago," he said, pointing to the saloon behind me.

I charged through the saloon doors and flew up the flight of steps. When I reached the landing, I saw Greta and Ingrid standing gawking into Suzie's room. Their faces were as white as the dolls on the shelf.

"What's happening?" I asked, just as Greta's eyes rolled to the back of her head, her knees buckled and fainted.

"Greta!" Ingrid shouted and dropped to her knees to attend to her unconscious friend.

I stepped over Greta and looked into the room. Sprawled like a rag doll, swimming in a pool of crimson blood, lay Suzie. I put my hand to my mouth, and stammered, "What the fuck?"

With each step closer, my eyes led me to the source of her blood. Suzie's head was tilted back, exposing a deep slash to her neck, where the wound was still pulsating and oozing blood.

"Who did this?" I turned to ask Ingrid.

"I don't know. We were downstairs and heard a scream and came running."

I put my hands over my face, unable to look again. I pushed my way past Ingrid and stumbled my way downstairs.

"I heard screaming," Sheriff Siringo said charging into the saloon with his guns drawn. "What the fuck is going on?"

"Someone murdered Suzie," I stuttered.

"Where?"

I lifted my arm and pointed. "In her room."

It took nearly all day before the sheriff allowed us to remove Suzie's body. It was obvious that someone had entered the saloon, knew where to find Suzie and slit her throat. But the sheriff insisted on a thorough investigation of the crime scene.

*

"She would have liked for the reverend to have said something," Ingrid said in between tears, as the wooden coffin I had purchased from the Sunrise Lumber Mill was lowered into the ground in the Point Comfort Cemetery.

I nodded, wishing the same. But unfortunately, Suzie had no chance to ask for forgiveness of her sins before her demise, and even if she did, the reverend wasn't around to hear her confession.

Never before had I felt such an emptiness inside me. It was as if my heart was ripped out. The last time I remember crying, was when I was

262

twelve years old and hearing the news that my grandmother had died. That too was a heart-wrenching day, for she was the only person who was able to protect me from my abusive father.

While tears flowed, each of us took turns with the shovel, dropping dirt onto the coffin. This small cemetery in the woods should not have been Suzie's final resting place. I wish I had told her that I imagined that one day, when we were older and living off our savings, we would have settled down in Chicago, got married and started a family.

Once the last scoop of dirt was laid on top of the grave, the solemn group of Henry, Cameron, the girls, and myself, headed back along the trail to the saloon. I looked at Greta's swaying hips and thought she would be the likely successor to Suzie as madam. Perhaps in a day or so, once things settled down, and we scrubbed the blood from the crime scene, I would tell Greta the good news.

Just as we were about to step from the trees and onto Front Street, two men blocked our path. Ingrid screamed, put her hand to her mouth and said, "That's them, the two who Suzie shot!"

No wonder Henry couldn't find the damn bodies; they weren't dead. These two, who I had never seen before, were pockmarked with shot wounds on their faces and arms, and their dirt-encrusted clothes were blotched with dried blood. It wasn't until the clouds slid by, and the sun shone through the foliage, that I saw that both men were wielding hunting knives in their blood-stained hands.

"It was you two who killed Suzie," I said.

One of the men smiled, displaying a mouth of rotten teeth, and brandished his knife, with the sun glistening off its blade. "You'll need to dig a few more graves," he growled, taking a step toward us.

Just as the girls screamed, two gunshots exploded, and both men stood frozen for a moment, with a round bullet hole suddenly appearing in each of their foreheads. They were dead before their bodies collapsed to the forest floor.

Standing off to our right was Sheriff Siringo, with a Pinkerton-issued Colt 45 gripped in each hand. By the sound of it, he took two simultaneous shots with his Peacemakers, hitting his targets at the spot where their eyebrows meet.

When we got back to the saloon, Sheriff Siringo stopped me before I stepped inside. "Lucky for you, and everyone else," he said, cocking his head to Henry and the girls who were walking ahead, "I was out looking for you. Cap Lathrop is throwin' around accusations like he was calf roping, and you're the bull. He says you're behind the disappearance of the reverend, Tommy, and the *LJ Perry*. I'm gonna need you to come down to my office and answer some questions."

I shook my head. "After what I've just been through? Come on now, Sheriff, I'm the Mayor of Sunrise, don't I get a little leeway here?"

"I'm afraid no one is above the law. Not even you, Mr. Mayor."

CHAPTER FIFTY-FIVE—MAJOR AUSTIN LAWRENCE

"It is good to see you, Nicholai," Major Lawrence said, stroking his red beard.

"It is good to see you too, Teacher," Nicolai smiled, putting his right palm over his chest.

"Tell me. Why have you come?"

"We are looking for Tommy."

"Has the chief's son gone missing?"

Nicholai nodded.

The major held his hands out and said, "No one has come this way that I know of." He spoke in a native tongue to the men, presumably asking if anyone knew the whereabouts of Tommy. The men whispered among themselves for a moment, but apparently no one had seen them.

Major Lawrence shook his head. "What's he done?"

I lifted my hand like I was back in school. "Reverend O'Hara is also missing, along with Cap's schooner, the *LJ Perry*."

The major puckered his brow and said, "What's happened to the reverend?"

I shrugged. "We think Mr. Vega is behind all of this. Do you know him?"

Major Lawrence made a fist and shook it. "I have heard stories of that cursed man. Let's hope that his day of reckoning will be soon."

I rose from the stump, looked at Nicholai and said, "Well then, perhaps we should push on. There's no time to waste."

"Nonsense," the major said. "You won't get far with the tides at this hour. That canoe will get swept down Cook Inlet and end up in the damn gulf before you know what happened. Tonight, we will be honored to have you as our guests. You can leave in the morning."

They offered us one of the elevated huts we had seen when we beached our canoe, to spend the night in. The inside of the hut did not appear as ramshackle as its dilapidated exterior. Liam and I each had a hammock to sleep in, which, unlike the ones onboard the Bertha, didn't smell of puke. There were no windows in this compact, ten-foot-square, single-room house, probably because of the harsh weather and strong winds common to Fire Island.

A hard knock startled me. I turned to look through the open door and saw Nicholai's smiling face. He had climbed the ladder from the mudflats below and now just his head was poking above the floorboards. "Major Lawrence invited us to the circle, come now," he said and dropped from view.

"Hey, Nicholai, what about something to eat?" Liam shouted after him. "We're starving."

The campfire in the center of the circle burned strong. They passed around a wooden bowl, filled with small pieces of smoked salmon.

Although salmon fishing was a strong part of the culture in Alaska, ironically, since arriving in Hope, I had salmon only once at the café, which was broiled in Ella's oven, and remembered it to be delicious.

When the bowl reached me, I popped a chunk of the fish into my mouth and bit into it. As I did, a delicious sensation consumed me. I closed my eyes, allowing the sweet and salty flavors to coat my throat. Unaware that the talking had ceased, I opened my eyes to find everyone's eyes upon me. Smiles and laughter broke the silence. The major clapped his hands together, and said, "We are pleased you like it, Sam."

Liam was chewing and pointing to his mouth, nodding vigorously. When he finally swallowed, he looked around for the bowl, and jabbing at it with a finger, he exclaimed, "Can I have more?"

We washed down the salmon with delicious herbal tea brewed over the campfire in an old brass tea kettle and served in simple wooden cups. Even though it was after midnight, the summer sun hung over the inlet, casting a soft light upon the fish camp.

In a few hours, we would be off, searching for the reverend and Tommy. But in the meantime, there was this mysterious elderly white man, dressed like someone from my bible storybooks, with the military rank of Major, holding our attention.

I raised my hand.

"You're not in school, Sam," the major reminded me.

I looked up to my hand and dropped it. "Sorry, it's a habit. Can I ask about your rank as Major? Did you fight in the civil war?"

A bright smile lit up the major's face. "I did. I led the Battle of Carlisle."

Before I could confess that I did not know of this conflict, he held up his palm and said, "I'm sure that you've learned of the Battle of Gettysburg in school?"

"Of course. We had to memorize President Lincoln's Gettysburg Address."

The major wagged a finger at me and said, "On that same fateful day of that infamous battle, a mere thirty miles to the southwest, we fought at the Battle of Carlisle. History neglects our struggle, but I'll never forget it.

"Our regiment was joined by a local militia, led by Baldy Smith, and together we defended Carlisle against Major General Stuart and his cavalry. Four days and nights, we held off the Confederates from taking the city. Eventually, the general gave up and retreated. He and his men joined up with General Lee's army at Gettysburg," the major smirked, and said, "it was my small contribution to the war."

"But what brought you to Alaska?" Liam asked.

The major's eyes gleamed at Liam's question.

"That, Liam, requires me to start my story before the war. Would you like to hear it?"

Liam nodded and looked at me. I too was fascinated to learn Major Lawrence's story.

The major stroked his beard, and I think I saw a tiny moth flutter out. He crossed his legs, exposing his hairy shins as the flaps of his animal-skin robe flipped open. He took a sip of his tea and began.

"I was born in Utica, New York in 1832. My father owned a newspaper called *The Mechanics' Free Press*. On the morning of my seventeenth birthday, I was helping Father set type to run the press for the headline that day, which comprised only one word, and it was printed in caps, three times across the front page. It read," he said, holding his hand up in the air, and jerking it three times, "GOLD! GOLD! GOLD! And that one word changed my life forever.

"The next week, I packed my bags, said farewell to my parents, who were upset with my departure, and boarded a commercial ship traveling west along the Erie Canal, headed for Youngstown. Once there, I bought a ticket for passage onboard a steamship that took me through the Great Lakes and eventually I managed my way overland to Independence, Missouri where I joined up with a wagon train heading for California. Three months later, through treacherous conditions, we arrived at the American River on the base of the Sierra Nevada Mountains near Sacramento.

"During that year of 1849, men from all over the world flocked there, traveling great distances. They scaled mountains, crossed oceans and fought hardships, hoping to find gold. These people became known as the Forty-Niners."

"Yes, we learned about them in school," Liam interrupted.

269

"Well, you're looking at one of 'em," said the major, jerking a thumb into his chest.

"And did you find gold?" Liam asked.

"I did, and became a wealthy man, at least for a while. In the spring of 1873, disaster struck. I lost my entire fortune when Jay Cooke, an investment banking company, went belly-up, when its plans to build a transcontinental railroad called the Northern Pacific Railway failed, bankrupting the company and making my investment worthless.

"Destitute, I returned home to Utica for the first time since I left twenty-four years earlier. Mother and Father were old, but they took me in, happy to see me again.

"Within three years, both of my parents died. For the following thirteen years, I lived a dull existence, alone in the home of my birth. That was until the summer of 1889, when, at the age of fifty-seven, I read in *The Mechanics' Free Press*—Father's newspaper that he sold upon his retirement—of an account by a miner who discovered gold in Resurrection Creek.

"This news gave me a rebirth, a new purpose, and a chance to reclaim the lost glory of my youth. It didn't take me but a few weeks to purchase passage on the Transcontinental Railway to San Francisco, and once there, board a steamship headed for Cook Inlet.

"Before I knew it, I was placer mining the banks of Sixmile Creek, and just like I did at the American River in California, I was lining my pockets with gold. But this renaissance was short-lived because I was attacked and mugged by two men living in what we would soon know as the city of Sunrise.

"They used something to hit me hard and must have thought I was dead, because they dragged my body to the creek, and tossed me in. The second I hit the icy waters, I came to and realized my predicament. I grabbed on to a hefty branch floating alongside and tried to swim to shore. But the currents were too strong, and within minutes it swept me into Turnagain Arm and on my way into the swift-moving currents of Cook Inlet.

"I was near freezing and would have soon lost consciousness and drowned, had it not been for two Dena'ina fisherman in canoes who rescued me and brought me here to Fire Island, and I've been here ever since."

"That's amazing," Liam said.

"It is a gripping story, but you didn't tell us how did you become their king?" I said, pointing to the wooden throne.

"He is not king," said a woman's voice from behind us.

I turned and saw an elderly native woman walking our way. Her silver hair was long and straight, providing a frame to a round face featuring crevice-deep wrinkles. She wore a similar long animal fur coat to the major's, with a belt cinched around her narrow waist.

Suddenly the Dena'ina men chanted the word *shunkda, shunkda*, over and over.

I looked over to Nicholai and asked, "What are they saying?" as the old woman entered the circle.

"The word *shunkda* means mother."

She approached the major who sat like a statue, his eyes glued to this woman called Mother. She flicked her fingers at him in dismissal, and the major quickly removed himself, allowing her to take the throne.

Mother looked at Liam, and then at me, and said, "Major Lawrence tells a sad story of the white man's greed and ignorance, handed down from generation to generation like a poisoned inheritance. The Dena'ina people teach our children how to honor our relationships with the plants, and animals that we share the earth with. These lands are not a resource for us to plunder, but an heirloom that we must treasure and preserve for our future generations."

Mother's words rang true in my ear, and I hung my head. After all, the purpose of my excursion this summer was to find the gold, claim it from the earth, and call it mine. What right did I have to disturb the balance of the natural world, though my effect was small compared to people like Mr. Wible and his powerful Hydro-Giant, ripping and tearing into the creek banks, leaving open wounds and gashes in its wake?

CHAPTER FIFTY-SIX—EARTHQUAKE

Opening night at the Hope Saloon was nothing like the grand one at the Gold Digger's. In fact, it was an unmitigated disaster. Some people stopped by, but mostly out of curiosity to see what was going on. With the other three girls remaining behind at the Gold Digger Saloon, Greta and Ingrid stood on what used to be the Hope General Store's front porch, trying to lure customers in with their alluring outfits and womanly charms, but instead instigated sneers and snide remarks.

If Suzie had been alive, I'm sure she would have found ways to entice these stuck-up men of Hope. But just the thought of her stirred up a grief that I'd been trying to subdue, and I knew I would never be able to find another woman quite like her.

It was apparent that even though the reverend was not physically in Hope, his influence lingered on in the community. These people would not succumb to the temptations of whiskey, women or winnings as quickly as I thought they would.

The bottle of whiskey I was nursing provided no relief to my disappointment, though I was determined not to let this first night's results dissuade me. People's memories were short, and if the temptations I offered were powerful enough, they'd soon forget about the reverend's ridiculous rants about sinning.

I walked out onto the front porch to check on the girls, and just as I pushed my way through the newly installed saloon doors, I saw Ella climbing the steps. She walked over to Greta and held up three fingers, inches from her face and growled, "You girls have three seconds to remove yourselves from here."

Greta and Ingrid looked at me, frightened. I cocked my head toward the saloon doors, and they quickly obliged and scooted indoors.

"It's good to see you, Ella. Can I buy you a drink?"

She shook her head and sneered, "I didn't come here for amusement, Magnus."

I held out my palms. "Please explain how I can be of service."

"You can shut these doors. The good people of Hope will never allow themselves to be tempted by Satan's saloon."

"Satan's saloon," I said, nodding. "What a great name."

Ella's face reddened, and her lips pursed. "What you need to do, is tell me where you've taken the reverend."

"Like I told the Sheriff earlier today, I had nothing to do with it."

"You should shake in your boots, Magnus, knowing the retribution that awaits you upon the reverend's return."

"Well, if there's nothing else, Ella, I need to get back inside," I said, swinging my arm toward the saloon doors.

"Do you think you can avoid the Lord's retribution?"

I offered a smug smile and turned away. Then, like divine intervention, the porch beneath my feet shook violently, and the windows rattled in their frames. Shouts of fright resounded from pedestrians along Main Street. Seconds later, the quake ceased, but my heart continued to thump against my chest.

"God sees all," Ella said, spun on her heels as if in triumph, and marched back to her café.

*

Once I got back to the Gold Digger Saloon, only Henry was left cleaning up. "Hey, boss, how'd it go?" he asked as I walked in.

"Not what I hoped for."

"Oh, sorry to hear that."

"Was there any damage here from the quake?"

"Earthquake?" Henry asked, looking up from the bar top he was wiping down.

"Yeah, an earthquake. About five or six hours ago. You felt nothing?"

He shook his head and said, "No, boss, I didn't feel a thing."

Too exhausted to probe further, I said, "I'm going to bed," and headed upstairs. When I reached the second-floor landing, I walked down the hallway to Suzie's old room. The door was closed, and I hadn't been inside since the day they murdered her. I closed my eyes, took a breath, trying to steady my nerves, and opened the door.

The only thing remaining of the bed was its wooden frame. The blood-soaked mattress, linens, and pillows were burned in a campfire down by the creek.

The room felt empty, not only for the contents that were removed, but for Suzie's beauty, charm, and charisma. She always drew attention when she was in a room, be it among a few people, or in a packed saloon.

I walked over to her dresser and opened the top drawer. Her clothes were still there, neatly folded. I picked up a delicate lace top and brought it to my face. Her favorite perfume still lingered upon it. I took it and sat down in the chair in front of her vanity table and looked at my reflection with tears rolling down my cheeks.

We had come far together since first meeting at the Miller House in Dawson and then traveling together to Sunrise. Suzie didn't deserve to die like this, carved into pieces. The more I thought about it, boiling anger replaced my anguish. Suzie's death at the hands of two vagabond, toothless prospectors, was Reverend O'Hara's fault for forcing the girls to move across the creek. The blood was on his hands; he got what he deserved.

But, now with the reverend gone, there were no valid reasons for keeping the girls in that house, unprotected from further harm. I would move them back into the saloon and deal with the pushback from Judge Cole and Sheriff Siringo. After all, as Mayor of Sunrise, it was my duty to protect its citizenry, regardless of their occupation.

CHAPTER FIFTY-SEVEN—BOUNTY HUNTERS

When I awoke the next morning, cradled gently in the cocoon-like hammock, I heard the soft lapping of water upon the mudflats just outside from our hut. I wiggled my way out, and stepped lightly toward the door, careful not to disturb Liam, who was sleeping soundly.

I stood upon the small porch of our hut, elevated over the still waters of the inlet, and looked north toward the mountains off in the distance visible in the cloudless, blue sky.

I was eager to find the reverend but perplexed as to which direction to go in. There were many places along Cook Inlet that Tommy could have taken Reverend O'Hara, and with the speed of the *LJ Perry*, they could have been hundreds of miles away by now.

Several of the Dena'ina fishermen were already by the campfire. I greeted them and was offered a warm brew from the kettle. As I sipped the herbal tea, Major Lawrence greeted me.

"Did you sleep well?"

I nodded. "Yes, thank you."

"It has been very good meeting you, Sam."

"Likewise, Major. It looks like you have made a nice life for yourself. This seems like a peaceful place."

The major nodded. "Mother spends every summer here on the island. She says it renews her connections to the spirit world."

"What do you do during the winter?"

"Mother allows me to live with her and her people at the Dena'ina village on Knik Arm, where I repay her kindness by teaching her children to speak, read and write English."

"Why would they want to learn English?"

"Mother says the white man is coming and for the tribe to survive, they must be able to speak the white man's language."

Just as Liam, Nicholai, and I were ready to push off from Fire Island, Mother appeared as if she had risen from the mist and stood before us upon the mudflats. I gaped at her, placed my palm over my heart, and said, "It's been an honor to know you. Your wisdom has touched me."

She smiled, returning the hand gesture with a slight bow. She looked over to Nicholai and pointed to the west and said, "Go to the Tyonek village. The holy man you seek is there and is unwell."

"How do you know this?" I asked.

"I have seen it in my dreams. The reverend is in the care of Sha-e-dah-kla. He is Shaman. He performs miracles, cures sick people."

I looked over to Nicholai, just as the color drained from his pink cheeks.

"What is it?" I asked.

He shrugged and said, "The Kniks have a troubled history with the Tyoneks."

"What do you mean by troubled?" Liam asked.

278

"The Kniks on the Arm have warred with the Tyoneks. Some years ago, the Knik chief offered, um . . ." he paused for a moment trying to think of the word, "a *bounty* for the killing of the Tyonek chief."

"Why would he do that?" I asked.

"The Knik chief believed that the murder of the chief of the Tyoneks was the fastest way to end the war. So, he sent his bounty hunters disguised as traders. Upon their arrival into the Tyonek village, a celebration of singing and dancing ensued, as was the custom among traders.

"Once the Tyoneks dropped their guard, the Knik bounty hunters massacred all the unsuspecting Tyoneks except for the chief's nephew, who escaped the carnage. He ran and warned his uncle the chief, that these men were imposters and were seeking to end his life. The chief acted quickly, sending his best warriors who killed the Knik bounty hunters."

I looked up to Mother and asked, "If the Kniks and Tyoneks are mortal enemies, won't Nicholai be in danger?"

"It is possible," Mother said. "But I will pray for the Tyoneks to offer their forgiveness."

Nicholai pursed his lips and said, "We must go."

"Are you sure, Nicholai?"

"I'm sure. The reverend needs our help, we cannot abandon him."

"Did you say that Tommy, the chief's son, captured the reverend?" Mother asked.

"He has. What does that mean for Tommy? He is also Knik," Liam said.

Mother raised a finger and said, "The son of a chief is quite a prize. Sha-e-dah-kla will prevent bad spirits from harming his people with his spider net. But you must go now to Tyonek, before it's too late."

I held out my hands. "Too late for what?"

"Sha-e-dah-kla takes his captives inland to secret caves, where you'll never find them."

"Do you have visions?" I asked, baffled by how she knew what was happening so far away.

Mother looked at me for a moment. Her eyes glazed over and became reflective like two tiny mirrors. "Do not ask me any more questions. You must leave now or you will never see them again."

Liam and Nicholai looked at me, and I shrugged. "Let's go then," I said.

Nicholai gave us a push off and, in one swift motion, leaped into his position at the stern. We waved farewell to Mother, Major Lawrence, and the Dena'ina fishermen, and began our journey across the Cook Inlet, heading southwest toward the coastal village of the Tyonek tribe.

CHAPTER FIFTY-EIGHT—SHORTAGES

The emergency meeting for the Concerned Citizens of Sunrise and Hope was called for eight o'clock. I entered Sunrise City Hall a few minutes past the hour and found already in attendance: Judge Cole, Sheriff Siringo, Simon Wible, Cap Lathrop, Ella Carson, and Hank Stanton representing the Alaska Commercial Company.

"We've been waiting for you," said Mr. Wible in an accusatory tone.

"My apologies. There was a problem at the saloon that needed my attention."

Mr. Wible shook his head. "Whatever your problem was is nothing compared to what we all may be facing if we don't come up with a solution to Cap's missing steamer."

I took a seat at the lone empty spot around the table.

Cap jabbed a finger at me and barked, "All of this is your fault, Magnus. Where's my fucking boat?"

"If you ask me," Ella blurted out, "you'll find your boat when we find the reverend."

I held my hands out. "Is the purpose of this meeting so I can be yelled at? If that's the case, I'm leaving," I said, pushing back my chair.

"Cut the shit, Magnus, and sit down," barked Mr. Wible.

I lowered myself back into my seat.

Mr. Wible began by looking directly at me. "There's a strong suspicion that Tommy, son of Chief Ephanasy, has stolen the *LJ Perry*, and has taken the reverend with him. The result of which has left the businesses in Sunrise and Hope without our last leg of transportation from the inlet into the Arm, and unless we locate the *LJ Perry* soon, we will face significant shortages of essential goods."

"At this point, I'm serving bruised fruit, brown lettuce, and stale bread at the café," Ella said shaking her head, and continued, "and another few days of this and all we'll be offering is salmon and moose meat."

Shortages was something I hadn't considered. Without my weekly shipments of corn, my whiskey business would come to a screeching halt.

"I need parts for the hydraulics, which if I don't get shortly, we'll be shutting down at least half of my operations," said Mr. Wible.

Judge Cole pointed a finger at Cap and asked, "Is there some other way to move goods?"

Cap shook his head. "I'm afraid not. I designed the Perry for Turnagain Arm. There's nothing that can haul loads, while being small and nimble enough to dodge the mudflats and outrun the tides."

"If I may?" Hank Stanton said, raising his hand. "As some of you know, I work for the Alaska Commercial Corporation, and last year, before we knew of Cap's services, we negotiated with the Tyonek natives to transport goods from their village on Cook Inlet into Turnagain Arm on their sailing scows."

"What's a sailing scow?" asked Mr. Wible.

"It's a flat-bottomed sailboat," began Cap, "and like the *LJ Perry*, it can navigate shallow waters."

"That's great, Mr. Stanton, but how does that help us?" asked Ella.

Mr. Stanton shrugged and said, "We can pay the Tyoneks for use of their scows to deliver our goods from the steamships. I can send a wire to my office in Seattle and inform them to notify the next steamship to anchor off by the Tyonek village. But we would still need to work out a deal with the Tyoneks for them to transport our goods into the Arm."

"And how would we do that?" I asked.

"What if we ask Chief Ephanasy if he would transport a delegation, in his canoes?" Mr. Wible said.

Judge Cole slapped his palms on the table, causing everyone to jump and said, "Great idea. Who's going?"

*

Later that night, while watching the activity on Front Street from my bedroom porch, I was having second thoughts about volunteering as one of the four delegates to travel by canoe out of Turnagain Arm, and across the treacherous Cook Inlet to the Tyonek village.

Regardless of my worries, an alternate form of hauling goods was needed. I had a lot to lose if Cap's steamer wasn't located soon. I couldn't even imagine what Tommy could have done with it. Suddenly, my grand plan to get rid of the reverend was having unforeseen consequences.

After we adjourned the meeting, the four people who agreed to go— Cap, Sheriff Siringo, Ella, and I—visited the Knik village to speak with Chief Ephanasy. Hopefully he would allow two of his braves to guide us in his canoes to the Tyonek village.

When we arrived, the chief greeted each of us warmly, placing his hand over his heart, but refused that honor for me. I shrugged to dismiss the intended insult. The chief gestured for us to sit in the circle surrounding a campfire that was being tended to by a young native boy.

"Does this visit have something to do with the reverend and my son?" he asked.

"Yes, Chief, how did you know?" asked Ella.

The chief pointed out to sea and said, "I already sent Nicholai with Percy and Liam to search for Tommy and the reverend."

We all shared a look of surprise with each other. "When did this happen?" asked Ella.

"Yesterday," the chief said dropping his gaze into the fire for a moment. When he looked up, he asked, "Are you also looking for my son and the reverend?"

"We are. But we also have another pressing need. Tommy has taken the Cap's steamer the *LJ Perry*," Ella said. "Many of the businesses of Hope and Sunrise are now in a crisis, as we cannot transfer our much-needed supplies and goods from the steamships that dock in the inlet. We are looking to negotiate with the Tyoneks about using their sailing scows to take the place of the *LJ Perry* since it's gone missing. That's why we're asking if we can we use two of your braves to escort us to their village."

The chief furrowed his brow and pursed his lips. His face turned a blotchy red as he stood up and jabbed a finger at me and said, "It was you

284

that poisoned my son's mind. Tommy is troubled, I know that, but he would never harm anyone."

I swallowed, and stayed silent.

The chief held his hands up, indicating he was done addressing me, but continued speaking to the others. "The Tyoneks are our enemy. I will not send my braves to their deaths because this man needs corn to make his whiskey," he said pointing at me.

"What will the Tyoneks do if they see your men?" Sheriff Siringo asked.

The chief held out his hands. "I do not know. It's been years since our last conflict," he said, sitting back down and returning his focus to the fire, which seemed to extinguish his anger. "But your offer may interest Chief Sha-e-dah-kla. He has been known to trade with the white man. You should know, however, that the chief is also a powerful shaman with a great spider net that he casts to catch bad spirits. If your intentions are good, he might allow my men to approach."

"But what if he doesn't?" I asked.

Chief Ephanasy grimaced at me and folded his arms across his chest. "There's the possibility that he may take you all prisoner. The Tyoneks have secret caves where they took Knik prisoners during the Indian Wars." He shook his head and said, "None have ever returned."

I looked over to Cap, Sheriff Siringo, and Ella, expecting to see my fear expressed in their faces. But no one seemed to be as frightened as me. "Are you sure you still want to go? This sounds dangerous," I pleaded.

"We're going, Magnus," Sheriff Siringo said boldly, dismissing my cowardice.

We agreed to rendezvous at the Hope Café at seven the next morning before making our way together to the Knik village. The chief agreed to allow two of his braves to guide our party to the Tyonek village.

I planned on packing my Colt 45, even though Chief Ephanasy warned against taking weapons.

"Do not take any guns," the chief said. "The shaman will know even if you hide them."

I laughed to myself, thinking how ridiculous all of this was sounding. This was nothing more than a collection of far-fetched Indian tales made up by the elders to frighten children. Perhaps the others would heed Chief Ephanasy's warnings, but I would not go unarmed. My Peacemaker would be safely tucked away in my pack.

The chief said that the trip to the Tyoneks would not be possible in one day because of something he called the cycle of the tides. "You must honor the tides or you will never reach your destination. That is why you must spend a night at the Dena'ina fish camp on Fire Island before continuing to the western shore of the inlet the next morning."

That night I lay in my bed thinking about the many dangers I was about to undertake. I replayed in my mind the chief's outburst about jeopardizing the lives of his braves in exchange for corn to make whiskey,

286

and wondered if risking my life was worth the reward. Yet, on the other hand, it was probably wise to show some responsibility for manipulating Tommy, and the consequences it incurred.

CHAPTER FIFTY-NINE—THE WALK

About an hour into our journey from Fire Island, the sun vanished behind swift-moving, black storm clouds. Liam pointed from his seat in the bow to a line of rain showers rushing toward us, and within moments of his declaration, we were in a downpour.

Accompanying the rains were driving winds, causing the flat waters of the inlet to turn choppy. Waves crashed hard against the canoe's sturdy birchbark shell. Nicholai shouted orders for us to keep paddling hard so we wouldn't capsize.

Just as I felt my arms were ready to give out from exhaustion, the rains and winds ceased, though we were still under silver skies. Nicholai permitted us to rest. I put my paddle across the canoe's frame and leaned on it, allowing my pounding heart to settle down. Sweat was pouring off me and blending with the ankle-deep rainwater sloshing back and forth in the canoe's bottom.

After a brief rest and a snack of tasty blueberries picked on Fire Island, we continued. With the stormy weather behind us, we moved easily across the light chop. Without the excessive physical exertion raising my body temperature, combined with the chill in the air created by the icy-cold waters of Cook Inlet, my teeth chattered.

Light rain soon returned. It was not nearly as troubling as the storm we just pushed through, but our canoe was taking on more water. When I turned and asked Nicholai if he had concerns, he shook his head and said not to worry.

It took some time, but my body temperature adjusted, and the chills passed. We pushed ahead, and after two or three more hours of steady paddling; we saw land. I could make out the rocky shoreline stretching in both directions, until it faded from view. Proving a backdrop to the coastline was a range of august mountains, their tops encircled by halos of clouds.

As we approached, the ominous cloud cover cleared along the shoreline, allowing the sun to beam its welcomed rays upon a small cove. We paddled into the desolate, natural harbor and beached our canoe onto the gravel shore.

It felt good to stretch our legs and look around.

"Where are we?" Liam asked.

"I'm not sure," Nicholai said surveying the area, "but I would guess the Tyonek village is further south from here."

We spent a few minutes exploring. There was not much to see, except for the woods and the vast Cook Inlet before us. I wasn't looking forward to getting back into the canoe.

"It's time to move on," Nicholai said, but took a moment to walk out on a sliver of a rocky outcropping that stretched into the inlet. He looked up and down the shoreline, rubbed his chin, pointed south and said, "Perhaps it's better to walk the rest of the way."

"Walk?" Liam asked.

With the warmth of the sun, and the fullness of the late summer foliage buffering the winds crisscrossing the inlet, walking sounded like a splendid idea.

"Yes," Nicholai said with a nod. "I recognize this place now," he said, gesturing to the cove. "I was here last summer hunting in these woods with Tommy. The Tyonek village is only an hour's walk that way," he said, pointing. "A stealthy approach by foot is wise, rather than gliding up by canoe and exposing us to a potentially hostile welcome."

We pulled the canoe off the beach, slid it under a healthy growth of Devil's Club and followed Nicholai. He took a few steps and turned to say, "The Tyoneks are expert trackers and will know of our presence if we're not silent."

I shared a moment with Liam, whose wide eyes expressed his anxiety. I reached over and put my hand on his shoulder and squeezed. "We'll be all right," I said, trying to muster some conviction behind my words.

We followed Nicholai down a worn footpath along the water's edge. A story, I believe by Jack London, popped into my mind and caused me to worry about our clumsy footfalls. In this tale, a native tribe was warned of a pending attack, because they heard the breaking of twigs under the heavy feet of soldiers as they approached.

What I found remarkable as we traveled down the coastal path, was how my senses, because of my nervousness, were aroused. Every flutter of a leaf, or the movement of a small creature, caused my head to jerk from side to side, while the waves lapping upon the shore were as audible as my thumping heartbeat. With this enhanced sense of awareness, if we were about to be discovered by the Tyoneks, I believed I would know the moment before we were in their presence.

CHAPTER SIXTY—SEARCH FOR THE *LJ PERRY*

Once we paddled beyond the Arm and out into the inlet, the storm came on quickly. I had been out at sea before in foul weather, but this was the first time I wasn't in a seaworthy craft like the *LJ Perry*. From my position, in between Ella in the bow and Alexander, our Knik guide, manning the stern, I did my best to keep my strokes constant and strong with Alexander's chants of, "PULL, PULL, PULL."

But regardless of our efforts, the strong currents forced our canoe off course, pushing us far south of Fire Island, our desired destination, and according to Alexander, ending our chances of turning back and reaching the island because of the severe winds, sharp currents and shifting tides. We also had another problem; we had lost track of the other canoe because of the driving rains and heaving seas. Alexander said we had no choice but to press on to the Tyonek village and hopefully spot Kusema's canoe with Cap and Sheriff Siringo.

I tried to get a peek of Ella's face, to see how she was enduring the stinging rain and mountainous sea swells. I had experienced nothing so physically challenging as this before, and there were several moments when I was certain we would capsize and most likely drown. But I never heard a single moan or whimper from Ella. Even when she turned her face, there was no evidence of the fright that had taken over my body like a swift-moving virus.

Then, just as quickly as the storm enveloped us, the black clouds passed us by and the skies cleared. We could finally take a break. I took my paddle and laid it crossways over the upper frame of the canoe as a support for me to collapse upon.

"Are you all right, Magnus?" Ella asked.

I lifted my head, though it felt heavy and said, "I'll be okay."

"Well, it looks like the weather has cleared," she said too cheerfully.

I pushed myself back up to my knees, tilted my face into the sun and closed my eyes. Its warmth provided relief to my racing heart, which I thought would burst from the combination of fear and exertion.

With our visibility improved, I looked about for the other canoe, and then turned to look at Alexander and asked, "How do you know which way to go?"

He lifted his paddle and used it to gesture ahead of us and said, "See the birds? I think we're close to shore."

Off in the distance were small fluttering shadows dotting the blue sky. If what he said was true, we were closing in on the western shore of Cook Inlet.

"Hey, I can see them," shouted Ella, pointing off to our left.

I quickly turned and saw off in the distance what looked like a canoe moving toward the shoreline. I kept my eyes glued upon it and within a few minutes could identify three figures paddling. It was Cap at the bow, Sheriff Siringo in the middle and Kusema working the stern.

The gap between us closed as we approached the shore, which was finally coming into view. I gasped and pointed at what was, without doubt, the *LJ Perry* tied to a dock, and several sailing scows beached at what appeared to be a native village.

I turned to ask Alexander and asked, "Is this the Tyonek village?"

He nodded and put a finger to his lips, reminding me to remain silent as spoken words carried quickly across the water. He turned to Kusema in the other canoe and gestured to him; and from what I could tell, they agreed to go ashore south of the dock.

I looked over to Cap, who must have been relieved to see his steamer in one piece. But why was it here and where were Tommy and the reverend?

We reached the mudflats just as the tide came in, which helped us maneuver alongside the tall rocky outcroppings. We tied up the canoes to the jagged stones and climbed up the steep face to its craggy top.

Kusema and Alexander quickly ushered us into the protective thick foliage, hugging the shoreline, and out of view.

While we huddled together, I said, "Let's just grab Cap's boat and get the hell out of here."

"But what about the reverend and Tommy?" Ella said, glaring at me. "They must be here and could be in trouble."

"We must find our brother," said Kusema.

Sheriff Siringo reached out and patted Kusema's back. "We won't leave without them," he said, offering his reassurance. "Now, according to what Chief Ephanasy said, our best bet to finding the reverend and Tommy is by seeking out their chief."

Once everyone agreed to the plan, our rescue party proceeded single file down a narrow footpath toward the Tyonek village. I secretly signaled to Cap for us to lag, and when we were out of earshot from the others, I whispered, "Listen, Cap, we're we risking our lives. Why don't we sneak away and grab your boat while we still can?"

Cap stopped short, turned to me, stuck a finger inches from my face and growled, "You're despicable, Magnus."

As he spun back around and marched onward with the group, I thought for a moment about commandeering the *LJ Perry* on my own, but without knowledge of operating the uniquely designed craft, I doubted I could make it too far before being captured.

It appeared I had no choice but to stick with the group for now. But before rejoining them, I slipped my hand into my rucksack and felt for my Peacemaker, which was still snugly tucked away. I smiled at my cleverness, and trotted to catch up with the rest of the party.

CHAPTER SIXTY-ONE—SIMEON

My imagined enhanced sense of awareness did little to warn me of the six
Tyonek warriors who were suddenly standing before us.

Nicholai held out his arms as a gesture that we meant no harm. The
braves slowly separated, forming a circle around us, preventing our
escape, if we foolishly tried to flee.

A tall man, with wide-spaced brown eyes, stepped before Nicholai
and said something in his native language. Nicholai nodded, placed his
hand over his heart, and after a brief conversation, turned to Liam and me
and said, "They are taking us to their village."

"Do they know anything about the reverend or Tommy?" I asked
while keeping my eyes on the Tyoneks.

"He would not say," Nicholai replied.

The Tyonek warriors spoke among themselves while they escorted us
to the village. It was hard to pick up any clues from their tone or intonation
of their words since their language was such a departure from any foreign
tongue I had ever heard. But I imagined that they were apprehensive to see
strangers approach through the woods as we did, especially with a Knik
brave leading us.

I was expecting to see a traditional native village, like the ones I read
about in my storybooks of the tribes from the southwest. But the Tyonek

village was not much different from what was in Hope. There were weathered wooden shacks and log cabins dotting a tree-barren plot of land. The pathways were muddy, because of the recent storm. But unlike Hope, there were no well-defined streets. The buildings were orientated haphazardly, with no apparent rhyme or reason.

The few natives we passed casually turned their heads to take notice of us as we entered a well-built log cabin in the center of the village. Just as we stepped inside, I shared a profound moment with an elderly man with deep, leather-like wrinkles. While it was not more than a second or two, his eyes locked onto mine, and I heard his words, though he remained silent. *"We have been waiting for you, Percy."*

When I realized what had just occurred, I wanted to stop, but I was already being pushed through the doorway. Inside was a single room about the size of the Hope Café. I took a quick look around and noticed a cluttered collection of fishing gear, colorful woven blankets and an assortment of worn, faded clothing tossed about. The sharp smell of smoked salmon mingled with other pungent odors, and there was chatter and laughter from the small children running about.

Liam, Nicholai, and I were ushered into a circular arrangement of blankets and odd-shaped cushions. We sat down, side by side and the same warriors that captured and escorted us to this meeting place, turned away and left us alone.

"What's going on?" I asked Nicholai.

He shook his head and shrugged.

With no one to observe us except the four children around the ages of five or six, and a couple of old women cooking by the stove, I stood up and looked around. It was apparent that several families lived and slept in this one-room house. I wondered how they managed in such a small space, thinking about my parent's home in San Francisco, where the salon alone was nearly as large.

"Would you care to join me, Percy?" said a voice from behind me.

I turned to see a young, beardless man, not much older than Liam or me. "Oh, you're mistaken," I said, walking over to the circle, "my name isn't really Percy, it's—" and before I could finish, he held up a palm forcing me to halt my words.

"Please, Percy, take a seat so we can speak," he said, gesturing to where Liam and Nicholai were already seated.

Once I took my place in the circle, he began. "Welcome to our village. My name is Simeon, first son to the Chief and Shaman Sha-e-dah-kla, who is now with your holy man in the healing cave. I am sorry to say that the reverend is close to death, and Shaman has not yet been able to reverse the illness. We've been waiting for you, Percy, and should waste no more time."

"The reverend is dying? What happened?" I asked.

Simeon shrugged. "It's best we waste no more time."

I looked over to Liam and Nicholai and said, "All right, should we go now?"

Simeon wagged his finger and said, "Only you, Percy. They must wait here."

"But why?"

"We do not question Shaman wisdom."

"But what about Tommy? Where is Chief Ephanasy's son?" Nicholai asked.

Simeon raised his arm and waved his hand to summon a brave waiting outside our circle. "Alexander will take you to him."

Liam looked over at me, his lips pursed and forehead wrinkled.

"I'll be fine," I said, trying to sound confident.

"Come," Simeon said, standing up. "We must go to the caves now."

CHAPTER SIXTY-TWO—TOMMY'S STORY

We hadn't walked but for a minute along the footpath before a dozen spears, with sharpened flint-knapped stones bound to their ends, were pointed at us by fierce-looking warriors. Our group instinctually huddled together, as the young native men closed in upon us.

One warrior, not among the tallest, but wide and muscular, growled something fierce-sounding in his language. Alexander answered him, leaving me to wonder about the differences in their dialects, but when they conversed, I realized they could communicate without issue.

"We're being taken to their village," Alexander said.

"Just tell them we've come for the *LJ Perry*, and we'll be on our way," I said.

Alexander turned to me and said, "I believe Tommy is here, and they are taking us to him now."

"But what about the reverend? Is he here too?" asked Ella.

"He said he cannot tell me anything more. We'll find out soon enough," Alexander said.

He led us into a log house with a thatched roof, and as we walked through the door, standing before us was Tommy. He looked pale and out of sorts, and squinted at us, as if he wasn't sure who we were. Alexander and Kusema quickly embraced him.

"What have you done with Reverend O'Hara?" asked Ella.

Tommy rubbed his forehead and took a deep breath, exhaled, and said, "He jumped into the inlet and nearly drowned. I pulled him out and brought him here to the medicine man. He's trying to save him."

Ella grabbed his shoulders and shook Tommy. "He jumped from where, Tommy? Why did he jump? Where is he now?"

"And why did you steal my boat?" Cap blurted out.

Sheriff Siringo stepped forward and said, "Let's give Tommy a chance to answer." He placed his hand on Tommy's shoulder and said, "Now, Tommy, tell us from the beginning what happened."

Tommy turned around and walked over to a large tree stump partially draped with an animal hide and sat down. He held out his hands, inviting us to join him on the floor, which we all did.

I took the moment to remove my pack. I felt for my Peacemaker tucked inside, and lowered myself into a cross-legged position on the wooden floorboards.

Tommy leaned forward, pressing his elbows onto his thighs, and began his tale.

"It all started when Mr. Vega offered me a twenty-ounce nugget," he said and paused.

Cap, Ella, and Sheriff Siringo all turned to look at me with gazes that seemingly attempted to pierce my heart with daggers of their anger.

"And what did Mr. Vega expect you to do for him in return?" Ella asked.

Tommy lowered his gaze, expressing his shame and said, "I was to force the reverend onto the *LJ Perry* and take him to the steamship out in the inlet, where we would sail to Seattle, and then put him on a train back to his home in Ohio."

I held out my hands, shook my head and said, "So what happened? Why are you here?"

Tommy took a breath and answered, "By the time we got close to the *Bertha*, the reverend started raving, insisting that he would jump overboard."

"Why would he do that?" Ella asked.

Tommy lifted his palms and said, "Because he refused to board the ship."

"So, he jumped into Cook Inlet?" Ella blurted out and added, "What did he think he could do, swim back to Hope?"

Tommy lifted his face for all of us to see his colorless cheeks, and said slowly, "He stepped out of my reach, looked up into the gray sky and said 'The almighty will protect me,' and leapt off into the inlet."

Ella's hand went to her mouth, and asked, "Then what happened?"

"I grabbed a rope and jumped in. By the time I reached the reverend, he had already gone under several times. It took great effort to get him back onboard the Perry, but by then the tide had pulled us far south of the *Bertha*, and I couldn't maneuver back."

"So, you brought him here?" Sheriff Siringo asked.

302

"There was no choice. He was unconscious, and I remembered about the powerful medicine man at the Tyonek village. I hurried here and when we docked, we were immediately greeted by these same warriors who brought you here. When I told them what had happened to the reverend, they called for the medicine man. It was only moments before he appeared, walking toward us along the narrow dock," he said, and paused a moment.

"Tommy, please continue," said Ella with little patience.

"He had such a pleasant face. I think it was his eyes—so soft and gentle," Tommy said.

"Where's the reverend now?" I asked.

Tommy smiled and said in a whisper, "He's with the medicine man who they call Sha-e-dah-kla."

Ella stretched out her arms and said, "What's happened to him, Tommy?"

Just then the door swung open and in walked Liam with a Knik brave that I recognized from Hope.

"Liam, what are you doing here, and where's Sam?" asked Ella.

"He's gone to find the reverend." Liam said, and saw Tommy. "It was you who brought him here."

Sheriff Siringo held up his hand. "Yes, yes, we've just been through all that. Apparently, Reverend O'Hara is under the care of a powerful shaman who is trying to save his life."

Liam nodded quickly. "Yes, that's true. Sam is on his way now with the chief's son Simeon. They have taken him to some sort of healing cave."

"What are we supposed to do?" asked Cap. "Just sit here?"

"Yes, Simeon asked that we wait here until he returns," Liam replied.

I slipped my pistol out from my pack, stood up, took a breath to gather my nerve, pointed my gun at the warrior guarding the door, and said boldly, "Or we could just get onboard the *LJ Perry* right now and have Cap take us home."

"Have you lost your mind, Magnus? Put the gun down. We're not leaving without the reverend and Sam," Ella said.

I laughed at her absurdity. "Well, you can stay here, Ella, if you like. Let's go, Cap," I said, signaling for the guard to step aside.

"No, we mustn't do that," Liam insisted.

Cap waved a hand and said, "If the reverend's in trouble, I say we go find him."

"I agree with Cap," said Sheriff Siringo, displaying his own Colt 45.

"Didn't Chief Ephanasy say no guns?" sighed Ella.

"Sha-e-dah-kla says do not bring guns," Tommy said.

Sheriff Siringo looked at his Peacemaker and said, "I go nowhere without them."

As we approached the door, the Tyonek warrior stood his ground before Alexander and spoke to him with great intensity and vigor.

"What did he say?" I asked.

304

"He said the white men are free to go, but we must stay," he said gesturing to his fellow Knik braves, Nicholai, Kusema, and Tommy.

I sighed with relief and said, "Great, let's go find the reverend and Sam and get the hell out of here."

CHAPTER SIXTY-THREE—SHA-E-DAH-KLA

"Percy is a made-up name. It was my father's idea," I tried to explain to Simeon.

"Shaman says you are Percy," he said and pointed toward a pathway that led to a small footbridge, bringing us to the other side of the stream and into the woods.

I shrugged, and figured it really didn't matter much if he wanted to call me Percy, and to be truthful, I didn't mind it. "How far are the caves?"

"Not far, but we mustn't speak anymore. We'll disturb the healing ceremony."

Simeon was not being truthful when he said that the caves were close by. We walked for at least another hour, which made me wonder why he insisted on my silence since we were still so far away.

We finally stopped walking when we reached the base of a rocky cliff side. With nowhere to go, and without permission to speak, I just looked at him and shrugged.

Simeon crooked a finger, beckoned for me to follow him, and ducked down behind an outcropping of large boulders scattered across the bottom of the rock face. I followed him and couldn't imagine how the shaman could transport the incapacitated Reverend O'Hara this great distance and around all these immoveable obstacles.

We ducked into crevices created by the rock scramble, and squeezed through narrow passageways, sometimes needing to crawl on our backs, or on our bellies.

I smelled the musty odors of the cave before we approached, and once we stepped inside, the nostril-biting smells only intensified.

Simeon and I exchanged no words as I followed him deeper into the darkening cave. I eventually had to stop walking out of fear, because I couldn't see my hand inches from my face and whispered, "Simeon, are you here?"

A puff of brightness, and a burst of the acrid smell of tar pitch, preceded the lighting of a torch by Simeon, and the illumination of a great cavern. Shadows from the flickering flame danced upon rocky and icy surfaces. Oversized icicles grew out of the cave's ceiling and dripped like upside down flameless candles. Their discharge formed a mirror image upon the cave's floor, where the icicles seemed to reach upwards towards their creator.

I remembered learning about these geological formations in school. The ones hanging from above were called stalactites, and the ones growing upwards were named stalagmites. Even though the black and white photos from my textbook taught me the names, they could not capture how majestic the formations appeared in the cave, as if they were living, plant-like things.

"You must go on alone, Percy. Shaman is just through there," he said, pointing to a small, dark crack in between a monumental sliver amid two stone walls.

"Through here? Are you sure?" I asked, not wanting to separate from Simeon.

Simeon nodded, handed me the torch, and said, "Shaman is waiting."

I took the torch from Simeon and said, "Will I ever see you again?"

"If it is meant to be," he said and gestured for me to move on.

In order to slip through the narrow crevice, I turned sideways and held the torch out in front of me. The passageway squeezed against my torso and was even too narrow for me to turn my head. My chest and back pressed against the stone, and I could feel its coolness through the layers of my clothing.

I tried to hold out the torch as far in front as I could, because a constant draft blew towards me, causing me to be covered in soot and smell from the now dwindling flame. I wanted to drop it, but I feared being in pitch blackness, so I held on tight and kept moving.

With no choice but to move forward, a strange thought popped into my mind that my woolen coat was being rubbed into tatters by the stone walls, and what plausible explanation I would offer Mother about what I did to my expensive coat; that is, if I survived my ordeal.

Just then, a powerful draft burst passed me and instantly extinguished the torch. My reflex was to shut my eyes, and when I opened them, instead of being in darkness, I saw a light flickering through the passageway in front of me. I dropped the torch and shimmied my way to it, and finally birthed myself out into an open cavernous space, where a large campfire was burning brightly.

"Ah, Percy, you're finally here," said a voice from the other side of the flames.

I stepped around the fire and saw the reverend lying unconscious upon an elevated stone shelf. An animal hide was draped over his body, and his face was as white as snow. Standing beside him was a small man, wearing a wool-like robe that ended at his feet. He had long, black hair, and the expression in his brown eyes was soft and welcoming.

"Is he dead?" I asked.

"Soon."

"Are you the shaman?"

He nodded and said, "I am Sha-e-dah-kla, Shaman and Chief of my people, the Tyoneks."

I looked about and gestured around me. "Why did you bring the reverend here?"

He shrugged and said, "This is my healing cave."

Still confused, I asked, "But why do you need me?"

"Oh." The shaman laughed. "I don't need you, I am fine," he said, patting his chest to prove his health. "It's the reverend who needs you."

I shook my head. "But what can I do?"

"I do not know, but this is what the reverend has told me."

"Reverend O'Hara has spoken to you?" I asked.

"You mean have the words come from his mouth?"

I nodded.

"No, he cannot speak, but I can hear his thoughts."

I looked at the shaman and shrugged in bewilderment.

"Do not worry, Percy. Now that you're here, you can help the reverend. I've prepared a tonic for you," he said, handing me a stone cup. "Drink this and lie down next to him."

I looked into the cup and saw a brownish liquid, with bits of plant leaves floating on top. "You want me to drink this?"

The shaman nodded. "Yes, yes, and please hurry. The reverend is losing his will to live."

I looked at the reverend and wondered what would happen to me if I proceeded.

The shaman put a hand on my shoulder, sensing my apprehension and said, "You can trust me, Percy."

I nodded and put the cup to my lips and drank. The shaman guided me to lie beside the reverend, and moments later, I was asleep.

CHAPTER SIXTY-FOUR—THE SPIDER'S NET

An old man with what seemed like bottomless wrinkles, greeted us. I amused myself by imagining if I counted them, like the rings of a tree stump, they would tell me his age. He held up his bony arms to gather in our group, and said, "I am Pavel. You will follow me. I will take you to the caves."

With no objections from any of us, we all nodded.

Like ducklings, we followed the energetic Tyonek elder as he moved swiftly through the village and out into the woods. We walked for what seemed like hours. Whenever one of us wanted to strike up a conversation or ask a question, Pavel would remind us, "You must remain silent."

Most of the time the journey behind Pavel was along a fairly flat pathway. But this changed when we stood before a towering cliffside that disappeared skywards beyond our view. Pavel put a finger to his lips and pointed for us to follow him behind fallen boulders, some as large as houses.

After ducking under rocky overhangs, and pushing our bodies through crevices that called for some serious gut-sucking, we emerged into a dark cavern.

It wasn't until Pavel lit a torch that we could see its magnificence.

"Oh my," Ella said, forgetting Pavel's insistence on our silence.

The sheriff took a few steps around the tall and tapered stone-like sculptures growing like plants from the cavern floor upwards, seeming to reach for their mirror images that hung above them from the ceiling of the cavern, and asked, "Where's the reverend?"

Pavel ignored the sheriff's question and instead looked about, like he was tracking a bird flickering back and forth. "You have caused a disturbance," he said, shaking his head.

"Because we spoke? I'm sorry. I was just surprised at all of this," Ella said, sweeping her arms outwards.

Pavel wagged a finger, pinched his eyes together, and said, "You were warned not to bring guns. Now you must wait here until Shaman removes his spider net."

"What do you mean? I see nothing," I said.

"Sha-e-dah-kla uses his net to capture bad spirits," he said.

"That's ridiculous," the sheriff said and walked about looking for some evidence of this mysterious spider net.

Meanwhile, Liam stepped toward Pavel, touched the old man's arm and said, "Percy and the reverend are my friends, our friends," he said, gesturing to Ella. "Perhaps we may go to them?"

Pavel shrugged. "You may try, if the shaman allows. It's through there," he said, pointing to a corridor-like passageway.

Liam picked up a dormant torch lying upon the stone floor, touched it against the lit one Pavel was holding, and it immediately caught flame. He held it out with an outstretched arm, reached for Ella's hand, and they walked into the darkened direction that Pavel indicated, disappearing from view.

I looked at Cap with a raised eyebrow and shouted, "Hey, wait up," and ran after them. Just as I reached the spot where they vanished from sight, something wrapped me in an invisible sticky web that prevented me from moving. "Hey, what's this?" I shouted.

"You are not permitted to go further," Pavel said, with a smirk.

I struggled to free myself, but the more I did, the more entangled I became.

Cap rushed over and touched my arm. "It's like a real spider's web," he said, pulling his sticky fingers apart.

"Why don't you go after them, Cap?" I said, while trying to undo myself from the netting.

Cap smiled, reached into his coat, pulled out a gun, and said, "Like you, I don't think I'll get too far."

CHAPTER SIXTY-FIVE—A HEALING

Piercing through my grogginess was a sweet voice that called out, "Wake up, Percy, it's me Ella."

"Ella?" I mumbled, trying to open my heavy eyes.

"Yes, it's me."

I reached out, took her hand, and caressed it between mine. "It's good to see you," I said, and as my vision cleared, I looked into her eyes and recognized the same woman who had been missing since that magical day we tossed stones into the water.

She smiled. "Liam is here too."

A hand slid under my back. "Can you sit up?" Liam asked, lifting me.

I swung my feet off the stone ledge and gripped onto my thighs to steady myself. "Where's the reverend?" I asked, suddenly remembering where I was.

"I'm here, Percy," said a voice.

Ella and Liam moved aside, and Reverend O'Hara stepped toward me.

"Reverend, you're all right?" I asked, looking at the seemingly healthy man standing before me.

"I'm fine, thanks to the shaman and you," the reverend said, holding out his arm to invite Sha-e-dah-kla to approach.

I pushed myself off the ledge and stood. "But what did I do?" I said, reaching out to grasp the reverend's outstretched hand.

He pulled me into him and wrapped his arms around me and whispered into my ear, "I passed, Percy, and you brought me back."

I pushed away from his grasp and looked into his eyes. "What do you mean?"

The reverend just patted my cheek and smiled.

There were so many unanswered questions. "Reverend, why are you here?"

"It began when Tommy tried to force him onto the *Bertha*," Ella said.

"Why would he do that?"

"Our friend Magnus Vega," Liam said, "offered Tommy a golden nugget for transporting the reverend to Seattle and then putting him on a train to Ohio. He wanted to get rid of him from Hope so he could open his saloon."

"And I refused to go," Reverend O'Hara boasted. "So rather than allowing Tommy to force me to board the *Bertha*, I jumped into Cook Inlet."

"And you nearly drowned," Ella snapped. "Tommy rescued him and thank goodness he was smart enough to bring him here to the Tyonek village."

"But I don't understand, Reverend, why would you risk your life and jump into the inlet?"

He looked at me with tears welling up and said, "Because I knew you would save me, Percy. All of this," he said, holding out his arms, "is as it was meant to be."

I shook my head. "But how did I save you?"

The shaman placed his hand on my shoulder and said, "The tea you drank sent you into the spirit world, where I could guide you to the reverend, who was beginning his great journey. It was then, that you, Percy, were able to return him back to the living."

My eyes darted between Liam, Ella, and the reverend, and I exhaled. "I don't know what to say, but thank God you're all right, Reverend."

The reverend nodded. "We always need to show our gratitude to the almighty, but today I offer it to you, Shaman, and to you, Percy Hope," the reverend said with a warm smile.

I embraced the reverend, and thought about his dreams. His foresight did seem to bear fruit. The pedestal he continuously put me upon during his sermons had caused me to cast them off as mere theatrics, but after today, I was beginning to think he may have been right all along.

Upon our return to the large cavern, we saw waiting for us a Tyonek elder, Sheriff Siringo, Cap Lathrop, and Magnus Vega, who was acting strangely by pulling at some imaginary thing stuck to his body.

"There you are," Mr. Vega said, frustrated with whatever was plaguing him.

"Reverend, you're alive?" Cap said.

"I am, thanks to the shaman and Percy."

"Percy?" Mr. Vega said with disdain. "You mean Sam."

The reverend wagged his finger. "His birth name is Sam, but here," he raised his arms, "in our world, he is and will always be Percy Hope."

Mr. Vega sighed. "That's fine, call him whatever you want. But can someone help me with this," he said, fussing with some unseen substance clinging to his skin and clothing.

The shaman laughed and shook his head. "You are not an honorable man. My spider net knows this. But you may go now, we do not want you here."

And with those words, Mr. Vega held out his hands and smiled. "It's gone."

It took us about two hours to walk back to the village. Once there, we rounded up the four Knik braves who were being held under guard by the Tyonek warriors, and we all boarded the *LJ Perry*. The shaman, his son Simeon, Pavel the elder and the Tyonek warriors all stood on the dock, offering their farewells.

"Tell your father, Tommy, that he's welcome here. We only wish to live in peace," the shaman said and placed a palm over his heart to emphasize his words.

"I will tell him," Tommy said, returning the gesture.

As we pulled away from the dock, I figured that this would be the last time I would ever see the great shaman Sha-e-dah-kla. There was no

317

doubt, after what I witnessed, that he was a healer, the likes of whom I would probably never meet again. Could it be, I considered, that the shaman was a direct hand of God, because who else could command such power to bring back someone who had passed on?

There was also the question of how he could transport the reverend's unconscious body all the way through the nooks and crannies that I had to squeeze and crawl through to reach the secret cave where he performed the ceremony. Also unexplained was the shaman's ability to wield his mysterious spider net that prevented Mr. Vega, Cap, and the sheriff from proceeding into the healing cave with their weapons.

I tried to make sense of these enigmas, but the only answer I could muster time and again was that the shaman had some divine connection to the almighty. How else could he wield such magical powers?

With Cap at the wheel and everyone onboard, we hurried across Cook Inlet, passing by Fire Island and the Dena'ina fish camp. I slid alongside Ella, who was grasping on to the handrail at the bow.

"That was some ordeal," I said.

Ella nodded. "I'm happy everyone is safe."

"Listen, I want you to know that I am sorry about what happened at the saloon. It was a mistake. Can you forgive me?"

Ella turned to me and said. "It's not about forgiveness, Percy. You know my beliefs. A man and a woman must save themselves for marriage."

I nodded, trying to accept that it was over with Ella, and said, "I understand. But I hope we can at least still be friends."

Ella patted my cheek. "Of course, Percy, we will always be friends."

When we arrived back at Turnagain Arm, I couldn't help but think, as we pulled up to Hope, that it would soon be time for Liam and me to go home. Our return passenger tickets to San Francisco were for September the fifteenth, two weeks from now, still ample time to offer heartfelt farewells to my friends.

My time in this rabbit hole was ending, and I had to admit, even though I was heartbroken over Ella, I was looking forward to returning to my normal and boring life as Samuel Rothman.

CHAPTER SIXTY-SIX—JUSTICE

I stayed onboard with Cap and the sheriff after dropping the others off at Hope and then headed off to Sunrise, eager to get back to the Gold Digger Saloon. From the time we left yesterday morning until tonight, I had been gone nearly two full days. Hopefully, there would be no costly mishaps to remedy in my absence. Thank goodness Cap's steamer would be back in operation, and our weekly deliveries of corn to make our whiskey would once again be arriving. But beyond all of this, I was looking forward to a good night's sleep in my bed.

"Thank you, Cap," I said, stepping onto the Sunrise City dock. "I'm happy things are back to normal."

"Hold it right there," Sheriff Siringo said from behind me.

I turned around and saw his Colt 45 pointing at me.

"Hand over your Peacemaker," the sheriff demanded.

I glanced over to Cap, who was tying up the *LJ Perry* to the dock, and then back to the sheriff. "What's this all about?"

He thrust the gun forward, and said, "Just do what I say, Magnus."

I exhaled, realizing there would be a price to pay for my malfeasance. I reached into my pack, pulled out my gun and handed it over. "Is this necessary?" I pleaded. "Haven't you ever heard the saying, Sheriff, that all's well that ends well?

"I have. It's from a play by William Shakespeare, which has nothing to do with you. You're under arrest, Magnus Vega, for the abduction of Reverend O'Hara and the theft of the *LJ Perry*."

"But how's that a crime, Sheriff, if the reverend has been found and the *LJ Perry* back in service? Thanks partially to me," I said, trying to claim some credit.

"Crimes are also based on intentions, regardless of the outcome. But it's not for me to decide. Perhaps you can convince Judge Cole in the morning. In the meantime, you'll be spending the night in the Sunrise jail," he said, pointing down Front Street.

"But what about my saloon? At the very least, I need to stop by and make sure things are running smoothly."

The sheriff shook his head. "My concern is for the safety and welfare of the people of Sunrise, not your saloon."

*

When morning came, I was awakened by Sheriff Siringo shaking me.

"Get up, Magnus, Judge Cole is waiting," he said, his voice piercing through my grogginess.

"What time is it?" I muttered, rubbing the crust from my eyes.

"It's nine-thirty, now get yourself ready. You have five minutes," he said, handing me a cup of black coffee.

"Thank you, Sheriff," I said, cradling the cup between my two hands.

Judge Cole's chambers were a brief one-minute walk down the hallway from the jail. Along the way, we passed what I was expecting to be my former office, as more than likely I would be removed as the City of Sunrise's first mayor.

"Mr. Vega," Judge Cole said looking up from his desk, as the Sheriff escorted me into his chambers, "what shall we do with you?"

I stood in front of his large desk, with Sheriff Siringo standing alongside.

"Please take a seat," the judge said pointing to the chairs.

I sat down, while the sheriff remained standing, his arms folded across his chest, maintaining a solemn-looking expression.

"You have created an awkward situation," the judge began.

I squirmed in my seat, feeling anxious about what he would say.

"Your trial is a foregone conclusion. With the evidence and first-hand witnesses, there's no doubt that you'll be found guilty. The problem, however, is your sentencing. As you know, we don't have the facilities to incarcerate prisoners for any extended period of time," he said and took a moment to light his cigar.

I rubbed my sweaty palms on my trousers, anxiously waiting for the judge to continue.

He stood up to walk over to his window and looked out onto Front Street. He then turned to me and pointed with his cigar. "You'll receive your trial and I'll hand down your sentence for your crimes. You've committed multiple felonies, which would require a sentence of what could be several years."

"Several years?" I repeated and swallowed hard.

Judge Cole took a puff from his cigar and nodded. "So, until we figure out what to do with you, you'll stay in the jail."

I rubbed the back of my neck and exhaled. "But when will you know?"

Judge Cole shrugged, tilted back his head and blew a healthy stream of cigar smoke up to the wooden ceiling. "I'm sure there will be a meeting soon to discuss the options."

"But what about my saloons? How will they run without me?"

"Oh right, that reminds me," he said, walked over to his door, opened it up and said, "Mr. Wible, please come in."

I twisted in my chair to look behind me and saw Mr. Wible enter.

"Good morning, Mr. Vega," he said.

"Mr. Wible," I replied, confused by his presence.

"Please take a seat," Judge Cole said, gesturing to the empty chair next to me. As Mr. Wible sat down, the judge continued, "Under our city charter, we have the right, meaning the City of Sunrise has the right under law, to take over any commercial enterprise or property when its owner or landlord has become detrimental to the community."

"Is this true?"

"Have you read the city charter?" the judge asked.

I lowered my eyes and shook my head.

"The City of Sunrise also has the right, once it has taken legal possession to sell it to someone fit, able and willing to run the said business or property."

I looked over to Mr. Wible, who returned my gawk with a satisfied smile. "Let me guess, you've taken over ownership of my saloon and sold it to Mr. Wible."

"Yes, that's right. We transferred ownership of the Gold Digger Saloon this morning to Mr. Simon Wible," Judge Cole said.

"Can I ask what the purchase price was?"

"Oh, I believe it was for one dollar. Isn't that right, Mr. Wible?" he said.

Mr. Wible smiled and nodded.

CHAPTER SIXTY-SEVEN—THE CHURCH OF HOPE

Erik Andersson had constructed a well-built and thoughtfully designed church. The congregants of the Church of Hope were thrilled with the structure. Today was not only going to be the church's first service in the new building, but it would also be my last, as my departure for home was less than a week away.

The reverend took a few days to fully recover from his ordeal, but when I saw him earlier, on my walk over to the Hope Café for breakfast, he looked well.

Liam and I moved back to the miner's bunkhouse in Hope after we heard the news of the arrest of Mr. Vega and the city council's clever maneuvering to gain control of the Gold Digger Saloon and sell it Mr. Wible for a dollar.

Though Mr. Vega was a thief and a scoundrel, he knew how to operate a saloon. Mr. Wible, from what the prospectors were sharing with us, was having a difficult time keeping the place running smoothly. With Suzie also no longer around, the girls were fighting among themselves for the best customers. Henry was having trouble getting parts for the still, and with Mr. Wible's hands-off managerial approach, there were more disputes at the poker tables.

There was word that he was considering shutting it down and sticking to his gold mining ventures and outfitting store.

Another beneficiary of Mr. Vega's incarceration was Mr. Jones, who regained control of his general store, and was planning on reopening in a few days. I promised to give him a hand with the restocking of the shelves.

I had not seen Ella since we returned from the Tyonek village two days ago, when it was made clear that any chance for romance was over. But as I was admiring the church, I saw her coming out onto the porch of the café. We locked eyes and she waved for me to come over. I hurried over and she asked me to come inside. We sat at a table and she said, "Greta was in Hope the other day picking up a few of her things Mr. Jones was holding for her while he was converting the Hope Saloon back into his store. I was sweeping the front porch of the café when she approached. She said she wanted to talk to me about the night you spent with her. I replied saying you mean when he lost his virginity? She nodded and told me she had a confession," Ella said, with a barely imperceptible smile before continuing. "She said you never had sex with her. Apparently, you drank too much and passed out, and when you woke up, she made a big fuss, telling you what a great lover you were, and you believed it really happened, though it never did."

I looked at Ella, and rubbed my chin, not knowing how to respond as I had no recollection either way of that night with Greta, but it sounded like a reasonable explanation.

Ella leaned in and kissed me on my lips, and said, "I'd like to spend more time with you before you head back home."

"You would?" I muttered at a loss for meaningful words.

"That is if you want to," she said, with her hands on her hips.

I nodded with too much vigor, causing Ella to chuckle.

Though Ella invited me to share her bed, she would still not permit anything more than just cuddling and kissing. I was fine with this, but at the same time now found myself torn as to what to do with my impending departure less than a week away.

I didn't want my romance to end. I could either decide to stay on in Hope for the winter, or bring Ella home with me to San Francisco. I could imagine my parent's vitriolic reaction introducing my *shiksa* girlfriend. They would send me and Ella back to Alaska on the next steamship.

Hopefully the answer would make itself obvious by the time the *Bertha* was set to sail.

*

The next morning, after breakfast, Liam, Ella, and I walked together to church. After Liam's experiment with the Asatru religion and the disturbing sacrificial ceremony that Ella and I interrupted, he was happy to join us. "Just give me that plain, old, boring religion," he quipped.

The Church of Hope was filling up when we entered. From what I could tell, there were at least twice as many congregants than usual, even some people I'd never seen before in church. The excitement for the new building was palpable.

Reverend O'Hara had reserved three seats up front for us. "I want you up close," he told me that morning during breakfast.

On our way up the center aisle to our seats, people stopped to thank me for my donation that covered the cost of construction of the new building, but mostly for saving the reverend's life. Many people were still calling me Percy, even though this charade was debunked weeks ago. I attempted to display grace in exchange for the appreciation, but I couldn't help but think the real motivation for my gift to the church was nothing more than a way to impress Ella.

Just as we were about to take our seats, Ella smiled and said she wanted to go to speak to a friend and would return.

With Ella out of earshot, Liam leaned in next to me and said, "What are you going to do about her when we leave?"

"About Ella?"

Liam nodded.

"I don't know." I shrugged. "She's planning to stay the winter."

"Don't you want to invite her to San Francisco and introduce her to your parents?"

"I want to but I don't think that's a good idea," I said, lowering my voice. "They would never approve of her."

"Because she's not a Jew?" Liam said with a smirk.

"Shh. Not so loud," I said, looking around.

With my heart now pounding like a Tyonek war drum, Ella returned to her seat, grabbed my hand, leaned in close to me and smiled. I returned the smile, but it felt forced and I wondered if she could pick up on my sudden nervousness from Liam's truthful observation.

With dozens of confusing scenarios bouncing around in my head, the door off to the side of the altar opened, and in walked Reverend O'Hara. The congregation hushed into silence as he stood before us, his eyes closed, his hands clutched together in front of his chest.

The reverend cut an august image, wearing a pure white robe with a gold cross and chain hanging off his neck. He stood poised in front of a white linen cloth draped over a wooden table, upon which sat a golden cross, flanked by two tall golden candlesticks, featuring white candles, burning brightly.

With the congregation primed, Reverend O'Hara opened his eyes and smiled. He took a moment to sweep his eyes up toward the church's geometrically shaped rafters supporting its peaked roof, then he gazed upon the people standing along the back and side walls and finally, those seated upon the dozen rows of the newly constructed, long wooden pews.

"I am humbled to stand before the people of Hope and Sunrise on this sacred day. A day that I must confess, I thought would never come."

I snickered at the irony of a public confession by the reverend.

"While we are a community not lacking in wealth, it wasn't until a gesture by a young man, with nothing but a few dollars to his name, who donated his miraculous golden discovery, that made all this possible," he said, holding out his arms.

Hands from behind me patted my back. I turned, grinned and nodded, expressing my gratitude for the acknowledgments.

"This young man," the reverend continued, now looking at me, "deceived us, however. He told us his name was Percy Hope, a Catholic from San Francisco. But we later learned that this was not the truth."

A buzz of muffled conversations swept across the sanctuary. I swallowed hard.

"Though we are aware of his true identity and upbringing, I want you to know that I am not here to lambast him," he said, taking a step toward me. "Does it matter what name we call ourselves, or what religion we are born into? Are we not all God's children?"

Comments of praise for the reverend's words filled the sanctuary.

The reverend, with an outstretched arm, pointed at me. "Percy Hope has provided our city with a worthy name. Percy Hope has given our community a beautiful church," he said, lifting both arms upwards. "Percy Hope has freed us from the temptations of the evil Magnus Vega," he said, encouraging the congregants to a rousing expressive response that required him to rein it in before he continued. "And when I stood before death's door, it was Percy Hope who came to me in the spirit world, and brought me back to my people of Hope and Sunrise."

Liam leaned in and whispered, "How's it feel to be a living saint?"

I put my hand to my forehead and sighed. "It's true I did all those things, except bringing the reverend back from death. That was the shaman, not me. I'm not worthy, nor do I want such praise."

Liam looked around at the people nodding and pointing and me, and said, "Well it seems they're of a different opinion."

I looked at him, my eyes bulging from their sockets, and I said, "Maybe it's time for us to go home."

CHAPTER SIXTY-EIGHT—NOME

"How you doin', boss?"

I opened my eyes and saw Greta and Ingrid standing at my cell door. "Girls, what are you doing here?" I said, sitting up from my bunk.

"We came to visit you," Greta said.

"How are things going at the saloon?"

Ingrid flicked her wrist dismissively and stuck her thin face in between the jail cell bars and said, "Not so good. Mr. Wible is what Henry calls *a fish out of water*. Which means—"

"I know what it means, Ingrid," I interrupted.

"Oh, sorry. But it's true; he does not understand what he's doing. When will they let you out of here?"

I exhaled and dropped my head. "I'm afraid not soon. They set my trial for tomorrow, and it's a foregone conclusion what the verdict will be. But the problem is, they don't know what to do with me. They may just leave me in here to rot."

"We've got to figure a way of getting you out," Greta said, looking behind her for the sheriff.

"And where will I go? They might as well let me out of here. Without my saloon, I have nothing."

Ingrid wagged a finger at me. "Don't you get depressed. Greta and I have some money saved, and Henry does too. We've been hearing from our customers that many of the prospectors are planning on leaving Sunrise and heading to some place called Nome.

I shook my head and said, "It's the same far-fetched story I've been hearing for weeks."

"No, apparently it's true. The word is that these men, the *Three Lucky Swedes,* people are calling them, though someone said they're actually from Norway, struck gold a few weeks back. They're sayin' there's gold buried in the sand along the beach."

"Is that so? Sounds like a perfect place for a saloon," I said, with a sigh because of the missed opportunity.

Ingrid crooked her finger for me to come closer, and said, "I have something to tell you."

I rose from my bunk and took the two steps toward the jail cell door. "What is it, Ingrid?"

"Mr. Wible has been talking to us about Nome."

"And why would he do that?" I asked.

"He wants to move his mining operation there, and thought it would be a good idea to take your whiskey still, along with the furniture and gaming tables and open up the Nome Saloon."

"Are you serious? How in the world does he expect to do that? He can't even run this one," I said, turning my back on the girls and sitting down on my bunk.

"That's why we're here. Mr. Wible said he wants you to run it," Ingrid said with a wide smile.

"Wouldn't that be great? But as you can see," I said, holding out my arms, "I'm locked in a cage, with no way out."

"Well, boss," Ingrid said with a broad smile, "Mr. Wible has a plan about that too."

CHAPTER SIXTY-NINE—FREYA

I had to admit to myself that since the Church of Hope's inaugural service, I was living a celebrated life. Any of the previous doubts regarding my sinful behavior were excused, except for that one night with Greta at the saloon when I drank to excess. Though many assured me that this was a forgivable sin to commit, in exchange for avoiding 'ungodly relations with a working girl.'

The *Bertha* had docked in Cook Inlet for the last time this season, and Cap was busy transporting passengers, merchandise, various groceries, and foodstuffs back and forth along the Arm.

It was only three more days until the *Bertha* would pull up anchor and set sail for San Francisco with Liam and me onboard. Even with this, my relationship with Ella was blossoming into a serious romance. We spent nearly every hour of every day together. I stopped prospecting for gold, and helped her out in the café. In between lunch and dinner, we would hike along the surrounding trails and along the creeks. We slept together, though she still refused to allow me to go beyond kissing and some exploratory touching.

When I brought up the dim prospects of our future together, she would dismiss such talk by saying, "Let's just wait and see what happens, Percy. Perhaps a little more time will provide an answer."

Ella asked if I minded that she called me Percy instead of Sam. She explained, "It's what I enjoy calling you."

When I jokingly asked what name she would like me to call her, she surprisingly said, "I would love if you called me Freya."

"Freya? Isn't that a Norse God name?"

"You mean Goddess, Percy."

"Goddess, my apologies. What was she the Goddess of?"

Ella smiled, tilted her head in that alluring manner that always stirred my blood and said, "Freya was the Goddess of love, beauty, fertility, war, death, and gold."

Her words stirred my loins. I blew a long exhalation from my puckered lips, like a steam engine on a locomotive. "That's quite a list of duties for just one Goddess."

Ella tutted at me and said, "They're not duties, Percy, they're the essence of the Goddess Freya. It's who she is."

"Does that mean since you want me to call you Freya, it's also who you are?" I said toying with her.

She looked at me with her soft blue eyes sparkling in the afternoon's reflection of the sunlight, and said, "Yes, it is who I am. Will you call me Freya from now on?"

"Sure, if that's what you want."

She leaned forward, grasped my hand and said, "No, Percy, it needs to be what *you* want."

I didn't understand what the difference was, but if she wanted to be called Freya, I'd be happy to oblige. At this point, my loins were a boiling cauldron. "All right, Freya it is."

She smiled, pulled me close and kissed my lips—as if this sealed the deal.

CHAPTER SEVENTY—WIBLE MAKES A BARGAIN

"Get up, Magnus," Sheriff Siringo shouted.

"What is it?" I moaned. "I just fell asleep a little while ago. This damn bunk is like sleeping on the floor."

"Then you should be pleased to hear that Mr. Wible has arranged for your release," he said, twisting the key into the jail cell lock.

I pushed myself up to my feet, rubbed the sleep from my eyes and watched the cell door open. "I don't understand. Why would he do that?"

"Why don't you ask him yourself? He's waiting for you in the saloon," he said, and offered a grand gesture with a sweeping arm, allowing me to stumble past him and out to my apparent freedom.

My sudden and unexpected discharge from jail caused double takes and whispers from the people of Sunrise as I walked along Front Street. When I passed by Bakersfield Outfitters, I caught my reflection in the front windows of the darkened store and realized that my disheveled look gave an appearance that I may have escaped from jail.

I ran my fingers through my greasy hair and tucked in my shirt. A bath was in order, but first things first. I needed to see why Mr. Wible had arranged for my release. Perhaps it had something to do with heading up to Nome as Ingrid had hinted at.

I took a deep breath before pushing open the saloon's swinging doors. Once I stepped inside, boxes and wooden crates greeted me in small piles arranged around the saloon.

"Good morning, boss," said Henry, his face appearing in between two crates on top of the bar.

"What's all this?" I asked.

"I'm packing things up. Mr. Wible says we need to have everything boxed and crated by the end of the week. We're shipping everything to Nome."

"Where is he?"

Henry pointed toward the stairs and cringed, obviously knowing his words would be painful for me to hear. "Um, he's up in your room."

"Thank you, Henry," I said and took the staircase.

I reached the door that I would previously enter without hesitation and sighed before I knocked.

"One minute," said a female voice.

Was that Ingrid's voice?

A moment later the door opened and standing in a white nightgown was Ingrid. "Hi, boss, come on in, Simon is waiting for you on the deck," she said, slipping past me and heading for her room she shared with Greta.

I walked into my former bedroom, which had been claimed by Mr. Wible, evident by his trousers crumpled on the floor, next to his mud-caked boots. Apparently, he didn't have the same respect for cleanliness that I had.

"Good morning, Mr. Wible," I said, stepping out onto the deck bathed in the morning sunlight.

"Ah, Mr. Vega, please come join me. Would you like coffee?" he said, his feet propped up on the railing, and dressed in a wrinkled, linen sleeping gown that had slid up exposing his beefy, hairy legs.

"Yes, I would, thank you," I said, and lifted the handle of the ceramic coffee pot sitting on a silver tray and poured.

"You look terrible," he said, scratching the day-old stubble on his chin. "I've arranged for Greta to draw you a nice warm bath and give you a shave after we have our little chat. Then you can get yourself some sleep, because you're going to need it."

I took a sip of the coffee, which tasted delicious after the belly-wash crap they served me in the city jail. "Can you tell me how you arranged for my release? I was facing sentencing today."

"There is no need to worry about that any longer. The City of Sunrise has dropped the charges and released you into my custody."

"Your custody? What does that mean?"

"Sheriff Siringo reached out through his network of Pinkerton Detectives to see if there was a municipality in the states that would consider incarcerating you, but none were. So, you became a burden to our city. Until I proposed a solution," he said and took a sip of his coffee, while I waited to hear what was in store for my immediate future. "I made a deal with the City of Sunrise to pay them a thousand dollars for your release, in exchange for you to never step foot anywhere along the Arm ever again."

"A thousand dollars?" I asked in awe of the sum.

"That's right, and don't worry about the money, you're going to work it off at our new venture."

"What's that?" I asked, not sure of his meaning.

"We're moving to Nome. Three lucky Swedes have discovered gold."

"Yeah, I heard that they're actually from Norway."

Mr. Vega wagged a finger at me. "That's right. So, we're packing up and moving out of Sunrise. We've mined this place clean, there's nothing here left but flakes."

"And you want me to come with you?"

"How else would you pay me back?"

I frowned and said, "Can you tell me more? You mentioned a new venture—what do you have in mind?"

"You'll operate the Nome Saloon for me. I've already purchased a building on Frontier Street."

"If you don't mind me asking, how long will it take to pay you back the thousand dollars?"

"Well, that depends on how well the saloon does. If all goes well, you could have your freedom by this time next year."

"And when is this all going to happen?"

Mr. Wible clapped his hands together and smiled. "Now, it's happening right now. You saw we're already packing things up downstairs. I've arranged with Cap to take us, the whiskey still, and whatever else is worthwhile in the saloon, along with my mining equipment down to Dutch Harbor—that's an island out on the chain of the Aleutian Islands. There we'll transfer to a steamship heading north to Nome."

"We're going up there in the winter?" I said, now realizing the impact of what was happening.

"Yes, we are. We need to get a jump on the competition. These are exciting times," he said, rubbing his hands together.

"I don't know what to say, except thank you," I said, though I wasn't sure I meant it.

Mr. Wible smiled, took a sip of his coffee, and said with a smirk, "You're welcome."

I sighed, stood up and said, "Is it all right if I take my bath now?"

"Why don't you take Suzie's old room until we ship out in a few days."

"Suzie's room?" I said, and an image of her with her throat slit open, lying in a pool of blood, emblazoned itself upon my mind. For a moment, I considered returning to the jail cell, and trying my luck with the law, instead of with Simon Wible.

CHAPTER SEVENTY-ONE—A VIKING DINNER

The way things were progressing with Ella, it excited me that tonight would be the breakthrough I was hoping for. The past few nights she allowed me to go further than I had before. I even touched her breasts by slipping my hand under her shirt. But when Ella casually brushed over my privates with the back of her hand, I was sure she was ready to go all the way.

Earlier in the day I asked Liam if he would prepare a special meal. I wanted tonight to be perfect. Liam raised his eyebrows sarcastically and said, "Don't worry, Casanova, I'll think of something."

By the time we sat down to eat, the last customer had left and Liam served us our dinner. He placed the tray before me laden with a strange arrangement of raw food, and two glasses filled with a red liquid. I shook my head and said, "What's all this?"

Liam shrugged and pointed to Ella.

"This is what I asked Liam to prepare for you," she said. "I also have something special for us to drink."

"Have a nice evening, you two," Liam said with a smile and left the café.

I took a moment to look at the plate before me. Arranged on it were a good-sized slice of uncooked, bloody moose meat, a chunk of raw salmon topped with pink fish eggs, and an assortment of grains sprinkled across the plate. But there was no plate of food for Ella. "Are you not eating?"

"According to custom, the woman does not eat, only the man," she said.

Before I could protest, Ella held up her glass and said, "Let's toast to our special night, Percy."

I squinted my eyes, trying to get a grasp of what was happening, but dismissed it as something from her Viking traditions. At this point I would have eaten dirt if that was required to make love to her. "All right, Ella—" I barely got out, before she fired back like a shot from a gun.

"You mean Freya! You promised to call me Freya."

I nodded quickly. "I'm sorry, I mean, Freya," I said, and held up my glass.

She put it to her lips and drank. Her full pink lips turned blood red, and she looked at me with a glint in her eyes that nearly melted me. "Come on, drink up, it's a traditional wine that we serve on special occasions."

As I swallowed the warm, honey-like concoction, an immediate warmth rushed over me. "That was delicious," I said, suddenly feeling light-headed, and a horrible thought occurred that I would pass out like I did with Greta, and sleep through another chance of ending my long days as a virgin.

"Eat up, Percy," she said and cut my bloody moose meat with a knife.

I struggled with the moose, but ate small bites of the fish, eggs, and grains. Satisfied, Ella rose, took my hand and said, "Come, Percy, it's time."

I got to my feet and followed Freya into her bedroom, where she told me to lie down, which I gladly did.

She sat on the bed next to me, and gently touched my face and said, "Take one more sip, Percy."

I lifted my head as Ella tilted the cup, and poured the honey-wine down my throat, and by the time my head rested back upon the pillow, I was asleep.

CHAPTER SEVENTY-TWO—THE NINTH

"Come inside quickly," I said to my brother.

"Is he out?" Rolf asked as he stepped in through the kitchen door.

I nodded. "He's in my bed."

Rolf gave me a quick nod, acknowledging that our plan was in motion. "Let's wrap him up in the blanket and I'll lift him into the wagon."

"Oh no, we'll both do it. I don't want you to drop him."

We covered Percy in a woolen blanket, and when I slipped my hand under his back to lift him, there was a moment when I thought he was awake. But it was just a moan and a hint of a smile.

We had just over three hours to get Percy to the ceremonial site before the ninth hour. With Rolf at the reins, Percy lying unconscious in the wagon, and me seated alongside him, we made our way through the pathway along the Arm and to the secluded beachhead tucked just before Six Mile Creek.

The fast-moving shadows created glimpses of light upon Percy's serene face. He was a sweet boy, and I was tempted to give of myself, but as the *Ninth*, Percy had to be a virgin.

Just a few days ago I thought we would not find our Ninth. But when Greta came to me and confessed that Percy had never touched her, my heart soared. Percy was still a virgin, another miracle among miracles.

I first learned about Percy the day Reverend O'Hara told me about his dream of a young man coming to our town that would touch all of our lives. Not just by giving the town its name, but that he would also affect the people of Sunrise, Chief Ephanasy and his braves, the Dena'ina tribe of Fire Island, and the Tyonek warrior clan. What was unforeseen by the dream, was how Percy, under the spell of the great shaman—Sha-e-dah-kla, brought Reverend O'Hara back from the dead.

There was no doubt that Percy was the Ninth. Such raw, untapped power was what Thor craved, and what I was about to offer.

One problem I still needed to deal with was that the Asatru ceremonial protocol called for the male priest to accept the blood of the Ninth, instead of the priestess. This meant that Rolf would perform the sacrifice. But this was something that I, Freya, disagreed with, and was prepared to do whatever was necessary to carry out my duty to the God Thor.

When we reached the beachhead, the six congregants of the Asatru Church had already formed a circle under the canopy of the tree, where eight freshly killed, male animals were now hung. They were waiting for the Ninth.

So it was, on the ninth hour of the ninth day, in the ninth month, that we hung the human, virgin male, our ninth sacrifice to the God Thor.

CHAPTER SEVENTY-THREE—THE WEDDING

I'm not sure what woke me up; it could have been the rope rubbing its way through my skin and cinching together the bones of my wrists and ankles. But when I came to, my head was covered with a burlap bag, and from what I could make out through the openness of the fabric's weave, I was hanging off a sturdy tree branch like a lamb, bound and ready for slaughter by the butcher.

I tried to shout out, but a gag in my mouth muffled my screams.

Where is Ella? I jerked and twisted my bound body to see, but the more I did, the tighter the knots seized me.

Then I recognized Rolf's voice. He began reciting that same poem that Ella and I heard when we spied on the Asatru sacrificial ceremony two months ago. As Rolf spoke the words, I squirmed and shook at my bindings, trying to loosen them. "Rolf," I tried to scream. *Why would Rolf do this to me?*

"Thunder rolls and lightning strikes, my hammer flies across the sky.

Gods of weather, chariots of storm, masters of rain and torrents,

Son of the strength of Mother Earth,

I ask you to grant me that strength for myself.

You whose tree is the mighty oak,

348

O', Thor, grant me unending sturdiness.

Let me not break beneath the blows of misfortune.

You who are the guardian of the common man,

You who care for the farmers and workers,

Look upon me here in this place where I am only one of many and

protect my steps.

Make me resilient and mighty as your own arm,

Make me unbreakable, you who are a friend of Man.

I ask for one small part of the vigor of the right arm of Thor,

That I might brave the tempest and stand firm in the gales.

Thunder rolls, lightning strikes, and my hammer flies across the sky."

When he finished, I could make out he was walking toward me, while the Asatru congregants chanted, "Thor, Thor, Hahrd-hoo-gahd-ur, Thor, Thor, Ah-sah-Thor," over and over.

Suddenly the bag was pulled off my head, and I saw slain animals hanging from branches just like I was. As Rolf stepped closer, I saw his eyes as two golden slits in his blood-washed face. He raised a butcher's knife above his head, poised to open me up like the other slaughtered animals bleeding out around me onto the black gravel beach.

Just as he was about to swing the blade and pierce my body, I closed my eyes, in fear of my pending doom. But it never came. Shouts of protest caused me to open them, and I saw Rolf lying beneath me, a large gash exposing the innards of his belly, and standing over him, with a curved, blood-stained machete was Ella.

She turned and took a step and stood under me, both hands grasping the long, curved blade. A golden, jewel-encrusted headband, like a crown, sat upon her head of long blonde hair that cascaded upon her shoulders. She wore a long, wispy white gown, now splattered in Rolf's blood, tied with a golden belt pulled taut around her waist.

Ella lifted the knife upwards, looked up into the heavens and spoke, "I am Freya, Goddess of love, beauty, sorcery, fertility, war, gold and of death. I offer this sacred, virgin man—Percy Hope—to you, my love, as my wedding gift. I give him to you, so we can be joined as husband and wife, as it was meant to be from the beginning of time, Thor and Freya."

I convulsed hard at the ropes, no longer concerned with the raw wounds around my wrists and ankles. The jerking motion caused me to swing violently, causing Ella's blow to strike awkwardly, missing my torso, but slicing a gash through my forearm that opened up and gushed blood.

"Stop moving," she screamed at me, and lifted her arms to strike again.

Suddenly, from beyond my field of vision, someone grabbed Ella and tackled her to the ground, subduing her.

"Let me go," she screamed. "Tonight is my wedding night. I must sacrifice the Ninth."

It was Erik Andersson, who was pinning Ella's arms to the ground, forcing her to release the weapon. "It's over, Ella," he said.

Erik instructed one of the Asatru men to bring a ladder over. My bindings were cut, and I was lowered to the ground. Someone saw to my gash, placing a cloth over it and wrapping a tourniquet around my arm to stop the blood flow.

Erik helped Ella to her feet, and she looked over at Rolf, lying in a blackened puddle of his blood. She screamed and fell on top of him. "Who has done this?"

"It was you, Ella," said Erik. "I saw you as I approached from the trees," he said pointing.

"That is not possible," she cried, and leaped for her machete, lying where Erik had tossed it aside.

Ella grabbed its handle, then ran toward me. In one swift motion, she swung the blade backwards, and just at that moment when she was about to swing it forward, a gunshot rang out, jerking her body backwards like she had run into a wall.

I turned to see who fired the gun and walking out of the shadows was Mr. Vega.

"It seems I came just in time, Percy," he said, patting me on my back.

I stepped over to Ella and kneeled down beside her. She was still alive, though, coughing up blood. I grabbed her hand, and she returned a gentle squeeze and smiled.

"Why, Ella, why did you do this?"

She shook her head slowly and said, "I am Freya, you are the Ninth, tonight is my wedding night."

"No, you are Ella, and I am Sam, and I was in love with you," I said, feeling my eyes well up.

Her eyes drifted away from mine, and her gaze settled beyond me, into the heavens. "I'm coming, Thor, I am coming, my love." And with those words, she passed.

CHAPTER SEVENTY-FOUR—A MAGNUS SURPRISE

"I never had time to ask you, Mr. Vega, how did you happen to walk by the Asatru ceremony last night?"

"I was heading over to Hope to see Tommy. I still owe him this," he said pulling out a golden nugget and placing it on the table. "That's when I saw a fire flickering off the trail, and for some reason, I was suspicious, so I tied my horse up and found my way to the beach and that's when I saw Ella poised like a samurai warrior ready to slice you in two. My reaction was," he paused to think of the word, "reflexive. That's the best way to describe it. I didn't think, I just drew my Peacemaker and fired, and good thing I did."

"Oh, hi, Percy. How's your arm?" asked Greta, interrupting Mr. Vega's explanation.

I looked up from the table and saw Greta coming down the staircase and said, "It's sore, but the doctor said it should heal fine."

"Good," she said and came over. "You know, Percy, I told Ella that we never, um," she hesitated, "you know, because you fell asleep."

I felt my face blush. "Yes, thank you. Ella told me, though it probably would have been better that you didn't tell her."

Greta scrunched up her eyes, apparently confused by my remark. "But we can make things right," she said with a smile, showing off her dimples, and pointing upstairs. "No charge."

I looked over to Mr. Vega, who was making a walking motion with his fingers, encouraging me to accept the offer. "That's very nice of you, Greta, but I think I'll pass."

"Oh, that's too bad," she said and gave me a kiss on my cheek, and looked over at Mr. Vega. "I guess I'll get back to packing things up."

"All right, Greta, I'll give you a hand in a bit. I just need to wrap a few things up here."

"Ah, look who's here, it's Percy Hope," said Mr. Wible, walking into the saloon. "What are your plans, Percy?"

"Liam and I are heading back home tomorrow. I guess I'll go to work for my father in his store," I said.

"Listen, why don't you and Liam come with Mr. Vega and me to Nome? The gold's just lying there in the sand. No more of this hydraulic blasting. It's easy pickings."

"That's kind of you to offer, Mr. Wible, but I think it's time to head back to my old life. My parents are probably worried sick. I was supposed to write home each week, and I think I managed two or three letters the entire summer."

"Well, if you change your mind, you'll know where to find me."

"Thank you, sir," I said.

Mr. Vega leaned over the table, picked up the nugget, handed it to me and said, "Would you mind doing me a favor, Percy, and give this to Tommy?"

I felt the nugget's heft in my hand, and it reminded me of the early days of the summer when Liam and I placer mined Resurrection Creek. Even though it was only three months ago, it felt like a lifetime. So much had occurred since then. I nodded and said, "Yes, I would be happy to."

"Thank you," he said, and pushed his chair back. "Well, that seems to be it then."

I rose to my feet and extended my hand. "Mr. Vega, I would like to thank you for saving my life. Honestly, after everything we've been through, you're the last person I would ever imagine saying those words to."

"You're welcome, Percy," he said grasping and shaking it. "There were times, I admit, that I would have liked to see you gone from Hope. But our paths crossed for a reason, and I'm glad I could save your life. Yours is a life worth saving."

Mr. Vega held on to my hand a while and said, "I want you to know, whatever your real name is, you will always be Percy Hope to me. Hell, that damn city is named after you, and will be long after we're all dead and buried."

"That is, if it doesn't disappear from the map after all the prospectors leave," added Mr. Wible.

CHAPTER SEVENTY-FIVE—THE LAST SUPPER

The reverend not only allowed Ella and Rolf to be buried in the Point Comfort Cemetery, he also said a few words, even though they weren't Catholic. He preached of the seven deadly sins, a common theme of his, which seemed appropriate for these two so-called *heathens* lowered into the ground.

As we walked together back to Main Street, I thought about the reverend's words and how Ella, who knew all seven of the deadly sins by heart, had violated each one to her doom, and nearly to mine. I had no doubt any longer why these sins were called *deadly*.

The reverend and I were headed for the café where Liam was preparing a farewell meal for our friends before we sailed for home.

"We never talked about what happened with the shaman," the reverend said, and pointed to a wooden bench in front of the church.

I took a breath, nodded and sat down alongside him. He leaned forward, put his elbows on his knees, and turned his head to look at me. "I was dead, I know I was. But then you appeared and called out to me. Don't you remember?"

I shook my head. "After the shaman asked me to drink his concoction, I fell asleep and have no memory of what happened until I woke up."

"It was most remarkable," the reverend began. "You appeared before me so clearly, just like you are now. You reached your hand out and said

356

that it wasn't my time and I should come back with you. I grabbed it, and the next thing I knew I was in the healing cave of the shaman."

"I'm sorry, but I don't remember."

He patted my knee. "That's all right. Maybe that's the way it's supposed to be."

I placed a hand upon my cheek and said, "I've been having a hard time making sense of the spiritual world after all that has happened this summer. I nearly lost my life to Ella's delusional obsession of Thor, but was saved by the sinful Magnus Vega, who tried to get rid of you for his illicit ambitions, which resulted in you returning from the afterlife by a shaman-guided Jew!"

The reverend looked at me and smiled. "The purpose of any spiritual path is not about knowing the absolute truth. The answers we seek might never be found, but we cannot stop looking. It is this continuous journey of our life that leads us closer to the mystery of the almighty."

I sighed, trying to comprehend the reverend's words.

"Now," the reverend said, slapping my knee again, "let's get to the café and see what Liam has cooked up for us in his that dirty skillet of his."

*

When I stepped onto the porch of the Hope Café, I immediately felt the absence of Ella. As much as I tried, I could not understand her secret obsession with the God and Goddess, Thor and Freya, and her misguided

357

idea that by sacrificing me as the Ninth, would unite them in some ethereal matrimony.

But what disturbed me the most was how I was manipulated into her crazy scheme. From the first time we met, her plan of stringing me up onto that branch as her ultimate sacrifice was already in motion. Ella went to great lengths to distract me from any suspicion that I might have harbored. She presented herself as a devout Catholic and encouraged me to attend services at the church and pretended to act infuriated at her brother's bizarre behavior during their mock Asatru sacrifice, apparently staged for my benefit.

Ella must have thought all was lost when she learned that I lost my virginity at the Gold Digger Saloon, and then felt great relief when Greta told her it was a ruse, and I was still a virgin, ripe for sacrifice.

Still, I would never forget those tender moments, when I would gaze upon her beauty, in what I thought was love, even as I realized now that it was nothing more than the deadly sin of lust, which nearly killed me.

I could see that there were several people in the café, waiting. But a sudden surge of sadness washed over me, forcing me to sit down on the steps. I felt a cold sweat, rolling down the back of my neck, and a dizziness that forced me to drop my head down below my knees to keep me from passing out.

I realized that I had never witnessed death firsthand before, and after this summer, I have been a part of three lives lost: Stan, Rolf and Ella, none of which I could take blame for, but all of whom I felt obliged to honor and mourn, regardless of their faults or misdeeds.

It took a few minutes for the dizziness to pass, and for my strength to return. I stood up, took a deep breath and entered the café.

Liam had arranged the individual tables in the café into a large square, as a way for everyone to see each other, while we dined on his delicious fried moose steak, onions, and potatoes.

By the time the reverend and I entered, nearly every seat was taken.

"Ah, Percy and Reverend O'Hara," said Mr. Jones, who rose to greet us, "it's good to see you both. Please come and join us."

Seated around the table were Chief Ephanasy and his son Tommy, along with his braves Nicholai, Alexander and Kusema, and Erik Andersson who was rising from his seat to greet me.

"Erik, I'm happy you're here. If it wasn't for you, I would have been sacrificed to the God Thor."

Erik smirked and nodded. "That you would have. It was a good thing I saw Rolf and Ella putting you in the wagon," he said, pointing toward the café's back door. "This concerned me, so I followed them. It took me a bit of time to catch up, but when I arrived at the Asatru ceremonial site, I saw Ella was about to cut into you, and that's when I leaped from the woods and tackled her to the ground."

I pulled Erik toward me and embraced him. "Thank you, Erik."

Erik offered me a humble smile. He took a deep breath and said loud enough for everyone in the café to hear, "I would like to apologize for getting involved with the heathen Asatru religion. It was a foolish mistake to allow myself to believe in such ridiculous fantasies. Would you please forgive me?"

I looked over to the reverend for his council, who said, "Forgiveness, Erik, is the fragrance that the violet sheds on the heel that has crushed it."

"That's incredible, Reverend," I said. "Is that from the scriptures?"

"No, that's a quote from the American writer and philosopher Mark Twain."

I always believed that Erik was a good man. Plus, he wasn't the only one duped by Ella and Rolf. "I forgive you," I said, and we embraced once more.

After dinner, while offering my farewells, I approached Tommy who stood beside his father. "It's good to see Tommy back home," I said to the chief.

The chief nodded and patted his son on his broad shoulder and said, "I am pleased to have him back."

"Mr. Vega asked me to give this to you," I said, and handed Tommy the golden nugget.

Tommy took it in his hand, looked over to his father, and then handed it back to me. "I don't want it."

"Why not? This can buy many things for your people," I said holding the nugget squeezed between two fingers.

Tommy held out his palm. "I was offered this once before, and I should have refused. Our people lived on these lands long before the white man arrived and never felt the need to rip its gold from the earth. Tell me, Percy, what good has it brought you?"

I looked at the chief, who smiled broadly at his son's words.

I shrugged and said, "Then what will I do with it?"

Chief Ephanasy put his hand on my shoulder, and said, "Take it with you, and when you find someone in need, give it to them."

CHAPTER SEVENTY-SIX—HEADING HOME

Liam and I stood topside, leaning over the railing, watching the late summer sun dipping over the landscape of the western shore of Cook Inlet.

"I will miss this place," I said.

Liam nodded. "We've earned a lifetime's worth of memories."

"I don't even know what to say to my parents."

"You're not going to tell them everything?" Liam asked with a grin.

I turned to Liam and folded my arms and said, "Are you going to share your exploits with your father?"

Liam shrugged. "There's nothing I did that I was ashamed of, plus he would enjoy the stories."

"There are plenty of stories from these last three months to write a book," I said.

"Well, why don't you?"

"What do you mean?"

"Write a book about our summer."

I nodded and processed the idea. "Maybe I will."

Liam held out his hands like he was holding a book and said, "You can call it *The Alaskan Adventures of Percy Hope*."

I shook my head. "No, I'll call it *Liam and Percy's Amazing Summer Vacation*," I said, and we both burst into laughter.

*

We were informed the previous night, that if we wanted to watch the *Bertha* sail into the Port of San Francisco at sunrise, we should be topside by six-thirty. Eager to get off the ship, both Liam and I were standing along the railing's edge with our valises, a half-hour earlier than that.

The darkness faded once the first sliver of orange peeked over the buildings on the far side of the harbor. As the sun rose, several long bands of dark clouds slid across the sky forming illuminated shards of sunlight that pierced skywards. I smiled and exhaled with relief that I could find my way out of the rabbit hole, to this glorious return home.

"We made it, Sam," Liam said, looking straight ahead.

"Yes, we did," I said, just as a memory flashed before me. "I just remembered a dream I had last night."

"Was it about Ella?"

"Not funny."

"Sorry, Sam, tell me your dream,"

"I drank the shaman's tea and instead of falling asleep, I saw how I brought the reverend back from the dead."

"Are you serious? What happened?"

"Reverend O'Hara was walking along a pathway, like the one that connects Hope and Sunrise. I was following behind him, calling his name, but he kept walking. I ran to catch up and placed a hand on his shoulder. He spun around so fast that he startled me and shouted, 'Leave me be!' There was anger in his eyes. He turned back around and kept walking.

"I ran and stepped in front of him, forcing him to stop. I put both hands onto his shoulders and said, 'It's not yet your time reverend, please come back with me,' and pointed in the direction from which we came. He showed no understanding of my words, nor do I believe he knew who I was. Then words from the shaman came to me. 'Tell him who you are.'

"I squeezed his shoulders tight and said, 'Reverend, this is Samuel Rothman, don't you recognize me?' But he just gazed beyond me, as if he was being summoned by a greater force.

"'Tell him your name,' the shaman insisted.

"I paused a moment, realizing what he meant. I grabbed his cold hands and forced him to look at me. 'Reverend, it's me, Percy, Percy Hope, you must come with me'. Upon hearing those words, the cloudy film coating his eyes cleared, and he saw me.

"'Percy, is that you?'

"I nodded. 'Yes, Reverend, it's me Percy. You're going the wrong way. We need to go back.' He nodded, and I took him by the hand. We took only one step back to where we came from, and in the next instant, I found myself in the cave waking up from my journey, and there you were, along with Ella."

"Do you think that's what really happened, or was that just a dream?" Liam asked as the Bertha docked along the long wooden pier where we first boarded her, three months earlier.

I shook my head. "That's hard to say, but the reverend recovered. Perhaps he would have done so, regardless."

Liam looked at me, shook his head and said, "People don't recover from death, Sam."

"Look, there are my parents," I said, spotting them on the deck waving. "And there's your dad standing next to them."

Liam and I waved back enthusiastically. We lifted our valises and walked over to the gangplank to disembark. As we walked down the incline to the boat dock, Liam said, "Just before we left Hope, Reverend O'Hara pulled me aside and asked me how I enjoyed my summer. I told him it was wonderful, except for my regret that I didn't strike it rich."

I stopped walking and looked at Liam. "Did the reverend have anything to say?"

Liam smiled and nodded. He said, "It is not what we possess that makes us rich, but what we can do without."

CHAPTER SEVENTY-SEVEN—MOTHER & FATHER

"I don't understand, Sam. Are you telling me they named the city after you?" Mother asked me for the second time.

"Yes, Mother. They named it Hope City."

"This is incredible," Father said puffing on his cigar like a chimney. "Just because you were the first one to step off the boat?"

"So now this place is called Hope City?" Mother asked again.

"That's right, Mother."

"Enough of that," Father said, tapping a clinging flake of ash off his cigar, "let's talk about the reason you went to Alaska. Tell me, Son, did you discover any gold?"

During the journey back home on the *Bertha*, I thought about Father asking me this question and decided that there were too many parts of the story that would upset him. He wouldn't have approved of the grubstake deal I made with the Company, giving them seventy-five percent of whatever I discovered. He would have become apoplectic upon learning that I donated the only golden nugget I found to the Catholic church, and there was no way I could tell him about the twenty-ounce nugget I carried back with me now, and that I was planning on giving to some unknown person in need, as Chief Ephanasy had suggested.

I shrugged my shoulders, and said, "Sorry, Father, neither Liam nor I had any luck."

Father's eyes opened wide. "All this time prospecting, and you found nothing?"

"I didn't say that. I found many things, just not gold."

"Leave the boy alone, Ben. Just thank God he's home, safe and sound," Mother said wrapping her arms around me and kissing my cheek repeatedly.

Father pointed his cigar at me and said, "All right, Sam, so you've come back empty-handed, that's fine. But you say you found things. What sort of things did you find?"

I sat up tall and tried to speak with purpose. "I found that man's desire to rape and pillage from the earth, to enrich oneself, is a foolish quest."

Father shook his head and blinked his eyes. "I don't understand."

"Before the white man came, gold laid about like any other stone, and the natives left it there, undisturbed."

"Because they're foolish savages," Father blurted out.

I shook my head. "No, Father, they're not fools or savages. They believe that whatever is in the ground, should stay in the ground. Everything is a living being, even the stones."

"That's nonsense," Father said, motioning his hand dismissively at me. "Man is the master of this earth and is here to exploit its resources to improve our lives. This is called *progress,* Samuel, unless you want to live like one of those primitives you're talking about."

"They're not primitives or savages, and from what I saw, these people are more evolved than the greedy stampede of prospectors trying to shake the earth loose of its treasure."

"You're young, Samuel, and you can afford to romanticize this fantasy of being in harmony with nature, especially when you're living under this roof. But one day you'll wake up and realize that you need to make a living for yourself, and when that time comes, I pray that it's not too late."

CHAPTER SEVENTY-EIGHT—JACK LONDON

Regardless of my disagreements with Father, he still expected me to work in the family store while taking classes at San Francisco State University. I had enrolled in several writing courses, hoping to become a journalist or a novelist.

I worked evenings from five to nine. We were closed on Shabbat, but opened on Sundays, which was my day to work the store alone. Father was hesitant about leaving me by myself for the full day, but I convinced him he should take the extra day as he was getting older and needed rest.

Sundays were not a very active day, especially in the morning. Many of our customers went to church, and it wasn't until the afternoon when the store got busy. But from ten in the morning until two in the afternoon, I had time to write.

It was the third Sunday in October, at eleven thirty in the morning, when Jack London, the writer, walked into Rothman's General Store. I was sitting behind the counter, with my writing pad out and working on the opening chapter of my book, *A Summer of Hope*.

"Excuse me, young man," a man said, capturing my attention.

I looked up, surprised that I didn't hear anyone come in. "Oh, I'm sorry, sir. How can I be of service?" I said, hurrying around from behind the counter.

"Do you sell Samson rope?"

I nodded, stepped around the counter and realized that I recognized this man. "Aren't you Jack London, the writer?"

"Have we met?"

"Yes, but just for a moment. My name's Sam Rothman. You spoke last June at our high school graduation."

"Oh right, you're talking about Mission High School."

"Yes, and you told us we should do something exciting with our lives, or we would end up like a dead mosquito."

"I did," he said with a smile, and looked around at the very boring store we were standing in. "So, tell me, young man, what have you done with your life since graduating high school?"

"Well, right now I'm going to the university. I want to be a writer like you, Mr. London."

"Is that so? What are you going to write about?"

"My first book will be called, *A Summer of Hope*. It's about my visit this past summer to Hope, Alaska."

Mr. London shook his head. "Never heard of this place. Where is it?"

"It was just named Hope, which I had something to do with. It's about a third of the way up Turnagain Arm."

Mr. London shook his head. "I'm not familiar with it."

"Would you mind if I asked you if you thought my story was worthy to write a book about?"

Mr. London raised a hand with a finger pointed into the air. "I have a better idea; let me ask you a few questions about your story, and that will determine if it deserves to be told."

"All right," I said, with my heart pounding away, excited at the opportunity.

"I'm assuming you're writing an adventure story?"

"I am," I said with a smile.

"That's what I thought. Are there many instances of conflict, or danger?"

I thought about being nearly cut in two by Ella at the Asatru sacrifice. "Oh yeah, there's danger."

"Good. What about the story, is it a battle between good and evil?"

I thought of Magnus Vega, as evil as they come. Perhaps I could consider myself as the one who battled evil, but there were other virtuous and righteous characters, such as the reverend. "The battle between good and evil is the heart of the story, Mr. London."

"You must remember to make the hero of your story relatable to the reader."

That I knew would be easy to do, since it was me.

"And you mustn't forget to include twists and turns. You always want surprises to amuse the reader."

Certainly, learning that Ella was a follower of the Asatru religion, and her misguided belief that she was Freya, destined to marry Thor, if she could sacrifice a human-male-virgin, would fit that brief. "I believe my story has those elements."

"And if your story is good, then the writing needs not only to be descriptive but also concise. If it is all of this, then you must offer your reader a way to read more of your work."

I thought how Mr. Wible, Mr. Vega, and their entourage were now in Nome, laying the foundation for the next gold rush. "If I'm able to write this book, Mr. London, I think there's another one in me, if I go to Nome next summer."

Mr. London took a step closer, put a hand on my shoulder, gave me a determined look and said, "Just remember, Sam, you can't just sit by and wait for inspiration. You must go after it with a club."

CHAPTER SEVENTY-NINE—THE DIRTY SKILLET

"What do you think?" Liam said standing alongside me, nearly in the middle of Market Street admiring his new sign.

"It looks good," I admitted.

Liam had just hung the sign advertising his new restaurant. I not only loved the name but also got a chuckle from its slogan.

THE DIRTY SKILLET

LIFE'S TOO SHORT FOR BORING FOOD

"I want you to know that I plan on paying you back, Sam."

I wagged a finger at him. "Oh no, you won't. You remember when I offered the nugget to Tommy, he refused it, and the chief said that I should give it to someone in need. Well, Liam, you were in need, and here we are."

We stepped back onto the sidewalk and entered the restaurant. Tonight was the grand opening and Jack London said he would appear to support Liam. Since my encounter with him at Father's store, I had been working once a week with Mr. London on editing my book, *A Summer of Hope*. He'd been a great help, enlightening me on the subtleties of great writing, things they don't teach at the university.

"You're a good friend, Sam," Liam said, as we stepped inside.

The restaurant accommodated only six tables, which Liam thought would be fine, as he didn't want to take on too much risk. I told him not to worry, because once customers got a taste of his beef and potato stew, there would be a line down Market Street waiting to get in.

Liam and I took seats at one of the tables next to the window.

"You think you're going up to Alaska next summer, Sam?"

"That depends if I'm able to get my book published. Mr. London thinks I have a good chance, and if that happens, come June of next year, I'll be in Nome doing research for the next book."

Liam sighed. "That sounds exciting. I wish I could go with you, but now I'm stuck here, at least for a while."

"This is a dream come true, Liam. You should be proud of what you could accomplish," I said, holding out my arms.

"Aren't you worried that what we experienced in Hope last summer might never be equaled in our lifetime?"

I sat back in my chair and looked out the window onto Market Street. This question had haunted me ever since we returned and was amplified in the writing of my book. I turned back to Liam, sighed and said, "You know some people say that falling down the rabbit hole, like Alice did in Wonderland, was a metaphor for losing control of one's life. And I have to say that during our time in Hope, I felt that my life was not my own. Events moved swiftly, as if I was just a passenger along for a wild ride. Nevertheless, I lived those months unbridled from life's worries, even when I faced mortal danger. Do I dare test those boundaries again, Liam?"

There was silence for a good minute, allowing the question to hang above us like black storm clouds over Cook Inlet, until Liam looked at me, reached across the table, clasped his hand onto mine, and asked, "What would Jack London say?"

THE END

About the Author

Neil Perry Gordon achieved his personal goal as an author of historical fiction with his first novel—*A Cobbler's Tale*, published in the fall of 2018. With over fifty, four and five-star reviews praising the story and his writing style, he released his second novel—*Moon Flower,* the following year. In the fall of 2019, the metaphysical fiction sequel to A Cobbler's Tale—*The Righteous One,* was published.

His creative writing methods and inspiration have been described as organic—meaning that he works with a general storyline for his characters and plot, rather than with a formal, detailed outline. This encourages his writing to offer surprising twists and unexpected outcomes, which readers have celebrated.

His novels also have the attributes of being driven by an equal balance between character development and face-paced action scenes, which moves the stories along at a swift page-turning pace.

Ready for 2020, Neil Perry Gordon once again explores the historical-fiction genre with two new novels: *Hope City* and *The Bomb Squad.*

Hope City is the first in a series chronicling the 1898 Alaskan adventures of the protagonist—Percy Hope. While *The Bomb Squad* tells the World War 1 story of Max Rothman an American patriot, protecting the homeland from the German spy, Dr. Harold Schwartz.

The author has attributed his love for the creative process from his formative years spent *learning-to-learn* at the Green Meadow Waldorf School.

Readers can learn more about Neil Perry Gordon, by visiting his website and blog at: www.NeilPerryGordon.com